Sticks and Stones

Susie Tate

For Lou and Emma.

Contents

Chapter 1

Silent tears

THE FIRST SENSATION THAT DYLAN REGISTERED WAS THE warmth under his hand. As he swam up towards full consciousness he also noticed the softness on his face and the delicious smell surrounding him. His head was buried in soft, wavy, blonde hair with an incredible, yet weirdly familiar, fresh citrusy scent, and as he looked down he saw that his hand was splayed possessively over a toned female stomach.

He groaned. Why oh why was he always as horny as a three-balled tomcat? Whoever it was he'd shagged last night, he knew it would bite him in the arse. If he weren't careful he would succeed in alienating the entire female staff of every hospital in South Wales before his rotation was over. The last three months he had been at his most prolific, spurred on by the mind-numbing boredom of Elderly Care.

Could he make a stealthy exit without waking her up? As he started shifting on the bed he felt her begin to stir. So much for a ninja-style-stealthy-minimal-confrontation-escape. He closed his eyes in resignation, and felt the stabbing pain behind them and the telltale badger-mouth, which explained his memory loss and latest stupidity.

Why didn't he stop at a few social wets? Especially on a mess night out. Another wave of recognition swept through him as he breathed in the citrusy scent, and his eyes shot open. He started sweating what was most likely pure alcohol as he stared down in horror at the woman who was now turning to nuzzle into his shoulder and drape her arm across his stomach, making a little low noise of contentment.

Christ, he'd really gone and ruddy done it now.

Or had he?

He wracked his brain for his memory of the night before. Lou and Frankie had been completely smashed. He remembered doing a couple of shots with them, telling Lou to dial it down and being poked pretty painfully in the chest for his trouble. He remembered snogging that physio he'd had his eye on for a while, but getting distracted by all the blokes around them openly leering at Lou and Frankie on the dance floor.

From that point on, everything was a little hazy. He had a few flashes of half carrying Lou through the bar whilst being furious with her for getting in that state and essentially cock-blocking him, seeing as he had to drag her home.

Her breasts were pushing up against his chest now, and her leg had draped itself over his under the duvet, which only served to intensify his alcohol sweats. Dylan wasn't blind, he knew that a half-naked Lou was most men's idea of a wet dream – and yes, of course, he himself had on occasion had the odd impure thought when it came to her.

To be honest there were very few females that Dylan hadn't at some stage visualized having sex with. Even his piano teacher when he was twelve, Mrs Allcock, despite her greying hair, dodgy front teeth and penchant for congealed, bright red lipstick, was not completely safe from the odd dirty thought (although Dylan thoroughly blamed her name for the direction of his daydreaming whilst trying to muddle through his scales under her watchful, heavily made-up eye).

But this particular female, who was currently plastered over his front, was very much off limits. There was a huge difference between thinking about doing something (or someone) and actually doing it (or her).

Weirdly in the last three months since working with Lou, he had been having more and more disturbing thoughts about her. He blamed her proximity and the sheer boredom of the job he was being forced to endure. Hell, the daily multidisciplinary team meeting was enough time for Dylan to construct an elaborate fantasy involving a much more amenable Lou than was typical, and a conveniently empty treatment room / office / registrar computer room / the floor beneath of the ward clerk's desk / the store cupboard on the geri's ward.

Okay, so it had recently become somewhat of an obsession with Dylan, but that didn't mean that he should ever have actually followed through. Lou was a big pain in the arse, but she, together with Frankie, were his best friends. Yes, it was a bit weird to have female best friends, but Mike (his male best friend – and not male partner, as might be suggested by the whole female best friend thing) lived in London now, and the four of them had been inseparable at uni.

At first, after falling head over heels for Frankie, Dylan had pushed the foursome thing to spend more time with her. But after two years of getting nowhere he realized that he had three best friends who knew him better than anyone, and that two of them were female. And when he got over Frankie he was actually pretty pleased with the dynamic. Mike had a girlfriend from school throughout uni, and was so loyal and in love with her (they were now married) that he may as well have been a eunuch, so none of the four of them had ever shagged or even snogged. However much Dylan fantasized about sex with Lou, he wouldn't risk the friendship, and to be quite honest she would be a high-maintenance nightmare as a girlfriend. He liked quiet, slightly shy, softly spoken women, *not* obnoxiously posh, brash, foul-mouthed, feisty ball-breakers.

So terror flooded him as he watched her eyelids flicker open. She was smiling slightly, and looked so unbelievably beautiful, and somehow vulnerable, that for a moment he couldn't quite believe she was the same harpy he knew. She squeezed his stomach, and her head slowly tipped back so her eyes could meet his.

'Bloody hell,' he swore, his voice loaded with regret. Her smile faded and that look of vulnerability was quickly replaced by her familiar defiant, take-no-bullshit expression.

'Please tell me we didn't ...' he started to plead. Something flashed across her face, and for a moment she looked almost in pain, but her next words were said in a reassuringly careless way.

'Calm down, Dildo. As if I would allow my lady parts to have any contact with your disease-ridden toothpick-sized excuse for a weiner.'

He heaved out a heavy sigh of relief. He most certainly did not need another balls up to add to his cluster-fuck of a personal life at the moment.

'Babes,' he said patiently, 'you and I both know that the junk in my trunk is most definitely the real deal; you've seen it often enough.'

'Ugh.' Lou pushed away from his chest and sat up in bed next to him. 'Only because you and your rugby buddies are such narcissistic freaks that you think everyone in the bar wants to see you drinking pints with your trousers down, and then wrestling half naked on the sticky floor. You do know it smacks of repressed homosexuality don't you? All those showers and baths together –'

'Babes, calm yourself,' Dylan interrupted, patting her on the head. 'You don't want to get yourself worked up imagining all that lush man-flesh whilst we're having a cwtch* in bed. I wouldn't want you to pounce on me in my weakened state.'

'Gah! You. Are. A. Disgusting. Sick. Deluded. Pervert.'

'Don't get all gushy on me, babes, you know it only embarrasses me.' Lou snorted and crossed her arms under her chest as Dylan ran his hands down his face. 'My head feels like there's a Frenchman living in it.'

'Series Two,' Lou put in quickly. They were both well used to this game now, and if either of them ever missed a quote they would never hear the end of it.

'Episode?'

'"Chains."'

'Well played.'

They sat in silence for a moment staring at the opposite wall.

'Jesus, you've still got that collage up of our elective,' Dylan said suddenly, making Lou jump. 'That must have been eight years ago now.'

'Well, those views were gorgeous,' Lou said defensively.

'Yes, babes, yes they were,' Dylan replied, and Lou rolled her eyes at his smug expression.

'I mean aside from the loser whose fat head is blocking half the shot in some of them.'

'Some of them?' Dylan spluttered. 'I think you'll find I'm the main attraction of that whole collage. In fact it's like a montage of me.'

He felt Lou stiffen beside him and he laughed. Above all things he loved to wind her up. Sometimes it felt like winding Lou up was his life's calling. He'd even found himself wishing that he were at Lou's flat winding her up of an evening when he was out with a girl. This for Dylan was beyond bizarre since he also considered sex one of his life's callings, and him thinking a night of guaranteed no action would be more fun than an (admittedly boring) evening ending in the horizontal tango was just plain weird. 'That beach was awesome, mind. All those freaky pink shells. Remember the time we watched the sun come up after we'd stayed up in that little beach bar?'

'Mmmhmm,' was Lou's only audible response, but he saw her nod her head.

'Where were Frankie and Mike again?'

'They were tired I think; you guys had just climbed Killy.'

'Pussies.'

Lou snorted, 'Yeah.'

Then Dylan had another flash of memory. A drunk Frankie swaying on the dance floor came to mind.

'How pissed was Frankie last night,' he said. 'She never lets herself get that steaming.' Dylan had practically made an art of watching Frankie over the years, and he knew that slamming back shots and letting drunk cardiothoracic surgeons maul her on the dance floor was not her style. Hardly surprising really, what with her mum and Papa Marco. He suddenly tensed with worry. 'She did make it home okay didn't she Lou?'

Lou sighed. 'I'm not a completely crap friend you know. I wouldn't have left her there in the state she was in. Truth was, Weasel Gankface got to her first and practically carried her home. Far as I know he's still here.'

Dylan let out a breath that he didn't even realized he'd been holding. Caring for and worrying about Frankie had become somewhat of a religion to him, and even though he'd given up long ago on her loving him back, it was still a tricky habit to break.

'He cares about her you know,' Lou said quietly into the silence that followed. 'You should tell her.'

'Yeah, I know,' Dylan replied in a small voice. Of all the stupid things he did at uni, keeping Frankie and Tom apart was by far the worst (and that was saying something seeing as he had once been caught rolling around in profiteroles and barking like a dog at the Dean's wife with his testicles hanging out, at one of the rugby balls).

'She'll forgive you,' Lou continued. 'You know she will, that's just her nature.'

Yup: sweet, caring, quietly funny, insightful, beautiful, forgiving.

Argh! He almost went to smack himself on the forehead.

Must not obsess over Frankie anymore.

It's been years.

Enough.

It seemed like Lou was going in for a reassuring hug, but she chickened out at the last minute and performed an awkward head pat instead, much like he had done a minute ago. For some reason Dylan found physical contact with Lou awkward, even more so over the last few months. His eyes drifted down to her pink lace-encased breasts (her nightwear was like something you'd expect a Vegas show girl to wear during a burlesque performance), and unfortunately he felt his body start to react.

'Right,' he blurted out, scrambling off the bed and making a grab for his phone. 'It's bloody half five in the morning. I better go sleep on the sofa or we'll have the piss ripped out of us all day. How did we end up like this anyway? We must have been really outers to fall asleep together.'

'Yes, well, at least neither of us remember too much about it,' Lou said stiffly. She had her arms wrapped round herself on the bed now, and wasn't meeting his eyes. Dylan had the nagging feeling that he was missing something.

'Look, babes, are you sure that nothing –'

'Of course not, you numpty.' She gave him a bright smile, which he thought looked somehow slightly forced. 'Don't get your knickers in a twist; you know I wouldn't touch you with a barge pole.' Dylan hesitated, then decided that his uneasy feelings were most likely the result of hangover paranoia.

'Oh, well, thank Christ for that,' he huffed out whilst pulling on his trousers and searching around for his T-shirt. 'That really would be the bloody last thing we need at the moment.'

'Yeah, absolutely,' Lou agreed, her voice sounding slightly raspy.

'You getting a cold, babes?'

'No, just standard hung-over-hedgehog-shat-down-my-throat,' she replied. 'Now can you please bugger off so I can get some sleep.'

'I'm going now ...'

'In a minute,' they both said together. 'Your turn of phrase is so predictable. I do hope that you and your countrymen realize that "now, in a minute" makes no real sense.'

Dylan held his hands up in front of him in surrender, finally located his T-shirt and pulled it over his head. Having dismissed him, he saw Lou turn away and sink back down under the covers.

He closed the door softly and was about to make for the sofa when his stomach started grumbling and he noticed the cake on the stand.

What did Frankie say about that cake-stand? he wondered as he sidled up to the kitchen counter. The bloody thing was huge; surely she wouldn't miss a couple of slices. He used a surprisingly lifelike sugar-flower to scoop up some frosting, and popped the whole lot into his mouth, before scouring the kitchen for some milk and a knife.

~

Lou waited until she heard Dylan leave, and then sat up. After staring blankly at the collage on her wall for a minute, she quietly swung out of bed and padded to the door. She carefully turned the lock, and after she was sure it was secure she crept over to her wardrobe. Standing on the mountain of clothes that had accumulated in the bottom of it, she reached up and extracted a small, dog-eared shoebox from a high shelf, which she took back to bed.

Once she was sitting up with her legs under the covers she took off the lid and started delicately pulling out the tattered photographs, which she laid out around her. At the bottom of the box was a small pink and white shell. She turned it over and over in her hands for a few moments, before gripping it firmly in one of her fists, which she brought up to her chest. With her other hand she reached for one of the photos and traced the shape of the face dominating it with her index finger, before grabbing the pillow that Dylan had been sleeping on and bringing it up to her face.

She hugged the pillow and inhaled deeply, letting silent tears track down her cheeks. For the longest time she remained absolutely still except for the deep breaths she took from the pillow as her tears started to soak into the material. Her eyelids started drooping as the first light of dawn began to shine through her window, and she finally succumbed to sleep lying in the middle of her photos, holding the small pink shell, with her face buried in the pillow she was still clutching like her life depended on it.

*cwtch – CUDDLE / HUG

Chapter 2

A great shame

DESPITE THE FACT THAT THE GRAND ROUND WAS IN FULL swing, Lou didn't do the standard open-the-doors-just-a-crack-and-slope-through-to-find-an- inconspicuous-place-to-sit-in-the-lecture-theatre. No, in true Dr Sands fashion she burst through the double doors, and beamed her mega-watt smile at the audience, who had all turned away from the interminably dull Professor Henderson to watch her entrance.

Dylan sat back in his seat and rolled his eyes. If anyone had made an art out of drawing a room's attention it was Lou. He looked back at her as he heard her stage-whispered greetings to people either side of the aisle, as if she was walking down her own personal red carpet and greeting her fans.

She flounced down to the front on her sky-high heels, and he had to suppress a laugh as she grabbed a handout from the desk in front of the lectern, winked at the Prof, and in another obnoxiously loud stage whisper, said, 'Sooo sorry to have missed the start, Professor, you know how I *live by* the *crucial* content of your lectures.'

As normally happened to any male in receipt of the full Louise Sands charm offensive, the Prof's eyes became unfocused and he nodded his head dumbly. With her long blonde hair flowing down her back and around her face, and wearing one of her fitted business dresses, which showcased her endlessly long legs, she could probably have told the Prof he was the dullest man alive and still have received the same reaction. Spinning round on her heel, she strode back up to where Dylan was sitting, scowled at him until he was forced to make room for her, and sat down with a flourish of her handout and a dramatic hair flick, which succeeded in sending the handouts of the bench above flying in all directions.

'Quite finished?' Dylan mumbled in her ear, inhaling her fresh citrusy scent and closing his eyes briefly against the impact. In the weeks since he'd spent the night in Lou's bed, he'd felt like he was going slightly insane. Her scent, the way she spoke, her smile, her laugh, in fact everything about her turned him on. After years of regarding her beauty in a rather abstract way whilst he obsessed over Frankie, it was like the shutters had been violently pulled away from his eyes, and he now found it difficult to focus on anything else in her presence.

'What are you on about now, Dildo?' she hissed out of the side of her mouth whilst maintaining a perfect smile for the Prof and her fans.

'Are you quite finished prancing about like the main attraction at Stringfellows during a bloody clinical meeting?'

Lou rolled her eyes, relaxed back in her chair, and crossed her arms under her breasts. 'As if you're paying any attention. Go on; tell me one fact the Prof has imparted that I missed.'

Dylan knew that there was a question in there somewhere, and that he was likely meant to answer, but unfortunately his eyes had drifted down to the fabric now stretched across Lou's breasts, and he'd lost focus.

'Um ...' *Cach** – what had she just said? With a great deal of effort he managed to drag his eyes away from her chest, and forced himself to look at the Prof instead, willing the blood to rush away from the relevant areas so that he would be able to leave the lecture theatre without embarrassment.

'Exactly,' Lou put in smugly, apparently pleased that she had won her argument.

Dylan hated losing to Lou. Over the years they had fought some epic battles. In their third year of uni Lou and Frankie had a house party which got hopelessly out of hand, and Dylan had decided to turn Lou's room into a 'virtual surfing experience'. This mainly involved a succession of drunken people trying to balance on the edge of the bed in a surfing pose, whilst beer from shaken-up cans was sprayed in their faces. Even three years later there had still been beer splatters covering the ceiling.

Lou didn't say much at the time; she merely removed her knickers from their heads (another essential part of the surfing experience) and ordered them to leave. She waited two months for the perfect retaliation. Much to everyone's bemusement she spent a whole night at the bar flirting with Bernard (a well-known bed-swamper) and buying him beers. At the end of the night she steered a very much worse-for-wear Bernard out of the bar and took him back to the flat Dylan shared with Mike. Using the spare key the boys had given her for emergencies, she manoeuvered Bernard inside and managed to direct him to Dylan's bed before he passed out.

When Dylan stumbled home at two in the morning he was confronted by a urine-soaked bed, and an unconscious Bernard with the words 'I WIN' written across his forehead. Needless to say, the girl from his tutorial group, whom he'd finally convinced to come home with him, was less than impressed.

Dylan rolled his eyes and tried to focus on the Prof again, who still seemed to be slightly dazed.

'Where have you been anyway?' he whispered, irritated that

she always seemed to get the best of him, but more irritated by all the attention that he could still see was focused on her after that display.

This was another odd change he'd noticed in himself over the last few weeks. He had started resenting all the male eyes that fixated on Lou wherever she went. Yesterday their new medical student had spent the entire ward round panting after her, and Dylan had nearly broken the guy's foot when he'd 'accidentally' run him over with the heavy notes trolley.

Lou flicked him an odd look, sort of a mixture of annoyance and resignation. 'Where do you think I've been? Mrs Talbot's faecal impaction wasn't going to sort itself.'

'Oh right,' Dylan muttered, shifting uncomfortably in his seat.

He *might* have been a little distracted on the ward round, and *might* not have made a note of any of the jobs that needed doing. In his defence he was still stewing over the revision hip he was missing out on that morning after Mr Jowett had told him about it last night at the pub. He *might* also have sloped off subtly after the round to sneak into theatre so he could assist. After all, surely there wasn't anything so urgent to do for the grave-dodgers that it couldn't wait until after lunch?

Suddenly he started feeling a tad bit guilty. He remembered that Lou was actually interested in the Prof's lecture, seeing as she wanted to specialize in stroke medicine. He also remembered how much Lou loved the free lunch that always preceded the weekly Grand Round. He had noticed that she'd lost weight over the last few months. Even her slutty drug-rep-on-heat dresses, which he knew she deliberately bought at least one size too small, were beginning to hang off her slightly.

Now that he thought about it, he realized that Lou often had to skip lunch to sort out the wards so she could get to clinic in the afternoon. He frowned. Maybe he should have made a bit more of an effort – but it wasn't his fault he was being forced to suffer through six months of a specialty he had absolutely no interest in.

Then again, when he thought back to this morning, he remembered that Mrs Talbot had been pretty uncomfortable ... He shuddered: manually disimpacting a patient's bowel was not what he signed up for as an orthopaedic surgeon. Anyway, Lou was tough as old boots; a few extra jobs here and there wouldn't really faze her. He glanced down at his watch and wondered if he could slope off again to assist Mr Jowett that afternoon.

～

LOU FLEW THROUGH THE DOORS OF THE OUTPATIENT department and smacked straight into Dr Hudson. As both women were carrying a set of notes, this caused an explosion of paperwork all over the waiting area.

Well this is just bloody typical, Lou thought savagely. The one person that she couldn't afford to piss off was lying sprawled opposite her on the dirty linoleum, her legs akimbo and glasses slightly askew (although her grey helmet of hair was, as ever, completely immobile).

'Louise,' Dr Hudson said in a surprisingly unruffled voice, despite her compromised position on the floor, 'I'm grateful, of course, that you finally decided to grace us with your presence.' She performed an impressively graceful leap up onto her feet, and started brushing off the back of her skirt whilst peering down her nose at Lou. 'But maybe you could aim for a slightly less dramatic entrance. I know drama is your thing, but we *are* trying to get through an extremely busy clinic here.'

As always with Elaine Hudson, Lou was made to feel about two feet tall. The woman seemed to have the unique ability to completely squash all Lou's confidence with a single strategi-cally placed acidic comment.

'So, so sorry Dr Hudson,' Lou said in a voice laced with mortification, whilst she scrambled around on her hands and knees collecting together all the papers and patient notes they had both been carrying, and separating them into two piles.

'Well, as long as it's all hands on deck now and I haven't suffered any permanent damage to my coccyx,' Dr Hudson continued briskly, then narrowed her eyes at Lou, who was now making a far less graceful (considering the height of her heels) ascent to her feet. 'It *is* all hands on deck isn't it? Where's "The Orthopod"?'

Lou didn't think she'd ever heard Dr Hudson call Dylan anything other than 'The Orthopod', and even that seemed wrenched from her as if the knowledge that orthopaedic surgeons even existed, leave alone that one actually worked in the Elderly Care department, was abhorrent to her.

'He ... um ... he ...' Lou furiously tried to think of an excuse for Dylan's absence. 'There was a lot of ward work,' she finished helplessly, trying to smooth down her rucked-up skirt whilst balancing the notes on her hip.

Dr Hudson frowned. 'Between the two of you, you should have been able to sort the wards and both help with the clinic. You're pretty senior now, Louise, you should be upping your game. If you ever want to have a chance as a consultant you've got to be able to delegate.'

Lou blushed and glanced around at the packed waiting room. Just bloody brilliant: humiliated in front of all the patients she was about to see.

Dr Hudson swept away past the reception having made her point, leaving Lou to trail dutifully behind her carrying both sets of notes. Five months ago she would have never been late to clinic, never had to miss the Grand Round lunch, never had to cover for a selfish, arrogant, lazy, drop-dead gorgeous ... no!

No!

Lou frantically tried to push the image of a half-naked Dylan in her bed out of her mind, but she knew from bitter experience that once she was on a roll it was impossible to stop herself: Dylan hung-over in their flat with the blanket over his head, looking so unbelievable cute that she actually had to pinch her arm to stop herself from rushing him, pinning him down, and covering his stubbly, red-eyed face in small kisses; Dylan's laughter and twinkling eyes after she'd walked into the mess and asked for 'Mike Hunt' (the name he had falsified on her paperwork as the new medical student that was supposedly joining their team); Dylan gazing at Frankie, a look of such longing on his face and such uncharacteristic sadness in his eyes, that it actually made her heart hurt.

'Late again, Sands?' A smug, nasal voice penetrated Lou's consciousness. She gave a small start and nearly dropped all the notes again. 'Daydreaming too. Not really out to impress at the moment are you?'

'Miles,' she said through her teeth. Right, time to focus and get back in the game. No way was this prick getting the best of her today. 'What's crawled up your arse? Run out of flies to pull the wings off? Or are you just on your period again today?'

'Whatever,' Miles sneered, two flashes of colour appearing high on his cheekbones. 'At least I'm punctual. I've already seen my first patient.' Lou glanced down at the notes he was holding, and snorted. Cherry-picking little bastard.

'Yeah, that must have taken all of five minutes. Try to pick off the top of the pile why don't you,' she said dismissively, dumping down the notes on the central desk, then picking up the massive tome that was the next in line. 'New patient' was written on a post-it stuck on the front, and as she lifted it she realized in horror that it was only Volume One. She could hear Miles chuckle as she struggled into her room, but kept her head high and didn't look back.

The fact that they were direct competitors had already made for a strained relationship. But things only really deteriorated badly after Lou dumped a cocktail in his lap on a mess night out last year. In her defence she had not been in the mood to have her arse pinched or be told she'd been 'asking for it for ages' by a slobbering, drunk, deeply unpleasant Miles. She knew that Miles had an inflated opinion of himself, and it wasn't as though he was unattractive looks-wise; but with his smug, self-satisfied personality Lou would have rather snogged a Dementor.

She dumped all the notes down and slumped into her chair to fire up the computer. Her stomach rumbled, and to her frustration she felt her eyes start to fill with stupid tears. She rubbed her nose furiously and swallowed hard as she heard the door to her room creak open. Looking up, she saw Gwen hovering at the doorway with a cup of tea and a plate of biscuits. Once Gwen had taken in Lou's somewhat dishevelled appearance, not to mention the tears in her eyes, she bustled in, shoved the biscuits in front of Lou on the desk, put a comforting arm around her shoulders and pressed her head into her ample bosom.

'Don't you mind that old dragon now, cariad*,' Gwen soothed in her thick Welsh accent, having obviously heard Lou's exchange with Dr Hudson in the waiting room. 'Drink your tea and I'll send in Mr Griffiths now, in a minute.'

In Lou's experience 'now, in a minute' could mean anything from a few seconds to a whole week. She gave Gwen a small, watery smile and whispered a shaky 'thanks', focusing on her tea.

Unbeknownst to Lou, Gwen tilted her head to the side and hovered at the doorway for a moment. Gwen was far older than she had admitted to medical staffing, or anyone else for that matter. She should have retired years ago, but she loved her job. One of the things she loved most about it was people-watching. All her life the people around her had fascinated Gwen and she didn't think she had ever met a woman more radiant and full of life than Dr Louise Sands. So Gwen frowned as she saw Lou's shoulders slump slightly. Lately something or someone was taking the shine off Lou's sparkle, and that, Gwen thought, was a great shame.

*CACH – SHIT

   *cariad – *darling, sweetheart*

Chapter 3

'You're a twp bugger, but I like you'*

'WELL, IT'S RIDICULOUS, THAT'S WHAT IT IS,' MRS TALBOT said crossly, shifting on her plastic chair in irritation and clicking her tongue. Lou tipped her packet of Malteasers towards her again and Mrs Talbot wasted no time in grabbing a handful. 'Bus drivers these days; they should be hung up in the town square by their balls for making us wait so long.'

'I think that might be a bit harsh,' Lou said mildly around her Malteaser, feeling a fresh wave of sympathy for Mrs Talbot's husband, who had (as his daughter-in-law put it) 'found the sweet release of death' last year after enduring nearly seventy years of marital bliss. Although, since then, dementia seemed to have largely taken the wind out of her sails – so much so that Lou was actually quite heartened by the cantankerous, slightly bloodthirsty streak that was making an appearance again today, if only briefly.

'Hey,' Lou looked up at the sound of Frankie's quiet voice, and smiled. Frankie was wearing a glazed expression and sporting a particularly dreamy look in her eyes as she pulled up another plastic chair and sat next to Lou.

Hurrah! At last something in Lou's life was going to plan. It looked like the little pep talk she had given Weasel had actually worked, and he'd managed to pull Frankie's head out of her arse and make her realize how he felt about her.

With Tom and Frankie, what should have been 'boy meets girl, they fall in love and boy marries girl' was unfortunately a case of 'boy meets girl, girl pines for boy, boy unintentionally humiliates girl in grotty student bar, boy and girl are kept apart by a crazy Welshman who's in love with girl'.

It was Boxing Day, and Lou knew that Tom had practically kidnapped Frankie yesterday to spend the day with his family after Lou let it slip that she was alone in the flat.

'Sooo?' Lou drew out the word and smiled at Frankie. 'Seeing as you look like a junkie after a fix, and you didn't come home last night, I'm thinking that things with Weasel Gankface are back on.'

Frankie looked at her, pressed her lips together, and to Lou's horror her friend's eyes filled with tears.

'What's going on?' Tom was suddenly in front of both of them, his arms crossed around his chest, and he was frowning down at Frankie. Lou saw red, and flew up onto her feet.

'I told you what would happen to your meat and two veg if you hurt her, Weasel,' she said in a threatening tone, making a small lunge towards him. Much to Lou's satisfaction, his face paled and he took a step back, his hands flying to cover his groin. He then reached to pluck Frankie up off the chair and held her in front of him.

Lou relaxed when she heard Frankie giggle and saw that her eyes, although glistening with unshed tears, were still shining with happiness. The sight of a big man like Tom using petite Frankie as a shield was enough to break through Lou's anger, and she smiled. Frankie stepped forward, away from Tom, and wrapped Lou in a firm hug.

'I'm happy,' she whispered in her ear, and Lou gave her a

squeeze. Lou looked over Frankie's shoulder at Tom, who was watching Frankie like a lovesick puppy.

'Don't fuck it up,' she said to him, and he smiled. 'What are you even doing here today, Weasel? You're not on call.'

He scuffed his feet on the ground and threw her a sheepish grin. 'I drove Frankie in and then thought I'd check on a few patients, get a bit of paperwork done.' He shrugged, and Lou's face softened. She knew for a fact that Weasel hated paperwork and would never voluntarily do it, especially on Boxing Day. Her guess was that he just wanted to be where Frankie was; at least until it settled in that she had really come back to him.

Despite this, after Frankie had turned to go, Lou caught his eye, pointed two fingers at her own and then one at him. He smiled, but she was pretty sure there was a small flicker of fear there too.

Lou sat back down next to Mrs Talbot, who flicked her an annoyed look.

'All this commotion at the bus stop,' she said snottily. 'Most unseemly – and why is everyone standing and walking in the middle of the road?' She was starting to get agitated, and Lou sighed, putting her hand over Mrs Talbot's papery one.

'We're in the ward, remember, Mrs Talbot?' she said softly, turning towards her. Mrs Talbot's confused eyes were now looking frantically up and down the ward corridor at the patients and staff.

'Well, I ... I need to go home. Dennis will be at a complete loss.' Her words were shaking slightly and both her hands were gripping Lou's in a vice-like grip. 'I don't feel so well, dear,' she finished in a small voice.

'How about we go back to your bed?' Lou said briskly. 'Get you a nice cup of tea and some biscuits.' Mrs Talbot brightened as Lou led her through the ward and settled her with her tea, turning on the pay-per-view telly.

'Punctuality is just not your thing lately is it, Louise?' The crisp voice pulled Lou up short when she came back out onto the ward corridor. Ugh! She'd been early today, and had already spent half an hour pretending she was at a bloody bus stop whilst she waited for the round to start. Dr Hudson would have to arrive the moment she had left the main ward.

'I was –'

'Save me the excuses, Dr Sands, let's just crack on.' Of course it would have to be Dr Hudson on call today; it couldn't be her own, more laid-back consultant, Dr Morris. 'Where is "The Orthopod",' she said ominously.

'Someone call for an orthopod?' Dylan replied, as he strolled round the corner wearing a Father Christmas hat. He came to a stop in front of them, and, with a flourish, produced two reindeer-antler headbands from behind his back. 'Merry Christmas! I've brought in something to get us all in the spirit.'

Grinning, he shoved one down onto Lou's head. Then, to Lou's horror, he breached the perfection of Dr Hudson's grey helmet of hair with the other headband and unceremoniously adjusted it. Dr Hudson's face had turned an alarming shade of red with barely contained rage, but Dylan, who either didn't register this or didn't care, merely gave her a small shoulder bump and winked at her with a cheeky grin.

'See, aren't you feeling more festive already?' To Lou's surprise Dr Hudson relaxed her furious stance slightly and pressed her lips together as if she was holding back a smile. Very few females of any age were impervious to his charm, and, as ever, Dylan played on this ruthlessly.

'That's all well and good, Orthopod,' Dr Hudson said, rolling her eyes at the sheer audacity of his impertinence, 'but do you think we can be festive and still do the ward round?'

'Sure,' Dylan offered magnanimously. 'Lead the way, boss.'

There was an awkward pause and Lou looked up to the ceiling, seeking patience.

'I think you'll find that that is your job, young man,' Dr Hudson finally said, and then turned to Lou. 'Seeing as "The Orthopod" has turned up empty-handed, other than novelty items, I'm hoping that you have a patient list underneath that magazine.' Lou glanced down at her copy of *Hello* and cringed; the ward round was turning into a complete disaster and they hadn't even seen a single patient yet.

'It's not for –' Lou started, gesturing at the magazine, but was cut off by Dr Hudson.

'Didn't I already say I wasn't interested in excuses?' she said sharply. Dylan shifted next to Lou uncomfortably and shot her an apologetic look. Lou closed her eyes for a moment in frustration: he knew he was supposed to print the list. It was about the only job she actually entrusted to him. Would it be so hard just to do his job and help her for once? She understood that he hated Elderly Care, or, rather, hated anything that didn't involve his hammer and power tools, but couldn't he make the slightest bit of effort? They were friends after all, and this might not have been his chosen career but it was hers.

Dylan's happiness *mattered* to her, weirdly almost as much as her own. It was galling to realize that he couldn't even muster enough concern for her to arrive five minutes early and print the bloody list out.

After an embarrassing wait whilst the ward computer took the requisite five hundred years to splutter to life and produce a list of patients, they started the ward round. Lou's irritation was gradually ratcheting up, as by the fifth patient she realized that Dylan's idea of note-taking today appeared to consist of the date, an odd word or two (one entry merely read 'poorly'), and his scrawled signature.

The referral cards he was filling out weren't much better,

with the clinical information on a gastroenterology referral consisting of 'dodgy tum'. And he was smirking as if it was all a huge joke as Lou ran around like a blue-arsed fly sorting everything out. Unfortunately this meant she missed loads of what Dr Hudson was saying and kept having to make her repeat herself (something it was clear that Elaine Hudson did not enjoy doing).

By the time they made it to the last two patients, Lou was completely frazzled. Mrs Jones had finally been decontaminated of MRSA and was on the ward next to Mrs Talbot. The two of them had been having a great time, seeming to have found a kindred spirit in each other as far as their general disdain for the staff went (there was much dark muttering about 'illegal immigrants'; they even referred to the New Zealand F2 working on the ward as 'that one from the colonies'), and the level of cleanliness, and above all the food.

Lou managed to shoot ahead slightly and slip Mrs Jones the copy of *Hello* she'd been carting round with her. This particular issue had an interview with Kylie Minogue that Lou knew Mrs Jones would love. When she was moved onto the ward, Mrs Jones made it clear that her ancient telly and video player were coming with her so she could continue to watch *Neighbours* circa 1980s on repeat. Her eyes lit up when she saw Kylie's face beaming from the front page, and she snatched the magazine from Lou, but not without giving her an uncharacteristic small smile.

'Finally a ffwcin* grown-up I can speak to.' Lou looked up sharply to see a large red-faced man barrelling towards them through the four-bed bay. She sighed, recognizing him as Mrs Talbot's son. His rather meek, reed-thin, brow-beaten wife was trailing behind him. 'I've been trying to see the top dog here for two bloody weeks but all I get are these pathetic minions,' he continued, gesturing to Lou and Dylan. 'I want to know how the hell you lot think we can pay for carers to come in?'

'Mr Talbot, I'm sorry but I already explained to you that as clinicians we have no influence over –'

'Zip it, you dumb ast*!' He threw out his hand towards Lou, but before he could connect she felt herself shifted back behind Dylan's big frame. Lou could literally feel the menace radiating from Dylan's body as he leaned into Mr Talbot's space. She was guessing that 'ast' was Welsh for something none too nice, and, with the way he said it, she thought she could take a good stab at the translation. The change from Dylan's usual persona as the standard relaxed, carefree joker was stark. Despite the other man's size he was no match for Dylan, who towered over him, his Welsh accent thickening in his anger.

'Cau dy ffwcin ceg*!' Dylan barked, and Lou noticed both Mrs Jones and Mrs Talbot suck in shocked breaths. His Welsh probably wasn't S4C pre-watershed material either. Mr Talbot shut his mouth and paled, having only belatedly registered the level of Dylan's anger.

Dylan leaned into Mr Talbot and started talking quietly, still in Welsh. Lou couldn't decipher any of the words, but she caught the flash of fear in Mr Talbot's eyes. After Dylan had finished, Mr Talbot beat a hasty retreat, dragging his mortified wife behind him. Dylan shifted back to easygoing as soon as Mr Talbot had rounded the corner, and smiled at Dr Hudson.

'He's decided that he'll make an appointment to discuss things another time,' he said casually, totally unruffled by the experience, whereas Lou could feel herself shaking. Dr Hudson sighed.

'Well, it's good to see that you're keeping the patients' families on side, Dr Sands,' she said sarcastically, and turned to Dylan. 'I know that some people may consider orthopaedic surgeons to be somewhat lower on the evolutionary scale; even so, I would advise that you handle potentially volatile situations with rather less Welsh obscenity and male posturing, and rather more restrained behaviour and hospital security.' Dylan shrugged. Dr Hudson rolled her eyes and went back to Mrs Talbot to listen to her chest. Mrs Talbot, however, was looking at Dylan like he'd hung the moon. She was obviously not her son's biggest fan. Ignoring Dr Hudson, she leaned forward in her bed and pulled Dylan down to her level, grabbing his face in both her hands.

'You're a twp* bugger,' she said loudly, 'but I like you.' She gave both his cheeks a couple of forceful pats before pushing him away. Dr Hudson went to start examining her again, but she shooed her away.

'Tea! Custard creams!' Mrs Talbot cried dramatically. 'What kind of hellhole is this place? Are we all to be starved to death?' Lou eyed Mrs Talbot's tea, which was only half finished and still steaming slightly, and the crumbs on her plate, and rolled her eyes.

*ast – *Bitch*
*Cau dy ffwcin ceg! – *shut your fucking mouth*
*ffwcin – *fucking*
*twp – *stupid, simple-minded*

Chapter 4

Bittersweet

Dylan heard himself growl, and jerked in surprise. What kind of freak stood around bloody growling at a New Year's Eve party? He didn't think he'd ever growled before in his life. Ash was looking at him as though he'd grown an extra head, and Dylan didn't blame him.

They'd been happily talking about the arthroscopic rotator cuff repair Dylan had managed to skive off to assist Mr Trompeter with (well, Dylan had been happy, although Ash's glazed expression may have hinted that he didn't find the conversation quite as riveting) when Dylan had caught sight of Lou talking to Richard-Slimeball-Morris. Her head was thrown back with laughter, and she had her hand resting on his chest. Rich was loving it – the creepy git – and Dylan could swear that he'd seen him smell her hair. The fact that watching Lou and Rich engaged in some seriously vomit-inducing verbal foreplay had actually made him growl was another indication that, as far as Lou was concerned, Dylan was losing his ever-loving mind.

'Kiss me,' Dylan heard Lou's voice whisper in his head, and his mind flashed to a vision of her face: lips parted, cheeks

flushed, beautiful blue eyes staring up at him with a look of such longing that he felt his chest constrict painfully.

'Goddamn it,' he muttered savagely, shaking his head to clear it of the image, and no doubt further freaking poor Ash out.

'You alright?' a confused Ash asked carefully. Dylan tore his eyes away from Lou as he heard another peal of her laughter ring through the living room.

Yet another image flashed into his mind: this time she was laughing into a pillow hysterically before turning back to him, framing his face with her hands, and saying through a wide, gorgeous smile, '*This* is why.'

'Why what?' he'd asked.

She'd searched his face for a moment before looking into his eyes and whispering, 'Why it was always you. Always.'

Christ, what the hell was wrong with him? The weird dreams he'd been having about Lou had started invading his consciousness during the day. It was just glimpses of her face as she lay in bed with him, and snatches of conversation. It felt like there was something his mind was reaching for but never quite getting to, and it was driving him nuts.

Ash looked back over his shoulder in the direction of Dylan's gaze, then the crazy bastard turned back to Dylan and smiled like a lunatic.

' "Love is blind but jealousy has 20-20 vision," ' he told him.

Dylan rolled his eyes, 'Okay, tell me that you did not just proverb me, you weirdo.' Ash shrugged and continued his freaky smiling.

'I like you crazy Welshmen and your strange courting rituals. It amuses me. I'm glad that you and Lou are going to provide me with entertainment now that Tom and Frankie have finally succumbed to the inevitable.'

They looked over at Tom and Frankie. Frankie was talking

to one of Tom's buddies, Stuart. Tom was standing behind her with his arms locked around her waist. Dylan didn't think he'd seen them more than a foot apart all evening.

Although it was so cutesy that it made Dylan vomit in his mouth a little, he was still glad that it had worked out for them. The gut-churning guilt of what he'd done at uni to keep them apart had kept him up at night since Frankie had moved here, and at least now it was all out in the open. As he looked at Frankie he realized that even though he felt drawn to her, it wasn't with the sharp, bittersweet yearning and intensity that it had been back then. He couldn't say when he'd stopped feeling that overwhelming attraction to her, but now the only pull she seemed to have was as his best friend.

'*Please stay with me.*' Lou's face and her whispered voice flashed into his mind again. Frustrated, Dylan brought the heels of his hands to his eyes and pressed in, trying to rid himself of the unwanted image. He was definitely losing it. Growling again, he grabbed the bottle of tequila next to him on the kitchen counter. The only receptacle he could find was a wineglass, so he poured in a good measure and slammed it back.

When he'd put the glass back down and was feeling the burn in his throat, he looked over towards the living room again and was satisfied to see a slightly disgruntled Rich standing on his own. He followed the direction of Rich's gaze to see an overexcited Lou jumping up and down on her sky high FMBs and trying to extract a reluctant Frankie from Tom's arms. Dylan listened to the sound system for a moment and realized that Lou must have slyly changed the music. 'Backstreet's Back' was now blaring out; she was always a cheese monster.

He was about to smile at her ridiculous antics, when he realized that every bloke in the room was also staring at her in fascination. In typical Lou fashion she was not wearing casual clothing appropriate for a house party. No, she had decided to wear a skintight, short, backless, red lace dress that left very little to the imagination, especially whilst she was bouncing all over the place. Shaking his head in disgust at the bloody cheek of all of them ogling his Lou ... Wait ... What? ... He reached for the tequila bottle again. What was going on? Since when was she *his* Lou? Men had been staring at Lou and her assets for all the years he'd known her, and he'd never had the urge to punch a wall before.

Lou seemed to realize that she wasn't going to win against Tom, and released Frankie huffily. Dylan watched as she spun out onto the makeshift dance floor in the centre of the living room, and started doing what she always did: dance like a psychotic (but sexy) stripper. He saw Rich push off from the wall and start to move towards her, and his control snapped. There was no way he was going to be able to stand by and watch whilst Rich danced with, and likely mauled, Lou. Dylan slammed back another shot and pushed past a bemused-looking Ash, striding over to catch Lou up in his arms just as she was executing a particularly raunchy but bizarre squatting-stripper move.

'Omph!' she exclaimed as she was hauled up against Dylan's chest. 'What the hell are you doing, you freak? You're inter-rupting my flow.'

'Babes, you do know that this is a house party and not Stringfellows?'

She rolled her eyes. 'You're just jealous of my sick moves.'

Dylan stifled a laugh. Lou was renowned for her insane dancing. Typical reactions were shock, confusion and possibly arousal (for the men and maybe even some of the women), but he didn't think jealousy featured that often.

As she tried to pull away Dylan pulled her closer and whis-pered in her ear, 'Come on, babes, stop being chopsy. Dance with me.' Lou rolled her eyes again, but he could see the small smile that was tugging at her lips as she started swaying in sync with him.

When he could feel that she had given in, he spun her out, twirled her a couple of times and pulled her back in. Lou and Dylan had many years experience dancing together. In their second year of uni he had convinced her to learn salsa with him at a bar in central London. Things were not progressing at all with Frankie, and he had decided that the way forward was lots of meaningless sex. In his nineteen-year-old brain he equated being able to dance with scoring more chicks – and he was right. He was surprised that Lou had agreed quite so readily to learn with him, but it had turned out to be a stroke of genius on his part. They always just clicked when dancing, and he could throw her around effortlessly to great dramatic effect. Back in uni he'd used their prowess on the dance floor to reel in girls he had his eye on. Turned out that seeing him dance confidently with a beautiful woman was a huge turn-on to others, and Lou didn't seem to mind.

∾

Lou let out a hysterical giggle as Dylan spun her faster and faster, and then pulled her back in against his chest. She took a big breath in to inhale his unique, clean scent. When they danced like this she could almost pretend that he was really hers; that they were made for each other. Over the years their moves had become so honed that the dance itself barely required any conscious thought at all. Lou had learnt simply to appreciate the time she was allowed to be held close to him, and shut everything else out (like the fact that there was usually some other willing woman waiting in the wings that Dylan was trying to impress).

She was used to the bittersweet thrill of being spun around

and ultimately pulled back in against his huge frame, and the amazing feeling of his breath against her face as he dipped her down practically to the floor. Unfortunately she was also used to the stinging disappointment when the dance was over and she lost his warm, strong body against hers. Then had to watch from the sidelines whilst he moved in on the unwitting female whom he'd made sure had had a front-row seat to the proceedings. Lou had always smiled through the pain, sometimes even giving him a cheeky wink and wishing him luck whilst her heart felt like it was breaking inside her chest.

As Lou landed on her feet after their well-practised finale of 'the lift' straight out of dirty dancing, and applause from the onlookers that had congregated around the outskirts of the living room, Lou steeled herself to plaster on a smile and act casual when Dylan made his inevitable, swift retreat. However, when she didn't lose the warmth of his body against hers, she looked up into his eyes and was confused by the weird, intense way he was staring at her. The applause faded but Dylan still held her close to him and searched her face, tucking a lock of hair that had fallen in front of her eyes behind her ear.

The music changed and he seemed to register where they were. He grabbed her hand and pulled her out of the living room as couples piled onto the dance floor. Once out of the room, Dylan led her into a relatively quiet corridor and turned to face her, looking even more confused than Lou felt.

He tore his hands through his hair, then paced away only to pace right back into her personal space. 'Lou, I ...' Lou frowned at him: he never called her by her first name. '... I ...' He was staring at her mouth. Her lips were parted and she was still panting slightly from the exertion of the dance, her chest rising and falling rapidly. His gaze dropped to her chest, then returned to her mouth before settling on her eyes. She watched as another wave of confusion swept over his gorgeous face; then he reached out and cupped her jaw with his hand, smoothing her pink cheek with his thumb.

Her eyes flared wide as she realized what was about to happen, but she was too late to question it as he crowded her back against the wall, slid his other hand up to the other side of her jaw, and kissed her.

In the back of her mind Lou could hear the faint voice telling her that this was a supremely bad idea, but with his big hands cupping her face, his lips on hers and his scent surrounding her, she found it impossible to be anything other than an avid participant in the proceedings. Seconds ticked by with Lou's heart in her throat as she kissed him back. When they finally broke apart they were both breathing heavily, their foreheads resting against each other.

'Thawasmazin,' Dylan slurred, and suddenly Lou registered the smell of tequila on his breath. Her belly hollowed and her heart sank into her boots. She wrenched her head away from his grip, hitting the back of it on the wall behind, and wriggled out to the side to step away from him.

The thud of Lou's head on the plasterboard seemed to sober Dylan somewhat. 'Shit, babes, you okay?'

And now she was back to babes.

Of course.

~

'You're drunk,' Lou said flatly, backing away further from him, and his brows drew together.

'Well it *is* New Year's Eve, babes,' he replied, his voice laced with confusion. What was wrong with him being drunk? Just then, a movement from the stairs caught Dylan's eye. He swung round to be confronted by a curious little face peeking through the banisters next to them.

'Hi,' Benji chirped cheerfully, apparently unconcerned that he'd been caught spying on them. 'What were you guys doing?'

Dylan closed his eyes in frustration at the interruption, and when he opened them Benji was still looking straight at him, his eyebrows raised imperiously as if demanding an answer. Dylan had come across Tom's nephew a few times now, and to say the five-year-old was a loose cannon was an understatement.

'We were ... um ... talking,' Dylan said evasively. 'Shouldn't you be in bed?'

'You weren't talking a minute ago,' Benji said, narrowing his eyes, 'and you were both making funny noises.' Dylan ground his teeth, wondering why, at midnight on New Year's Eve, he was being given the third degree by a kindergartener.

'Well?' Benji asked, lifting his eyebrows again.

'I'm going to go and get your mum and dad,' Dylan replied, feeling that this particular conversation had gone far enough.

'Okay,' Benji said nonchalantly, his too-intelligent eyes lighting with amusement, and a smug smile on his face. Dylan was about to turn back into the living room to find Rob and Sarah so they could put the little shit to bed; but at the sound of Benji's easy agreement, he paused.

~

BENJI WATCHED AS DYLAN SWUNG BACK TO FACE HIM. *HA! Now he's getting it*, he thought. If there was one thing Benji knew it was when adults were trying to hide something. He was guessing that Dylan would not want Mummy and Daddy to know that he had been cuddling Lou against the wall and making funny noises. Gathering information was one of Benji's specialties – as was negotiation.

'Benji, how about we keep all this between ourselves for now?'

Benji bit his lip to stop himself smiling: this was working out fantastically. '*Well* ...' he started, pretending to consider his options, 'I guess I *could* keep it a secret.'

'Great,' Dylan smiled at him. 'Well, no need to get your mum and dad then. Off you go to bed, I'll just ...' Benji watched as Dylan looked up and down the corridor, obviously not having noticed that Lou had left ages ago. Benji had noticed; but then there weren't many things that Benji missed.

'Keeping secrets makes me a bit hungry though,' Benji told Dylan, who had been starting to slope away. Dylan turned to face him again with a resigned look on his face.

'Just tell me what you want, Benji.'

'A bowl of those profiteroles I saw Mummy making with Auntie Frankie earlier, a Mars bar (Uncle Tom keeps a secret supply in the top left cupboard in the kitchen) and a can of coke (but not that yucky diet stuff Auntie Frankie drinks).' Dylan stared at him for a minute then looked up to the ceiling.

'Anything else?' he asked sarcastically.

Benji considered this for a moment. 'Throw in a bag of Haribo and we'll call it quits,' he said magnanimously.

'Fine,' Dylan bit out.

Benji smirked and leaned back against the stairs, happy with his victory. He had a feeling that if he kept a close eye on Lou and Dylan in the future, he might do pretty well for himself.

Chapter 5

Friends can kiss

LOU WAS BLESSED. SHE HAD AN AMAZING ABILITY, WHICH was widely admired throughout her time at medical school: she never, ever suffered with hangovers. This was indeed a blessing – but it could also be a curse. There were drawbacks to being the only functioning person the morning after the night before. One of the biggest was putting up with a load of hung-over zombies who seemed incapable of even making themselves cups of tea.

Now, Lou herself was a doer. She almost never sat around feeling sorry for herself (in fact the only times she really gave into self-pity was during her pining sessions for Dylan) and she certainly was not given to wasting whole days lying about channel-surfing in a onesie, sucking back fat Cokes and munching on crisps. Therefore it had always been in her best interests to attempt to revive her hung-over friends so they would be jump-started for the day.

As everyone knows, the best way to jumpstart hung-over people is with grease and stodge, and over the years Lou became renowned for her cooked breakfasts. So, despite the crying she had done the night before after sneaking out of the party and walking back to the flat alone, she'd woken up early and got to work on breakfast.

The front door slammed just as she was pulling a huge tray of sausages out of the oven, causing her to lose her grip for a second. Hot shooting pain went up her forearm as the tray clattered to the floor, together with the glass lid, which shattered on the tiles.

'Argh!' She jumped up clutching her forearm and looking down at the angry red weal that had already started to form. Lifting her foot cautiously, she tried to find a way through the sausages and broken glass that surrounded her. Just as she was about to attempt a leap to safety, she heard heavy shoes crunching through the glass, and turned her head in shock to see Dylan standing behind her.

He looked around at the destruction, then at her arm. 'I think the phrase rhymes with "clucking bell".' Even though he was the last person she wanted to see and her arm was throbbing uncontrollably, Lou still cracked a small smile.

'*Blackadder Goes Forth.*'

'Episode?' he asked as his large hands landed on both sides of her hips. She sucked in a huge breath, and then stopped breathing all together as he lifted her clean off her feet and into the air. He deposited her in front of the sink, away from any of the detritus, turned on the cold tap, and held her arm under running water.

'Babes?' he breathed.

One of his big hands was cupping her elbow and the other was holding hers to keep her forearm outstretched under the water. Lou shivered even though the water wasn't yet that cold.

' "Goodbyee",' she said finally, after pulling herself and her thoughts together.

'What?' Dylan's mouth was touching her temple as he stood behind her, and she could swear she felt his nose nuzzle her hair. She was suddenly very aware of how little she was wearing. Frankie might like to wear huge T-shirts (most of these used to be filched from Dylan, but Lou had noticed with some amusement that Tom had carefully replaced them all with his own) and tracky bums to bed, but Lou was a satin-and-lace kind of a girl. Dylan had always joked that she looked like some sort of burlesque queen about to put on a show rather than about to go to sleep, but now, with just her small, thin satin shorts and lacy vest top on, and Dylan's big body pressing her against the counter, it didn't seem so funny any more.

'Oh no!' Lou and Dylan both jumped as they heard Frankie's voice from across the flat. Then Lou felt the sudden cold at her back as Dylan stepped back and dropped her arm. 'What are you doing here?' Frankie continued, her voice still croaky from sleep. 'If you've touched that ruddy cake I'll –'

'Relax, Ladies,' Dylan said, seeming completely composed. (Neither Lou nor Frankie, to Lou's knowledge, had ever found out why Dylan called Frankie 'Ladies'; they could only assume it was a Welsh thing) 'I'm well aware of your complicated cake rules.'

'One rule, Dylan. *One rule*: don't eat the blinking cakes.'

Lou had been focusing on the water still running out of the tap and trying to control her breathing throughout this exchange. The pain in her arm had eased to a dull throb, but she could still feel the heat in her cheeks. Not much could make Louise Sands blush. She needed to get it together before she turned around, or Frankie would smell a rat.

'Oh my goodness me!' Frankie exclaimed, and Lou risked a look at her over her shoulder. Frankie had moved around the counter into the kitchen area and was staring at the glass and sausages on the floor. 'Jeepers creepers, Louey. You okay?'

Lou took in Frankie's rumpled appearance: one side of her dark hair was flat, the other looked as though it had been backcombed vigorously; she was wearing one of Tom's huge T-shirts, and ugly tartan pyjama bottoms; her eyes were bloodshot and she had no makeup on; and yet she looked, as always, completely adorable. She loved Frankie to pieces, but felt a familiar clench in her chest when she thought of how the only person she had ever really wanted preferred dark, natural and cute, to blonde, over-the-top and outrageous. Preferred someone who would say 'jeepers creepers' and 'goodness me' rather than a girl who swore like a sailor most of the time.

'What's all the goddamn shouting about?' Tom looked about as worse for wear as Frankie. He was basically wearing the same outfit as her, the only difference being that the T-shirt was stretched across his broad chest rather than falling down to his knees, and he hadn't had to fold the bottoms of the pajamas up several times. 'Jesus, Frankie, get away from the kitchen. Your feet will get ripped to shreds,' he barked as he rounded the corner.

Lou rolled her eyes. Frankie's feet were nowhere near the glass, but she knew Mr Overprotective wouldn't be happy until she was well away, preferably in another room, in case her precious feet should –

'Babes! Do not fucking move,' barked Dylan, just as Lou lifted her foot again to step away from the sink. She started, and her foot came down on a rogue shard of glass

'Bollocks!' Balancing on one foot, Lou was about to grab the other when she found herself lifted clean off her feet again and deposited on the kitchen counter, with a frowning Dylan inspecting the cut as though it were a potentially mortal wound.

'Frankie, get the first-aid kit,' he ordered.

'Oh for Christ's sake.' Lou attempted to grab back her foot

but Dylan kept a firm hold of it with both hands. 'It's probably just a little nick.'

'Well, as the only surgeon here,' Dylan said, causing Lou to look up at the ceiling, seeking patience, 'I think we should let me be the judge of that.' When Lou looked back down she could see Tom watching them closely. As she caught his eye a slow smile spread over his face, which only became wider with her answering scowl.

~

DYLAN LOOKED UP FROM HIS HUGE BOWL OF BACON AND eggs (Lou made the best scrambled eggs on the planet, something about adding some sort of fancy cheese) when he heard a loud crash against the door of the flat. After he had cleaned and dressed Lou's foot and Tom had swept up the glass, she had insisted on getting back to making breakfast.

Dylan himself thought that she should be off her foot, which she'd bloody well ripped open, but apparently he was making a 'ridiculous fuss'. She barely even let him clean and dress it (okay, so the bulky bandage he'd put on might have been overkill, but you couldn't be too careful), so there was no way she was going to be confined to the sofa. He had managed to get her to wear slippers, and was relieved when she put on a dressing gown as well; he wasn't sure how much more of her body on display in those ludicrously tiny pajamas he could take.

There was another crash at the door, and Frankie jumped down from the stool she was perched on at the breakfast bar to hurry across the room. As she opened the door three blond children fell through it onto the welcome mat. Fortunately Finlay, who was only two, was on the top of the pile, with the two older boys, Benji and Jack, underneath.

'I told you not to try to bulldoze the door,' Jack shouted at

Benji whilst scrambling to his feet. When Benji managed to get to his, Jack gave him a hard shove. 'You can't break down a door anyway, you're too small.'

'I am *not* too small,' Benji shouted back, giving Jack an equally hard shove. 'I'm big and strong like Mummy says.'

'You're so stupid. Mummy only says that to make you eat your broccoli and you fall for it every time 'cause you're stupid, stupid, STUPID.'

Benji stood stock still for a moment, his face screwed up and turning an alarming shade of red, before he pounced on his older brother. Finlay, who Dylan knew was partial to some rough-and-tumble, was delighted by this turn of events, and started jumping up and down and clapping, before launching himself head first into the fray. Frankie was dancing round the writhing tangle of boys, looking slightly lost. Tom, well used to his nephews' antics, carried on eating his eggs, completely unconcerned.

'Finlay, cuddle?' Lou called from the kitchen counter. Finlay's little blond head poked up from the mass of flying limbs, and after seeing Lou he scrambled to his feet, scampered across the living room, and barrelled straight into her legs shouting, 'Cuccol! Cuccol!'

Lou jumped off her stool and Dylan noticed her wince as her foot hit the ground. Christ, she was stubborn. Would it have killed her to put her feet up on the sofa for a couple of hours? At least then the wound could dry and have some chance of healing. He watched as she scooped Finlay up, nuzzled his hair, and, much to Finlay's delight, blew a raspberry into his neck.

'Eppa ig,' Finlay demanded through his giggles.

'Don't you dare, Lou,' Tom warned, his mouth still full of eggs. Finlay squirmed in Lou's arms until she let him down. He then proceeded to push her legs in the direction of the sofa.

'Eppa ig, cuccol, loc-loc.'

Before Tom could stop them, Lou and Finlay were cuddled up on the sofa, with Finlay happily munching on a Malteaser, and Peppa Pig on the telly. A long-overdue Sarah, with baby Thomas strapped to her front, came barrelling in just after they'd got settled. She stepped over Benji and Jack, who were still rolling around on the floor, without even sparing them a glance and moved in to give Frankie a warm hug with baby Thomas squished between them.

'I tried to –' Frankie started, indicating towards the boys, and Sarah shook her head.

'Best just to let them roll around for a while, I find,' she said briskly. 'Just have to make sure there's no –' she lifted the tall lamp near the door, putting it a safe distance away just before the boys were about to careen into it '– breakables in their way,' she finished.

'Hey, boys, lovely Lou.' She smiled as she surveyed the scene on the sofa. 'Spoiling the cute one again, I see. Oooh! Eggs.' She moved to the counter and grabbed Tom's fork off him. He made a low, feral-sounding growl in the back of his throat and attempted to shield his plate (Lou's eggs were just that good), but Sarah had the advantage of a baby strapped to her front, and short of elbowing a newborn in the face, there wasn't much Tom could do as she stole his food.

'Don't worry,' Lou chirped from the sofa, 'I'll make more for you and the boys, honey.' Finlay gave a mewl of protest as Lou shifted, preparing to stand. Dylan had no doubt that she planned on cooking another round of breakfasts, on her feet and with a toddler attached to her hip just for extra weight through her legs.

'Sit down,' he growled. 'I'll make them. Stay on the bloody sofa, you stubborn woman.' Everyone turned their shocked eyes to him. Even the boys stopped scrapping on the floor.

'You're going to cook?' Sarah asked, her eyebrows practically in her hairline.

'Yes,' he said, throwing out his arm in frustration, 'I'm going to cook; you and the maniacs are going to eat. What is *not* going to happen is Lou standing any longer on her *goddamn foot*. Got it?'

Dylan started clattering with various saucepans, not entirely sure how to approach this particular challenge. He could see everyone exchanging confused, curious looks out of the corner of his eye, but he chose to ignore it.

Just as he was about to serve some rather worse-for-wear eggs and burnt bacon, he felt a tugging at his trousers. He looked down to see Benji's small, intelligent face peering up at him.

'Do you look after Louey?' he asked. Everyone else was engaged in a lively *X-Factor* debate, which Dylan had been heartily glad to avoid, so this conversation was relatively private.

'What do you mean, squirt?'

Benji sighed with impatience, 'Mummy and Daddy look after Jack, Finlay, Thomas and me, and each other. Uncle Tom looks after Frankie, and she looks after him. I look after Stanley —'

'Who's Stanley?'

'My lizard.'

'Right, of course.'

'Well?' Benji prompted.

'Well what?'

Benji huffed again, squinting up at Dylan with an impatient frown, 'Do you look after Louey?'

'Look, Benji.' Dylan was raking his brain for a good explanation. 'She's my friend, so yes, I do look after her ... sometimes.'

'But not all the time?'

'No.'

Unfortunately Benji was not that easily put off. 'If you're her friend then why did you kiss her?'

This kid was like some kind of bloodhound. They should use him to question terror suspects; he'd crack them in no time.

'Friends can kiss,' Dylan told Benji.

'Not like you kissed Louey they don't. I know 'cause Annabelle Evans kissed me on the lips at school during kiss-chase, and everyone said that made her my girlfriend.' Benji's nose was crinkled in disgust; clearly this turn of events was not welcome.

'Lou's not my girlfriend, Benji.' Dylan could feel his patience slipping at this increasingly bizarre conversation, and the hollow feeling he had at this denial wasn't helping. Benji crossed his arms over his small but puffed-up chest.

'Just so you know,' he told Dylan. 'I've decided to marry Louey when I grow up. She's funny, she makes great eggs, she reads great stories, and she tickles really well.'

'Okay,' Dylan said slowly, fighting a smile. Benji's criteria for a wife might not be that extensive but Dylan thought he'd got a lot of the important stuff covered. 'Don't worry, little man, I won't stand in your way.'

Benji narrowed his eyes at him.

'So if I was to tell Mummy and Auntie Frankie about you kissing Louey ...'

Dylan sighed. 'What do you want kid?'

'Well, there *was* this new Hot Wheels track ...' The boy looked up at Dylan expectantly.

'Fine,' Dylan snapped, digging in his pocket and producing a pound coin. Benji looked at Dylan's extended hand with disgust.

'That wouldn't even buy a Hot Wheels *car*.'

Dylan huffed and fished out a tenner, but Benji just lifted one eyebrow (how a kid of five could pull off an eyebrow raise,

Dylan had no idea) and kept his arms crossed across his chest. Dylan swore under his breath and managed to find a second tenner in his wallet. Benji lowered his eyebrow, snatched both tenners out of Dylan's hand, and, after throwing him a supremely smug look, sauntered out of the kitchen to settle in next to his future wife on the sofa.

Chapter 6

Vicious

Lou looked across the conference room and smiled at Rich. He returned her smile very briefly with a tight one of his own, then quickly looked away. Well, that was just brilliant: she'd managed to piss off one of the nicest, most laid-back men she'd ever met.

They had both been dancing around the issue for weeks, with Rich making it clear that he was interested, and Lou responding to his flirting but never really letting it get any further. Before, there was always the old fallback of the fact that he was her boss as an excuse, but she had known that things were probably going to come to a head at the New Year's Eve party. Come January 3rd she would rotate to Dr Hudson's team, and so in Rich's eyes that path was relatively clear.

Lou had been sort of looking forward to taking things further with him, and had been trying to psyche herself up for exactly that over the last week. But when it came down to it, and the time came to actually bite the bullet and let him kiss her, she just couldn't do it.

She didn't understand why on earth he didn't float her boat. Objectively she could see that he was attractive, with his lean frame clad in a tailored suit, sandy, perfectly styled hair and deep blue eyes. But when she looked at him she felt ... nothing. He was good-looking, polite, respectful, and, most importantly, actually interested in her. In theory all of this should have been preferable to gorgeous but scruffy, cheeky, relentlessly teasing, and only interested in her when he was completely blotto; but when Lou tried to focus on Rich's attributes all she could think of was green eyes, dark hair, a far more built frame, and a mischievous smile.

She sighed as she tried to re-engage with the subject of the meeting. Trainees, was it?

'So that's why we've brought you all here today,' Dr Hudson was saying to Lou and the other registrars. 'I know it sounds a little harsh, but under the circumstances we all agreed in the consultants' meeting that there was little other choice. Unfortunately "The Orthopod" has behaved abysmally for the entire six months and –'

'What?' Lou interrupted frantically. What had she missed? Was Dylan in trouble?

'Do try to keep up, Sands,' Miles said smugly. 'They're trying to get your mate chucked off the training scheme.'

Lou's face paled and she started to feel a little sick. Chuck him off the scheme? For the first time she noticed a couple of orthopaedic consultants, Mr Kent and Mr Aird, sitting at the end of the table. Normally this meeting was just for medical consultants and registrars.

'In this instance an example needs to be made,' Dr Hudson put in. 'We can't have these arrogant orthopaedic surgeons waltzing in, disrupting the department and taking absolutely no interest whatsoever in anything not involving hammers and power tools. That is not the point of the joint training scheme.'

'No.' Lou was gripping the table in front of her and had half risen out of her seat. When she realized that all eyes in the conference room had swung to her, she sat back down heavily and felt her face flame. 'Um ... what I mean is ...' She thought frantically to try and come up with something, anything, to get Dylan out of trouble. He couldn't get kicked off the rotation: orthopaedics was his dream.

'He's made more effort than you think,' she went on, taking one of her hands off the table to cross her fingers on her lap. 'And ... and the patients love him.' At least that much was true. Dylan had charmed the socks off everyone, from patients to nurses and physios (bar a couple of bitter ones, having been given the morning-after brush off). Even Dr Hudson wasn't completely immune to his appeal.

Rich cleared his throat and gave Lou a kind smile. 'We understand that he's your friend, Lou, but the fact that he gets on with people doesn't excuse the persistent lateness, unexplained absences, and lack of effort when he does actually bother showing up.'

'He's had several warnings,' Dr Hudson added.

'Okay then,' boomed Mr Kent from the other end of the table (his voice seemed to be set to a range of different levels of posh boom: you could literally hear him across the whole hospital on a clear day). 'Jolly poor show of Griffiths, not denying that he should have bally well pulled his finger out. Tricky situation, he's a damn fine fellow and a chuffing good surgeon. I suppose an example should be made.' He shifted in his seat. 'But throwing him off the rotation seems a bit punitive. Couldn't we come to some sort of compromise?'

'I'm sorry,' said Dr Hudson, puffing up in her seat, 'but the same standards should be applied to "The Orthopod" as to our own trainees, and if one of ours had consistently and deliberately underperformed they would be out on their ear. I see no reason to make an exception for Dr Griffiths.'

Taking a deep breath and hoping that she wasn't flushing

her career down the toilet, Lou straightened in her seat and said, 'That's not necessarily true, Dr Hudson.' Elaine Hudson swung her furious gaze to Lou and looked like her head might explode at this level of insubordination. 'What I mean is,' Lou hurried on, 'we would consider a period of supervision, trying to get them up to standard.'

Dr Hudson's eyebrows shot up but it was Rich who answered. 'That's as maybe, Lou, but I doubt that anyone wants to babysit Dylan for any longer, and we don't have any spare training places.'

'Look, he's doing a fellowship over the next six months isn't he?' Lou asked Mr Kent, who nodded, looking a bit bemused. 'Well, couldn't he spend a couple of sessions a week in Elderly Care under supervision whilst he does the fellowship?' She turned to Dr Hudson. 'We *are* short staffed. Any extra help we can get can't be bad, can it?'

'Hmph, that depends on the kind of help,' Dr Hudson said, 'and anyway who's going to supervise him?'

Lou looked at all the other registrars in turn pleadingly. They all studiously avoided her gaze except for Miles, who looked straight at her with a smug smile on his face. She sighed. 'I'll do it.'

'Out of the question,' Rich bit out in an uncharacteristically sharp tone.

'Now just wait a minute, Dr Morris,' Dr Hudson interrupted. 'Lou might have something there. I hope your friend will be grateful, Lou; you've just saved his bacon.'

∼

'You bitch,' Dylan shouted across the mess. Lou jumped in her seat on the sofa and looked across the room to where Dylan was towering in the doorway, shaking with fury.

'W-what?' The heads that had turned in the direction of Dylan's outburst now swung to Lou as if watching a match on Centre Court. It was lunchtime and the mangy old sofas and chairs were crammed with doctors of all specialties. The promise of a little hospital gossip was enough to distract most from the telly.

'Don't pretend you don't know,' Dylan said, taking a step towards her, his fists balled at his sides. 'Did it occur to you that something would have to give if I spend two bloody sessions a week with the grave-dodgers? My research is now completely shot to shit, thanks to you.'

'Dylan, I –'

'Don't you dare give me any of your sanctimonious bullshit about how I should have taken an interest whilst I had the opportunity. As if wasting four months of my bloody life pill-pushing to grannies is going to help me be a fucking surgeon.' He slashed a hand through the air dismissively and took another step towards Lou, his finger now pointing at her. 'You're a selfish, spoiled, posh, vain, attention-seeking little brat.' Lou had now risen from the sofa, and he advanced towards her, disregarding all the curious stares. 'You've always irritated the shit out of me. I knew you were a nasty piece of work but I never thought you'd sink this low.'

Lou never, but never, cried in public. She could feel the prickling behind her eyes but she refused to let the tears fall. Fuck him. Louise Sands was not a shrinking violet; she was a Goddamn Amazon and she didn't have to take this kind of abuse. Pushing aside the pain of Dylan's vicious words and the fact that whilst she had been desperately in love with him for over a decade, he apparently found her an irritating bitch, she drew herself up to her full height, put her hands on her hips and swallowed the lump in her throat.

'How *dare* you talk to me like that,' she spat at him, moving around the sofa so that they were nearly toe to toe. 'You don't know what I've done for you –'

'Oh please, spare me. The dragon lady already gave me the whole "wonderful opportunity" speech. She made it clear this nightmare was your idea and that I had no fucking choice anyway.'

'No, Dylan, listen. You don't understand. I –'

'What don't I understand?' he snarled. 'What? Are you so desperate to spend time with me that you engineered an extra three months with me hanging on your coat-tails?' Lou blinked, then paled, taking a step back and hitting the back of the sofa. He'd come so close to the mark that she had started to feel a little sick. In truth she always looked forward to spending time with Dylan. There was nobody who could make her laugh as hard or who gave her a buzz by just being near them. 'Well, you might be beautiful on the outside, but you're ugly as sin underneath and I wouldn't touch you if my life depended on it.'

'I think you've said enough, Dylan.' Frankie stepped between them and gave Dylan a small shove (well, Lou suspected that Frankie hadn't intended it to be small, but even with all her weight behind it, it was never going to have that much effect on Dylan's bulk), looking uncharacteristically furious. Her intervention seemed to snap Dylan out of his angry tirade. He looked around at all the others in the mess, then back at Lou over Frankie's head. There was a flash of what looked like regret, maybe even panic, across his face before he turned away.

'Fine, take her side. See if I care,' he muttered before swinging around and stomping towards the door. But before leaving he turned back to Lou again. 'You know what? I think I can finally understand where your mum was coming from.' Lou's chin jerked back as if Dylan had struck her. She felt herself start to shut down.

He knew. He knew all about her family. He'd met them, for God's sake. He knew the way it was for Lou, the way it had always been.

'If you were this much of a pain in the arse growing up, no wonder she fucking hates your guts.'

Lou heard Frankie gasp next to her but it was like everything was coming through a dark tunnel. Dylan looked her up and down slowly and curled his lip. 'See you around, *Boss*.' With that parting shot, he swept through the doorway, slamming the door behind him.

Lou had thought that she was impervious to embarrassment of any form, but as she stood shaking in the middle of the mess with everyone watching her, and her nose stinging as tears threatened again, she realized that she may have been wrong.

Chapter 7

Blank

DYLAN WAS IN A FOUL MOOD. HE'D BEEN IN A FOUL MOOD for the last three days, since his appraisal and the fight with Lou. At first he was just angry with Lou. How dare she mark him down and make sure that he had to waste even more of his time granny-fiddling? He knew that he hadn't been the most helpful member of her team but he never thought she would punish him like this, effectively scuppering his chance of a research project. Without the project his CV didn't stand a chance, his career would be in the toilet. Mr Kent had explained the whole thing in his usual ham-fisted manner:

'Jolly bad luck, old boy, but seems you've got to spend a bit more time in purgatory before you can get on with the real stuff. That dolly-bird registrar came up with the idea.' (Mr Kent was completely unashamed when referring to any member of female staff as a dolly-bird, even to their face. This didn't always go down too well – Dr Hudson being a case in point. Despite being only in his fifties he seemed to be stuck a good few decades, maybe even a century, in the past.) 'Afraid that it rather puts the kibosh on the old research – but I offered it up to Percy and he jumped at the chance.'

Percy was not actually called Percy, but Mr Kent seemed to think it suited Luke better, and if Luke wanted to get ahead in orthopaedics, and Mr Kent wanted to call him Percy, then Percy it was. Dylan would just bet that Percy jumped at the chance. That research project would have been the key to a winning CV.

Unfortunately, now that Dylan had shouted at Lou in the mess in front of the whole bloody hospital, he was not only angry at her but at himself as well. Okay, so she'd royally screwed him over, but he shouldn't have gone crazy like that. He'd lost control and said stuff he didn't even mean. If he was honest he couldn't even remember half of what he'd said, such was his anger. But from the way both Frankie and Lou were avoiding him, and the hurt look on Lou's face after he'd let rip, he thought it was probably pretty bad.

Not that he had gone out of his way to see the girls either. Normally he would hang around their flat, or lately Tom's house, in the hope of a few meals and some banter. But instead he'd spent a miserable weekend either drinking with the other bone docs of an evening, or watching TV in his flat. He hadn't even been able to have sex to get his mind off the situation, and not for lack of offers: the stunning blonde surgical core trainee had been gagging for it at the pub.

The truth was, he hadn't actually shagged anyone in weeks. These bloody dreams were messing with his head. He thought it might be better not seeing her every day, but if anything it had made them worse. It seemed as though every time he closed his eyes a fresh image of Lou would pop into his mind; and now, not only was he confronted by half-naked visions of a happy, laughing Lou, but also by the awful look of pain on her beautiful face and the unshed tears in her eyes after he'd shouted at her.

As he strode into the rehab hospital and Lou looked up from the ward desk, he realized that this was yet another image that would haunt him: that of Lou's blank face, her normally expressive eyes wiped clean of any emotion. His gut started churning and he had a strange feeling of panic.

'Babes, I ... look, I'm sorry, I shouldn't have shouted at you in front of the mess like that. It was totally out of order.'

'Forget about it,' she said with a small formal smile that made the churning in Dylan's gut step up a notch. 'I'm sure you had your reasons. Let's just try to get through this, okay?' Dylan was about to say something, anything, to wipe that cool detachment off her face and get back to the Lou he knew, when she shoved a piece of paper in his hand just before they were interrupted.

'Right, kids,' Rich said as he sauntered up the desk, seeming oblivious to the tension crackling in the air. One of the many things Dylan hated about this guy was his habit of calling his juniors (bearing in mind that most of them were only a few years younger than him) kids. 'What's on the menu? Dylan?'

'Um ...' Christ. He'd forgotten to print the list again, or go through the notes, or ask the ward staff about the patients.

'Dylan,' Lou prompted, 'I think Dr Morris wants to start going through the list you've made.' She widened her eyes at him, and then nodded towards the paper in his hand. He looked down and realized that it was a patient list. No, not just a printed list, but one with notes in the margin next to each patient's name. All the information Dylan needed was there: reason for admission, social situation and progress, even down to level of mobility. It must have taken Lou ages.

Rich was looking at Dylan with a smug expression, obviously waiting for him to fuck up. Dylan looked back at Lou; she was now making big eyes at him and raising her eyebrows, looking adorably frustrated. He felt himself relax slightly; anything was better than her dead expression from a moment ago.

He cleared his throat. 'Right, so, first patient is ... Mr Townsend.' He checked the list and saw that Lou had written all the bed numbers in bold by each name. Looking surreptitiously around the ward, he caught sight of the number he needed and started striding over to what he hoped was the appropriate patient.

He glanced at Lou as he was reeling off the details from the list once they reached the patients, and his chest felt tight again. Gone was the animation in her features. Back had come the lifeless look from before.

As he continued to lead a seamless ward round (thanks to Lou's copious notes) he was getting more and more angry. If Rich put his fucking hands on Lou one more time Dylan swore he would punch him right in his lecherous face. For her part Lou wasn't exactly encouraging this, but at the same time she wasn't putting any effort into overtly discouraging it either. She appeared to have morphed into a strangely robotic version of herself, her usual vibrancy and spirit only making brief appearances for the patients' benefit.

'Hi, Alun.' She smiled at the next patient, whom Dylan recognized from the stroke ward. Alun's resemblance in both appearance and personality to Father Jack out of *Father Ted* was uncanny, the only difference being that he had a thick Welsh accent instead of a thick Irish one.

Alun was not an easy patient. He had obviously been incredibly independent before his stroke and he did not take the loss of this well. He came in after collapsing at home and spending nearly two days lying on his kitchen floor (his niece felt terribly guilty about not checking on him sooner, but considering his last words to her were 'Fuck off unless you've got whisky, you stupid cow,' it was understandable).

'Bugger off,' Alun muttered, and Lou beamed at him.

'Brilliant, Alun! You're speech is so much better.' Lou's face was shining with excitement, and Alun rolled his eyes, but Dylan could see the side of his mouth that wasn't permanently pulled down from the stroke was twitching slightly. Even this old bastard wasn't immune to Lou's charm.

'Hey, Lila,' Rich said from the end of the bed, and Dylan watched as the dark-haired physio he had hoped to avoid in the coming months approached them. Lila smiled at Rich and Lou, then flashed Dylan a look of annoyance. Dylan noticed Lou looking down at her hands briefly and taking a deep breath, before she looked up at Lila with an oddly strained smile.

'I see you've been working your magic, Lil,' Lou said.

The annoyance cleared from Lila's features and her pretty face lit with enthusiasm. 'He's mobilizing with a frame brilliantly,' she told them.

'Fuckin' ... frame ... bullshit,' Alun slurred from the bed, glowering at Lila.

'Now, Alun,' Lila chided. 'We've talked about this. The frame is your friend; it provides the extra support with balance and stability you need at the moment.'

Alun continued to glower at her, curling his lip, and Lila's enthusiastic expression faltered. Clearly done with any discussion of frames and mobility, Alun turned to Lou and grabbed the drug chart out of her hands with his good hand.

'Beer,' he said, pointing at the chart and scowling at Lou.

'Right – sorry, Alun,' she muttered, still smiling as she added a daily pint of Guinness onto the end of the drug chart, which had obviously been rewritten overnight, leaving out the most essential part (at least in Alun's opinion). After she was done Alun grunted in satisfaction, then scowled at all of them, barking, 'Now, Cachau bant*.' Dylan grinned and shook his head as the others looked at each other in confusion.

'I think he wants us to move on,' he told them. 'Oh, and he thanks you for your time.' Alun narrowed his eyes at Dylan, who decided to usher everyone out of the cubicle before Alun really lost it.

'Thanks for that, Lila,' Rich said once they were out in the main ward again. 'Do you have time to fill us in on the other patients?' Lila flicked another wary glance at Dylan, and he sighed.

'I'll go check if the sister is out of handover yet,' he said, moving away toward the ward desk and noticing Lila visibly relaxing. Maybe, just maybe he should have considered keeping his dick in his pants for once. It wasn't as though he didn't like Lila when he slept with her four months ago; it was just that something had been missing.

Oh, he gave it a go. They went out a couple of times and she even came over to the flat; but it just wasn't working for him. The clincher had been when they'd started watching *Anchorman* together. Ron Burgundy had told Veronica Cornerstone, 'I'm kind of a big deal. People know me.' Lila didn't even crack a smile. One of the funniest moments in film, and it completely passed her by. Now, when *he'd* first watched that scene he had nearly choked to death on his pizza. Lou had laughed so hard, Coke had come flying out of her nose, and disgustingly she had informed Dylan that she might have peed in her knickers a bit.

After that he'd known that things weren't going anywhere with Lila. He'd still thrown out a couple of *Blackadder* quotes to see if she could redeem herself, but she just stared at him blankly. When he thought back on things, it seemed that he never spent more than a few weeks – or days – with a woman before he decided that they didn't measure up. They didn't laugh the right way, were too prudish, didn't swear enough, didn't fill the room with their energy and vitality, didn't wear ridiculous heels at all times, didn't strut around like their life was a romantic comedy and they were the main character, didn't have clear blue eyes or long, thick, lush, wavy blonde hair ...

'Did you find her?' Dylan jumped slightly and realized that he had been staring at the ward desk for God knows how long. Lou was looking up at him with her head tilted adorably to the side in confusion. She waved her hand in front of his face. 'Hello, anyone there?' Her brows drew together in frustration and Dylan found himself thinking *that* was adorable too. 'Listen, surgery-boy, you've made it abundantly clear that you don't want to be here but please, please just pay attention for the length of the ward round. Once the boss leaves you can go back to theatre or whatever you like, okay?'

'Lou, I ...' Dylan shook his head in an attempt to clear it. Wasn't this all Lou's idea? Wasn't it Lou who told the bosses that he wasn't up to scratch? Why would she let him bugger off whenever he liked? Something didn't add up. 'I don't understand. What –'

'Look,' Lou interrupted, her tone fierce and her blank mask slipping to reveal what look alarmingly like pain in her features, 'you've made it quite clear that you don't want to be around me, and that all this,' she waved her hand at the packed rehab ward, 'is a waste of your time. Just put on a show for the bosses and then get back to your hammer and nails.'

'Lou, please. I've said I'm sorry and I meant it. I behaved like a complete twat, but I didn't mean –'

'I know what you meant.' Lou's harsh whisper cut through Dylan's admittedly feeble explanations, and he felt that weird, constrictive feeling in his chest again. He watched with no small amount of panic as Lou wiped the pain from her features and replaced it with the blank mask that he was finding more and more disturbing. 'Let's just forget it, okay? We'll get through the next three months with you spending as little time as possible "pill-pushing to grannies" as you put it. Put on a front for the bosses and then we can both get on with our lives.'

'Do you forgive me, babes?' He reached out to touch her arm, and then clenched his jaw so hard it ached when she flinched back from him.

'Of course,' she muttered, not quite meeting his eyes. Dylan clenched his jaw even harder.

Fine. If she wanted to shut down on him, that was fine. Two could play at that game. And if she was going to let him leave early and do all the work for him, he decided that was fine too. She was the one that had recommended this for him in the first place and royally screwed up his plans. So what if he'd been a bit cruel? It wasn't as if she was in love with him or anything.

*CACHAU BANT — *FUCK OFF*

Chapter 8

Indifference

LOU WAS EXHAUSTED. WHY SHE HAD BEEN STRONG-ARMED into coming to the pub was a mystery. She would have much rather let her thirtieth birthday slip by unnoticed. Which was weird for her: she had always been a birthday girl.

In fact, since leaving home, her twenty-first had been the only one she hadn't enjoyed thoroughly. It was a huge, marquee-based extravaganza at her parents' house and she should have loved every minute. But Dylan disappearing into the hay barn with Milly Jones hadn't been a highlight of the evening, and her mother had managed to get a few digs in (including 'the incident', which Lou tried not to remember). All the same, none of those occurrences were entirely foreign to her, and it had almost been worth it to see all her friends having a laugh together.

So, by all accounts, Lou should have been champing at the bit for a big party, but when Frankie pressed her she just shrugged it off and claimed she couldn't be bothered. Which actually wasn't far from the truth. The extra hours she'd been putting in were wearing her down.

Having a disinterested orthopaedic surgeon on her team for six months had increased her workload but she'd managed. But over the last few weeks, since they had threatened to remove Dylan from the rotation, she had been covering for him in an attempt to make him look good, and now she was really struggling.

To top it all off her yearly appraisal was coming up, and she didn't feel nearly as confident as she had in the past. There were two audits she had yet to finish, and a poster presentation she had to submit before she would be even halfway ready, and somehow she didn't think her performance evaluations would be that stellar either.

It wasn't just the work stuff that was exhausting, though; she was tired of hating Dylan. To go from loving him so fervently to hating him with equal passion was agonizing. She had come to the decision that indifference was the key, and had decided to look on the bright side: at least she'd finally been cured of her ridiculous crush.

She remembered every poisonous word he'd said to her in the mess with absolute clarity. Some of it she could have forgiven. He'd got the wrong end of the stick and he was angry, so some of the things he said were understandable – but not the stuff about her mother.

Not when he knew.

He knew what it was like for her.

That ... that she couldn't forgive. That was what broke her trust in him; broke her love for him. At least now she could move on. That is, if she could summon up the energy. Rich was still making it known in his subtle way that he was interested. And Lou had to give it to him: he was persistent.

'Happy birthday!' The chorus of voices assaulted Lou as she pushed open the door to the pub, and her head snapped up. The place was completely rammed. Every head was turned towards her and Frankie, who was beaming and bouncing up and down on the spot.

'I know you said you didn't want a fuss,' Frankie said, 'but I couldn't help myself. You would have never let me get away with no party on my birthday.'

Lou smiled at Frankie and tried to muster as much enthusiasm as she could, giving her a big hug and spying the huge cake balanced on a table in the middle of the pub. It was a massive, exact replica of Lou's favourite pair of shoes, complete with spiked, ridiculously high heel, red sole, and intricate design. Lou pulled back and looked at Frankie, cupping her face with her hands.

'I don't deserve you as my best friend you know,' she whispered, and she knew that, despite the noise in the pub, Frankie had heard her when her eyes filled with tears and she gave her a shaky smile. After that it was a whirlwind of hugs, kisses, old-lady jokes and the like.

'Hey, babes.' She turned to see Dylan standing in front of her, his hands shoved into his pockets. 'Happy birthday,' he said, offering a small smile. For the last month since their fight in the mess there seemed to be some sort of unspoken agreement between them: no more physical contact. After years of teasing and casual affection the difference was stark, but at the end of the day Lou thought it was probably for the best. A clean break was what she needed and that was exactly what she was getting. She summoned up the strained smile that she used with increasing frequency when he was around, and pushed her hair back behind her ears.

'Thanks, Dylan,' she mumbled, looking away quickly from his gaze, and heard him sigh.

'Come on, honey, time to do the candles.' Frankie was tugging on her hand and looking at Dylan warily. Lou had managed to convince her to speak to Dylan again after about a week of the silent treatment. She was pretty sure that Frankie had *never* given anyone the silent treatment, let alone for a whole week. So she was touched that Frankie would do it in her defence; but enough was enough. She didn't want to ruin Frankie's relationship with Dylan when it was already on shaky ground after Frankie had found out how Dylan had kept Tom and her apart at uni.

Unfortunately Lou had had to lead by example, and that meant she'd had to pretend that her heart wasn't broken, and force herself to be around Dylan as if nothing had happened. She lied to Frankie and the others, told them that the little scene in the mess was nothing and that she was over it, so they should be, too. How she felt about Dylan had changed, but she still cared about him and she didn't want him cut off from everyone.

'Okay, Frankster, lead the way.' Lou turned away from Dylan, but not before she saw Katie bounding up to him. This was another new development over the last month: Dylan, it seemed, had finally started a proper relationship. If Lou had still been in love with him she would have sunk into another pathetic Dylan-induced depression. Thankfully her emotions had settled into a comforting blanket of numbness, which she told herself was a relief. She was, however, confused by his choice.

Dylan had always seemed to go for shy, quiet types, and Katie was certainly not one of those; she was a small, dark-haired bundle of limitless energy, and, much to Lou's annoyance, completely adorable. Katie was a GP in Sarah's village and Sarah's best friend, and as such they had all met her occasionally over the last few months since Tom and Frankie got together. But Dylan had only started taking an interest in her during the last three weeks or so. Lou braced herself for the onslaught of cute verbal diarrhoea likely to emanate from Katie as she approached, but was shocked when another voice cut through the murmurings around her.

'Louise, there you are.'

No.

Please no.

'It's such a crush in here, we thought we'd never find you.' Lou turned and was confronted by both her parents. Her mother was brushing some no-doubt imaginary dirt from her pristine white silk blouse, and her dad was shifting on the spot in his Armani suit, looking uncomfortable in the small pub. Great. This party just got better and better.

'Mum? Dad? What are you doing here?'

'Don't looked so shocked, darling,' her mum said, frowning at her. 'It *is* your birthday. We popped into the flat earlier to see you, and Frankie told us about the party. So we thought why not pop along?' Her mum gave her a tight smile, then moved to air-kiss both her cheeks. Lou obediently went through the hollow ritual with both her parents, wondering why they would be showing so much interest this year after so many years of indifference.

Her twenty-first party had been an excuse to show off to all their friends, but since then they had lapsed back into the rather casual attitude they'd always had towards her birthday. Some years they sent her a card or even rang her, but to actually want to see her was rare indeed.

'But ... but ...' Lou didn't know if she could handle her parents, or more specifically her mother, on top of everything else.

'I'm really sorry, Mr and Mrs Sands, but we've got to cut the cake now.' Frankie had subtly inserted herself between Lou and her parents and was ushering Lou away.

'Don't you think you should change first, darling?' Lou hated how her mum managed to make an endearment like 'darling' seem like a sarcastic sneer. She managed to convey in just that one word how very far Lou actually was from being her darling.

'I think I look fine, mum,' Lou replied. 'Everyone knows I've come straight from work.'

Lou's mum emitted a ladylike but derisive snort, communicating exactly what she thought of Lou's outfit, and Lou was about to turn back when she felt a strong arm at her back.

'See you later, Mr and Mrs S,' Dylan threw over his shoulder as he propelled Lou forward through the crowd. Lou tried to push away, but he just pulled her closer to his side.

'Your fucking mother,' he growled under his breath.

'I thought you agreed with my fucking mother,' Lou mumbled, still straining away from him.

'I told you, babes, I didn't mean any of that bollocks I spewed.' Lou glanced up at him and saw that his jaw was tight, his eyes flashing with anger. She sighed.

'Let's not go over it again. What does it matter anyway?' They had reached the cake in the centre of the pub and Lou shrugged out of Dylan's grip.

'Fine,' he snapped. 'Right. What does it matter?'

～

DYLAN BIT THE INSIDE OF HIS CHEEK TO STOP HIMSELF saying any more as he backed away from Lou.

She tells him and everyone else she's forgiven him. Bullshit.

She says it doesn't matter. Bullshit.

She claims everything is fucking fine. Bullshit. Bullshit. Bullshit.

Christ, she was stubborn. He had always known this about her, but a whole month of cold indifference and blank expressions was impressive, even for her.

Frustratingly he couldn't even justify his current anger towards her. She was doing everything she could to see that he cruised through the two half days he was forced to spend in

Elderly Care. A list was thrust into his hand before every ward round, with all the prep work done and ready for him. He was encouraged to bugger off as soon as the boss was out of sight, and in truth the whole thing was being achieved with very little effort on his part. But it just wasn't quite sitting right, and he might even be starting to feel a tad guilty. After all, there must have been a fair amount of extra work involved for her, not only preparing him for all the ward rounds, but also doing all the jobs generated from the round by herself. But his weak attempts to stay on had been met with more blank stares and dismissive gestures, so he'd decided not to push it.

To be honest he was over the whole thing. So what if she thought she'd teach him a lesson and make him waste more time pill-pushing? He didn't care any more. All he wanted was for her to be back to her old self. No, he thought darkly as he looked over to where she was laughing her arse off with the group that had formed around her, she was her old self with everyone else; it was just him she was indifferencing to death.

He watched as Frankie pushed her way to the cake and lit the candles. The lights were dimmed and the whole packed pub sang a hearty 'Happy Birthday' to her, before she smiled her dazzling smile and started to bend down. He felt himself break out into a sweat, watching the graceful arch of her back as she lifted her head and pursed her lips to blow out the candles. One hand holding onto the edge of the table, the other holding the heavy mass of her blonde waves back from her face, as the light from the candles lit up her exquisite features.

Every movement Lou made was unconsciously sexy. She never walked anywhere; it was always a full-on strut. Her heels were never less than three inches, and whether her hair was up in a messy bun at the top of her head, showing off her slender neck and perfect jawline, or spilling over her shoulders and down her back, she always managed to look like someone's wet dream.

Glancing around the pub, he could see that he wasn't the only one fixated on the magnificent sight of Lou bending over. Of course bloody Rich's eyes were firmly glued to her arse. Even Miles, who openly disliked Lou, didn't seem to be able to help himself, and Dylan noticed with irritation that several of his orthopaedic buddies were eyeing her up, elbowing each other and giggling like schoolboys. Had Frankie actually put thirty candles on the goddamn thing? He felt his jaw relax when Lou finally straightened up, but was instantly back on alert as she was swept up in Rich's arms and swung from side to side.

He clenched his jaw and had to fight against all his instincts, which were screaming for him to storm over to them and punch Rich right in his smug, earnest face. And it was in that moment, watching her in another man's arms, that it finally clicked. The last month without Lou's friendship had felt empty. He truly had never realized how much of the laughter in his daily life was down to Lou, and having her vibrancy stripped away was like going from living life in glorious Technicolor to finding himself in black and white. Nobody actually quite got his humour like her.

Although she'd made it clear to everyone that the argument between them meant nothing, and that she was completely fine with him, he still hadn't felt right hanging out at their flat to the extent he used to. And anyway Lou always found excuses to avoid him whilst he was there, or, worse, she would be polite. He gritted his teeth. Lou was never bloody polite, and certainly not with him; she took the piss incessantly, challenged, argued with, teased, criticized, needled, judged, provoked, all the while laughing, snorting, scowling, never presenting the expressionless mask she wore whilst he was around currently.

He was stuck.

He felt compelled to be near her, but being around the new Lou was actually painful. He was desperate to get her back as a friend. Oh, he knew now that he wanted more than that; but with the state of play being as it was, he would take what he could get. From the disgusted way she'd looked at him after that kiss at New Year he was under no illusion that she wanted him that way, but he decided that he was going to do everything he could to at least win back her trust.

He even went as far as pulling the plug on his prolific shagging, which he knew from past experience she found totally gross, and was making an attempt at a settled relationship. Granted, things hadn't really progressed that far with Katie. He'd decided on her because, after his realization about Lou, he knew that the more reserved girls he went for in the past quite possibly weren't in fact what he was looking for. Katie was loud and fun to be with, like Lou, and he thought that if he could start something meaningful with Katie, maybe the incessant dreams and thoughts about Lou would abate. But in all honesty, he found it difficult to focus on anything Katie said or did, which he was guessing was not a particularly good sign.

As he started to lose the battle against his instincts and took a step forward, he felt a small hand on his arm.

'Hey, you okay?' Katie asked, smiling up at him. 'You look like you might puke or something.' Dylan tried to keep looking at her genuinely concerned, open face, but it was like his eyeballs had a mind of their own; he literally could not tear them away from the scene unfolding across the crowded pub.

'I'm fine,' he said, attempting to relax his jaw and stop grinding his teeth.

' "Avoid the company of a liar. And if you can't avoid him, don't believe him." ' Dylan rolled his eyes when he heard Ash's smooth voice from his other side, but was quick to focus back on Lou and Rich.

He noticed with satisfaction that she had managed to disengage from his rather tight grip and had taken a step back. Dylan's jaw unclenched, and he was just about to put his arm around Katie when he heard a high-pitched scream from Lou's mum at the bar. Her white silk shirt was covered in red wine, her face a mask of horror and revulsion.

Chapter 9

'The Mother'

EXACTLY NINE YEARS EARLIER ...

'You little bitch,' Dylan heard Mrs Sands hiss at her daughter, and then he flinched at the surprisingly loud slap that followed. Frozen in place in front of the bathroom mirror, his shocked eyes turned to the door, beyond which he was pretty sure he'd just heard Lou's mum slap her around the face. Whose mum actually did that sort of thing? Having been fussed over and spoiled all his life by his very Welsh but very warm parents, he had absolutely no experience to draw on.

'Mummy, I –' the sound of Lou's tiny, broken voice ripped through Dylan like acid. He'd never heard her sound like that. He'd never heard her sound even remotely cowed in the past.

'I told you what to wear, young lady,' Mrs Sands snapped, cutting Lou off. 'You will not embarrass me in front of all our friends by wearing *that.*'

'It's just a dress, Mummy.' Dylan strained to hear Lou's whisper. 'And it is my birthday.'

'You look like a slut, Louise, and not even an up-market one. Oh you might be Daddy's precious princess but you've never fooled me. I know what you are.' The amount of venom in Mrs

Sands's carefully enunciated words was shocking. 'I've always known that you are nothing but a selfish, spoiled, hateful little brat. And the fact that you would even consider wearing that outfit to a party your father and I are paying for just proves my point. Do you know how much this extravaganza is costing, Louise?'

'But Mummy, I said I'd just do something at uni for my birthday. I didn't want – *umph* ...' Dylan stepped forward quickly and grabbed the door handle when he heard the breath being knocked out of Lou, and a loud thump.

Both women turned to face him as he jumped into the corridor. Mrs Sands was gripping the red lace material at the front of Lou's dress and had her pushed up against the wall.

Dylan was only twenty-one years old. He'd been in plenty of punch-ups (he was from Swansea after all), but a mother hitting her daughter? So whilst he was dying to rip the poisonous woman away from Lou, he was instead frozen in absolute horror. For her part, after her initial surprise, Mrs Sands let Lou go and stepped away, calmly smoothing her immaculate black dress and offering Dylan a cold, formal smile.

'What ... what in the ... ?' He turned to Lou. 'Babes?'

'Ah ... the Welshman.' Mrs Sands's smile was more like a sneer now, and she shot Lou a knowing, cruel look that baffled Dylan. Lou looked panicked for a moment, and then hid it when she noticed Dylan staring.

'I'm so sorry,' Mrs Sands continued, her icy tone suggesting that she was anything but. 'If you were looking for the guest facilities, they are downstairs in the west wing, beyond the drawing room.'

Dylan knew exactly where the 'guest facilities' were. He was up on the first floor having a poke about the mansion so he could report back to all their curious mates downstairs. The last thing he'd expected from this woman, who had been formally polite to them all when they'd arrived that afternoon (stuffed into a collection of beat-up vehicles that were lucky to make the journey from London to the wilds of Hertfordshire), was her physically and verbally assaulting her daughter.

'You will change.' It wasn't a question, and from the way she was staring at Lou, Dylan could tell that Mrs Sands knew she'd won. When Lou looked back at her, Dylan noticed her mother's eyes flick over to him with some kind of silent message, and then saw Lou give her a brief nod. With one last pointed glance at Lou, she swept away in a cloud of expensive perfume, leaving Lou leaning heavily back against the wall, her head bowed in fierce contemplation of her fire-engine red shoes.

'Babes, I ...' He came unstuck and moved towards her as she straightened from the wall and one of her shaky hands came up to push her hair back from her face. 'You're bleeding!' He shot forward and placed a gentle hand under her chin to turn her head to the side, the other hand stroking her hair back from her temple. There was a small trickle of blood from her cheekbone. He could clearly see the handprint across Lou's face, and with rising nausea realized that the bleeding was from a small cut where Mrs Sands's ring finger had caught her.

Lou was avoiding his eyes, which was alarming, because Lou never avoided eye contact. *Not like Frankie,* he thought to himself with the familiar ache of longing that was fortunately dulling slowly as the months and years went by with no progress in that direction. Lou's hand came up to cover his own, which was now cupping her face, and she forced a small smile.

'I'm fine you know,' she said. She had tears in her eyes, but Dylan could sense that she would refuse to let them fall. He didn't think he had seen her cry once in the last three years. 'I'm used to "The Mother"; I grew up with her after all.'

Bloody hell. What a childhood.

'She is a massive bitch, mind,' Dylan told her, and to his

surprise a small laugh bubbled out of Lou. He relaxed slightly: this was the Lou he knew – she smiled, she laughed, she was outrageous, she had fun. She didn't talk in a small, broken voice, and she didn't cower away from a bully.

'Yes, you could say that,' she agreed, then looked down at her dress. Dylan knew about the dress: the girls had banged on about it the whole way down. He knew that they'd trawled London to find the exact one Lou wanted, and it certainly was very Lou: short, red, a high neck and long sleeves, but completely backless. He couldn't imagine a dress that would suit her more.

'I better change,' she muttered, her voice sounding small and broken again.

'What? No, fuck her. You wear what you want. "Laugh in the face of fear and tweak the nose of the dreadful spindly killer fish." ' Lou laughed again, not full-on Sands-strength laughter, but getting there.

'Series Two.'

'Episode?'

' "Bells"?'

Dylan frowned and shook his head.

'No! I meant "Potato",' she cried. 'You can't count that one; I'm off my game.'

'You know the rules: no re-dos, no rethinks, no second chances.' He realized that he still had his hand on the side of her face, and, even more shockingly, that Lou's hand was still firmly covering it. As if she could sense the path of his thoughts, Lou dropped her hand suddenly and stepped to the side along the wall of the corridor so that they were no longer in each other's personal space.

'Look, really, I better get cleaned up before I go down. You find the others, okay?'

'No, babes, I'll wait for you. Then we can go down together, see?' Lou's face froze for a moment, and Dylan swore that for a second she looked almost wistful before she cleared her expression.

'Please, Dylan,' she pleaded. 'Don't let her ruin any more of the evening. Look after Frankie for me. Mother would crush her; she can literally smell fear. Make sure that everyone stays out of her way and tell them I won't be long.'

Of course, he thought. Typical Lou behaviour: worrying about Frankie first and herself second. Dylan wasn't sure which of them loved Frankie more, and usually he encouraged Lou's protective bent, but this time he was annoyed.

He wanted to stay with Lou. He wanted to clean up the cut on her face and make sure it wasn't too deep. He wanted to make sure that her mum didn't come back for a second round. He wanted to make her laugh again and work towards making that subdued, cowed expression he'd seen her wear fade to a distant memory. But looking into her determined face he knew he was fighting a losing battle. She was nothing if not stubborn.

Up until the moment she walked into the marquee, Dylan had convinced himself that there was no way in hell that his Lou would be pushed around. No way would she change her dress. He was keeping an eye on her evil witch of a mother, so he now caught the slow, satisfied smile that spread across her coldly beautiful face. Following the direction of her gaze, he took in the sight of a completely transformed Lou. Her wild, flowing hair had been swept up into an elegant roll at the back of her head, and a dark blue, sophisticated floor-length gown had replaced the red dress.

She looked like a refined, well-bred debutante. Of course she was stunning – with Lou that went without saying – but her appearance was so far removed from the Lou they all knew and loved at uni that he could feel the confusion emanating from their group of mates en mass. Whoever this woman was, she was not their Lou; their Lou had left the moment her mother's hand connected with her cheek.

It turned out that she didn't reappear that night, either. Their normal party-animal Lou had morphed into a carefully polite automaton. She circulated amongst her parents' friends and the surprisingly large crowd of people her age that she'd told them on the way up were a mixture of boarding-school friends and others from 'socially acceptable' (or in other words filthy-rich) families. The Lou that got steaming with her friends, performed ridiculous dance moves, and snogged ludicrously inappropriate blokes was completely absent from the proceedings that evening.

She didn't even reappear when they left the next day: she spent the entire journey back to London staring out of the window from the back seat of her car after asking Dylan to drive, whilst Frankie kept up nervous chatter from the front and flicked concerned looks back at her. In fact it took a full week before they had their Lou back in full force.

PRESENT...

Dylan thought that he'd never seen Lou's face as devoid of emotion as it had been over the last month, but after remembering that awful party and the quiet Lou of the subsequent week, he realized he was not the only one who had had that effect on her. He felt his stomach hollow out as he came to the depressing conclusion that he was in the same category as Lou's hideous mother.

Christ. Had he actually used the awful knowledge that her mother was abusive (something she had made him swear never to tell anyone – not even Frankie) to hurt her? He wracked his brains trying to remember everything he'd said in his angry tirade, but as snippets emerged into his consciousness he had to force them back down or suffer a full on panic attack.

A hush fell over the pub, the scream having cut through all conversation. Glancing back to Lou, he saw that her head had shot up and she was focusing on her mother.

'Why on earth am I being subjected to this disgusting hovel!' Mrs Sands snapped at her husband. Lou starting moving towards where her parents were standing at the bar, and the crowd parted to let her through.

'Mummy,' Lou said as she laid a cautious hand on her mother's arm, 'are you okay?'

'Of course I'm not okay,' Mrs Sands snapped. 'I'm being jostled about all over the place.' The people standing closest to the bar started surreptitiously shuffling back. 'And now look at me.'

'Mummy, maybe you should –'

'Don't you dare tell me what to do, young lady.' Mrs Sands's voice was raised and her face was rigid with anger. 'I don't know why I let your father convince me –'

'Now, now, Evelyn,' Mr Sands cut in, sounding completely unruffled by his wife's outburst and the fact that they were the focus of practically the whole pub's attention. 'Let's try and get into the swing of things eh? We haven't seen our Lou-Lou in ages.' Mr Sands looked nearly as out of place in the pub as his wife in his tailored suit. They made an impressive couple: both equally glamorous and intimidating, despite their age, with Mrs Sands's blonde hair and botoxed features contrasting with her husband's distinguished grey and the lined, but still handsome, face. The Sands family's voices dropped and the noise in the pub started up again.

Dylan felt a small hand slip into his, and he started; he'd totally forgotten that Katie was there. Why did holding her hand feel so wrong? He looked down at her and forced a smile.

'Shall I go and get the wets in?' he asked, keen to get to the bar and yet not so keen to analyze why that was.

'Thanks, babe, white wine please.' Dylan winced at the endearment. Surely an endearment from a girl he was supposed to be dating should make him happy, not make him want to rip his ears off? He turned away from Katie to hide his expression. 'Ash?'

' "Beware of the idiot, for he is like an old dress. Every time you patch it, the wind will tear it back again." '

Dylan clenched his jaw. 'Okay, big man, as much as I enjoy the whole prick-with-a-proverb thing, I've no interest in riddling them out in the middle of a pub when I'm dying of thirst. You want a fucking wet or not?'

' "Against stupidity, God Himself is helpless." ' Dylan stared at him for a beat, took in Ash's knowing smirk, and decided to let the coeliwr* get his own drink.

As he pushed through the crowd to the bar he could feel a knot of anxiety forming in his stomach. For some reason the thought of Lou exposed to her parents on her birthday caused an almost panicky feeling to rise up to his throat.

*COELIWR — SOMEONE WHO PLAYS WITH THEMSELVES

Chapter 10

Self-confessed urophiliac

'I HAVEN'T SEEN YOU IN SO LONG, Lou-Lou.' HER DAD'S voice sounded thick, and when she looked up into his face Lou could have sworn that his eyes were wet. What on earth was going on? In an unprecedented move he reached for her and snatched her up in a tight hug.

After the initial shock she put her arms around him, giving him a squeeze and asking, 'Daddy? Is everything okay?' She could hear her mum clicking her tongue impatiently in the background, and leaned back to flick her a nervous glance. At a young age Lou had learned that any affection her father showed her would be met by strong disapproval, and often some form of retribution, from her mother. Her mother's intelligence, coupled with her ability to manipulate any situation to her advantage, meant that her revenge, whilst effective, was always under the radar. It was rare that her father actually realized what was going on between them – at least that was what Lou hoped.

'Yes, yes, of course I'm okay. Can't I hug my own daughter?' Lou studied him with her head tipped to the side as he moved back, and he had the grace to look slightly uncomfortable. She

79

could count on one hand the number of times he had hugged her since she was a child.

'Giles,' her mum's sharp voice cut through Lou's speculation, 'I really am completely soaked. I think it's time we left. Lou's here with her friends.' She made a show of looking around at the increasingly drunken, rambunctious crowd, sneering as if they were all drug-dealing ex-cons and not a group of professionals. 'She doesn't want us cramping her style.'

To Lou's complete shock her dad frowned in annoyance and shot her mum a filthy look. It was so at odds with the long-established power balance that it freaked her out a little.

Her parents stared at each other for a moment, something passing between them which confused Lou even more.

'Lou, we came down today because ... well ...' he rubbed the back of his neck for a moment, looking uncharacteristically lost. 'It's your brother. He ... we ... he's resigned from his job and we're having a little trouble contacting him.'

Lou stared at him for a moment. 'What did you do?' she asked, her voice hard.

'He brought someone home and ... and it was a bit of a shock for your mother, and things ... well, things didn't go well exactly.'

'You mean he brought his *boyfriend* home, Dad. His boyfriend of two years. How exactly was this a shock? You've known he was gay for the last five years. I was there when he explained *at length* about his partner last Christmas. I repeat,' she turned to her mother this time, 'what did you do?'

Her mother threw up her hands, scowling at Lou. 'Oh well done you. Well done for being *so* accepting, *so* understanding. Well, you, young lady, haven't invested twenty-eight years of your life in someone who is now completely screwing everything up. Giving up a perfectly good job in the city. He's taken up with some bloody charity.' Her mother might have been the only person to be able to say 'charity' like it was a dirty word. 'Now he says he wants to swan off to Africa of all the Godforsaken places.'

'Mum, he's going to be working for one of the largest aid agencies in the UK, and be allocating funds for an entire region. It's not like he's running off to join the circus.'

'Look, darling,' her dad said. 'We just want you to talk to him. Maybe convince him to let us speak to him. It's been over a month now since he cut us off and –'

'Dad, how long is it since you spoke to me?'

'Um ... I don't –'

'Four months. Neither of you have bothered to contact me for four months.'

All her dad could do was stand in front of her, his mouth working but no sound making it out. And seeing him at a loss for once was strangely therapeutic. Lou rolled her eyes, letting him off the hook.

'Fine, whatever. I'll do what I can.' At that point she was more than ready for them to just leave.

'Thank you,' her dad said with real feeling. 'We'll see you soon, darling.' Further shocking her, he pulled her back into another tight hug. 'I've missed you,' he whispered into her ear, 'so much.'

'Giles, you'll have to get the car,' her mum said as they were moving apart. 'I can't walk down the road like this.' Her dad sighed but looked resigned. He kissed Lou on the forehead and held her eyes for a moment, with his hands on either side of her face, before striding effortlessly through the crowd to the door.

'Thirty now, Louise.'

'W-what?' Lou stammered tearing her eyes away from her dad's rapidly retreating back.

'I said you're thirty now.'

'Right.' Lou frowned at her. 'I have kind of realized that,

Mum, this being my thirtieth birthday party and all. Ooh and the banner and balloons also might have given it away.'

'What I mean, Louise, is that you're thirty now and perhaps you should stop your slut antics and find a man to settle down with.'

It wasn't the first time her mother had called her a slut. Usually Lou was prepared to turn the other cheek, accustomed as she was to her insults and knowing that the arguments upset her dad and her brother. But Dad was getting the car, her brother was nowhere to be seen, and Lou was not feeling in the most tolerant mood. She was exhausted, and she decided that seeing Dylan with Katie tonight was enough of a blow to her self-esteem; she didn't need her mother chipping in as well.

'Get out,' Lou said through her teeth, leaning in so her face was inches away from her mother's. Her mum flinched in shock at first but then her features flushed with anger. Stepping even closer, she grabbed Lou's exposed upper arms, digging her long nails into her skin.

'What in the fuck is going on here?' Both women started and Lou's mum abruptly released her. They turned to see a furious Dylan towering over them. His eyes flicked down to Lou's arm and then went wide, his face losing all colour. Lou frowned and glanced down at her arm to see the angry red crescents her mum's nails had made, and the trickle of blood where one of them had pierced the skin.

'That's twice, lady.' Dylan put his hand in the centre of Lou's mum's chest and gave a small shove, causing her to go back on one foot. 'Twice I've seen you draw blood from your own daughter. Well, I'm not fucking twenty-one any more, and you're on my territory now, sguthan*. I suggest that you get the fuck out of here or I'll throw you out.'

'Oh, the Welshman,' she sneered back at him, and then continued in a fake high voice. ' "But Mummy, I'm not interested in any of the nice boys from the nice families. I've met someone at university, he makes me laugh, and he's got the most gorgeous Welsh accent, and I think I lo –" '

'Shut up!' Lou screamed. 'Just shut up and get out like Dylan said. You always ruin everything.' She glanced at Dylan to see that he was frowning, trying to piece together what her mum had said.

'Don't you dare speak to me like that, young –'

'Right,' Dylan cut in, grabbing Lou's mum's arm and marching her towards the door. 'As they say in Llandough, ciao for now.'

Unfortunately Lou's dad picked that moment to stride back into the pub and nearly collided with Dylan and her mum.

'What on earth is –'

'Listen, mate,' Dylan cut in, still holding onto Lou's mum's arm. 'Take your woman home and keep her away from my ...' As if realizing his slip, Dylan paused. Lou knew very well that she wasn't his anything. '... my ... my Lou. If I see her near Lou again, if I find out that she's even breathing the same air, I will not be happy.' Dylan let go of her arm and shoved her towards her husband.

'I told you,' her mum said in a fake shaky voice, 'complete ruffians. I told you this was a bad idea.

'What happened?' It was obvious that Lou's dad didn't quite know what to do at first, but, as his confusion cleared, he turned to look at his wife. 'What did you do?'

'Oh that's just typical,' she spat. 'What did *I* do? Never your precious daughter. God forbid that she could be anything but completely perfect. Noooo, let's just brush to the side the way she dresses and acts like a prostitute, the company she keeps, the way she treats her own mother –'

'Enough!' Her dad's face was red as he stared at his wife in revulsion. He turned to Lou, extending a hand. 'Lou-Lou?'

'Just go, Daddy,' Lou said quietly, unshed tears sparkling in her eyes. Her dad hung his head and for a second, looking utterly defeated before he sighed, saying, 'Come on, Evelyn. It looks as though you've done enough for one evening.' With a wary glance at Dylan, who was standing to the side with his arms crossed over his chest, he steered his wife through the crowd and out of the double doors.

The exchange had been loud and several people were now watching Lou and Dylan. All Lou knew was that she needed to get out of there before she lost it in front of everybody. The Sands family had provided enough entertainment for one evening, and the last thing she wanted was to add her tears to the whole mortifying scene. She knew she should probably say something to Dylan, but she was in no mood to endure any more embarrassment, and explaining her mother's words would be excruciating.

So, coward's way out it was, and she pushed through the crowd to get to the cardy that she'd left on the bar stool. Once she'd slipped it on and sighed in relief that her marked arms were covered, she felt large hands land on her shoulders turning her around to be confronted by a less than happy Dylan.

'I'm taking you home,' he told her.

His ridiculous bossiness actually made her smile despite herself. But her smile died as she saw Katie approaching the bar, craning her neck and obviously scanning for him. Lou's eyes dropped to contemplate her shoes and she vaguely registered how much her feet hurt; there was no way she would give up wearing four-inch heels, but it had to be said that after sixteen hours straight they smarted a little.

'Hey, guys,' an out-of-breath Katie said, drawing up next to them. 'Happy birthday, Louey.' She grabbed Lou round the waist, pulling her into a tight hug, as was Katie's way. Lou hugged her back; she liked Katie. It wasn't Katie's fault that she

84

had what Lou wanted (or what she thought she'd wanted before he became an arsehole), and anyway Lou was well practised at overcoming her jealousy as far as Dylan was concerned. For tonight though, Lou had decided that enough was enough, and when she pulled away she faked a grimace and put her hand over her mouth, saying, 'I'm sorry, guys, but I think I'm gonna be –' fake retch '– s-sick. I ...' and with that she turned and sped off towards the loos. At the last minute, and once the crowd had swallowed her up sufficiently, she hopped from foot to foot taking off her heels, and ducked down to scurry through the throngs of people.

Reaching the exit, she breathed a sigh of relief, but just as her hand made a grab for the handle it was enclosed by a much larger and far warmer one, and she was tugged forward through the door.

'What on earth –'

'Babes,' Dylan cut her off, not even bothering to look back at her as he dragged her along behind him down the pavement, 'no lip.'

'Dylan,' she shouted, trying to twist her hand free as she felt one of her feet step in something wet (the fact that there had been no rain that day did not bode well for the identity of said liquid outside a busy pub). 'Will you stop, you big Welsh lunatic; I'm not wearing any bloody shoes.' He drew to a halt so suddenly that Lou careened into his back and nearly lost her balance, but was steadied by Dylan's large hands enclosing her upper arms.

'Why in the fuck not?' he asked, frowning down at her. 'Jesus, sometimes I forget just how short you are.' Lou straightened to her full five foot six and glared at him.

'I'm not short; not all of us can be great, hulking, overgrown Neanderthals.'

'You're not tall either. You just prance around in those stilts all day so it seems like you are. Now, why aren't you wearing shoes? And why are you running away without saying goodbye to everyone at your own goddamn party? I don't think I've ever seen you make any entrance or exit that wasn't laced with more than a little drama.'

'Look, Dildo, I'm in no mood for the third degree alright?' Lou sagged slightly, and his hands tightened fractionally around her arms.

'And that voice,' he went on, frustration evident in his tone. 'Stop using that ffwcin voice.'

'What are you talking about? And what's f ... ffwcin? I hate it when you swear in Welsh.'

'I can't stand it, Lou.' He abruptly released her arms and stepped away, running both his hands through his already messy hair and looking down at the pavement. He took a deep breath, looking back at her, his green eyes boring into hers, and then stepped forward, right into her space, and cupped her face with one of his hands. Lou tipped her head back so as not to break eye contact, and her breath caught in her throat.

'Please, babes, I can't stand this small, lifeless voice from you. Nothing about you is small and lifeless.' His eyes flicked down to her chest before he looked back up with a cheeky grin on his face, breaking the tense atmosphere. Lou rolled her eyes but felt her mouth curve into a smile despite herself. Dylan was right. Louise Sands was not a shrinking violet. She was bold and brash and in-your-face. She didn't slink away from her own party, and she certainly didn't take any crap.

After shoving her heels back on and wincing as her wet foot squelched into the expensive leather, she straightened to her new, improved full height, shook out her hair and put both hands on her hips. Dylan's smile grew wider and what looked like relief flashed through his features.

'Let's get a few things straight, surgery-boy,' Lou said, all traces of small-and-broken swept away. 'You're going to pull your sodding finger out on the ward from now on.'

'Yes,' he replied immediately, and her eyebrows shot up, blatant disbelief colouring her expression.

'I will, babes, I promise. I'm a prick, I'll do better.'

His hands came up to cup her face, and he shocked her by bringing his forehead down to rest against hers.

'I'm so fucking sorry,' he whispered, the pain and regret in his voice almost painful to hear. 'Is that swearing English enough for you?'

Lou closed her eyes. There wasn't anyone on the face of the earth with as much power to hurt her as this man, but he wasn't to know that. How could he know how much he'd crushed her? She took in a deep breath and let it out slowly.

'I forgive you,' she whispered back, opening her eyes and meeting his. She'd said it before, but this was the first time it really meant anything.

'Thank you,' Dylan breathed as he took his hands from her face and pulled her in for a tight hug.

'Okay, Dildo, calm down,' Lou wheezed. 'Can't ... breathe ...' She felt the sudden bite of the night air as he abruptly released her, stepping back almost awkwardly and running his hands through his hair. Weird: Dylan was almost never awkward, seeming immune to any form of embarrassment most of the time.

'What ... um ...' he muttered, and Lou frowned in confusion. More awkwardness? Bizarre. 'What did your mum mean by ... um –'

Now, Lou had always been able to think on her feet. It was a natural ability that came in useful given her impulsive nature. So in a completely self-assured, derisive tone she cut him off. 'Don't get your knickers in a twist. So what if I had a bit of a crush on Ewan when I started at uni? It's all water under the bridge now.' Dylan crossed his arms over his broad chest and raised an eyebrow.

'You fancied Ewan Evans?' Lou nodded casually. 'Ewan Wet-pants Evans?'

She shrugged, 'His other charms overshadowed the whole personal hygiene thing. Not all of us are as squeamish as you.'

'The guy stank of urine, Lou. He notoriously put his dick away before he finished pissing, and didn't wash his hands. I watched the sick bastard do it a fair few times myself. The front of his pants had a constant wet patch.'

'You're so judgmental.'

'Babes. I'm not judging him. If he wants to stink of piss then he can be my guest. I'm just expressing doubt that you took one look-slash-smell of him and wanted to check out his urine-soaked knob.'

'You've just had a phobia of urine since I got Bernard to swamp your bed.' Lou smiled the smug little smile she could never hold in when recalling her victory, and Dylan's eyes narrowed.

'Bloody hell,' he said. 'First Bernard, and now Wet-pants Ewan. You've got some sort of twisted piss fetish. Golden showers and –'

'Yes, the smell of urine sets my heart racing blah blah blah,' Lou interrupted, waving her hands dismissively. 'I'm a self-confessed urophiliac. Ricky Martin and I would be in seventh heaven together. Now smell my foot.'

'Smell your foot? Is this another weird –'

'Just smell it will you.' She balanced on one foot and lifted the other as high as she could, grabbing onto Dylan to stop herself toppling over. 'You dragged me through a yet-to-be-identified liquid. Obviously I need to know what it was and whether I need to change my stocking. Of course if it *is* piss I will be in thrills of ecstasy all evening so I'll probably –'

'You're wearing stockings?' Dylan's voice sounded strangely hoarse and Lou looked at him in confusion.

'Yes, freak. You know I never wear tights or cotton underwear. Now smell my foot.' Two slashes of red appeared across Dylan's cheekbones, and Lou saw him swallow before he cleared his throat. She shook her foot at him again and even had to resort to poking him in the tummy with it to snap him out of his stupor. He grabbed her calf, took a deep breath and lowered his head to her foot.

'Nothing,' he said in a choked voice before clearing his throat again and releasing her leg. 'I mean, I think it's just water.'

'Oh well,' she muttered, shoving her shoe back on. 'Better luck next time I guess. Maybe I can sneak into the urinals and get some cheap thrills that way.' Dylan let out a strangled sound, which she thought might have been an attempted laugh at her joke, but his face still had a strangely faraway expression. She snapped her fingers in front of his nose, impatient now to get back to the pub, and furious that she had become the kind of woman who allowed a little bit of heartbreak and an unpleasant family member to run her out of her own birthday party.

'Come on loser. I need a drink.'

*sguthan – STUPID WOMAN

Chapter 11

My Louey

'RIGHT,' LOU SHOUTED, SLAMMING HER SHOT GLASS DOWN on the bar and stamping her foot. 'Who's dancing?'

The party had moved onto a bar with a live jazz band and, bizarrely, an open mic. The result was surprisingly good. Who knew that the pale radiologist who'd made it out of the bowels of the hospital for a rare night out had such a soulful singing voice? Or that the theatre team could give such a good rendition of 'Mack the Knife'.

Just as she was about to grab Frankie's hand and force her onto the crowded dance floor, the music was interrupted and a familiar, self-satisfied voice sounded over the microphone.

'Hello there, everyone. For those of you who don't know me, I'm Miles, and I work with an ... interesting woman who has a hitherto undiscovered talent.' Lou froze and turned towards the stage, her eyes widening and her face draining of all colour.

No, he wouldn't ...

'I must say I was surprised,' he went on, and Lou felt the urge to punch him right in his smug, smiling, annoyingly flaw-less face. 'She's not exactly known for hiding her light under a bushel; but it seems that she's been keeping a secret from us all, and tonight, as she's the birthday girl, I think she should finally let her talent shine through. Ladies and gentlemen, I give you Louise Sands.'

Lou's mind flashed back to a conversation she'd had with Gwen in Outpatients. Her worst fear: singing in public. It wasn't as if it was even an irrational fear. Lou was tone deaf, and not just in the fake self-deprecating way people say they are when they don't particularly fancy a singsong. Lou's singing was agonizing. Dylan had once likened it to the slow death of a constipated goat.

The whole bar erupted into applause, however, and Lou felt herself being shifted forwards through the crowd. She caught sight of Frankie's panicked face as she tried to push through the crowd after her, and noticed that Dylan had also moved away from Katie at the bar to start towards her; but she was powerless to stop being propelled forward. Before she knew it, she'd been pushed up onto the stage and was in front of the mic.

'What'd you wanna sing, love?' the sax player asked her, and she shot panicked eyes at him before looking back out to the seemingly vast crowd. Her hand shook as she reached up to clutch the mic, and she took a deep breath.

~

'I think maybe Miles has his wires crossed,' she started, and Dylan tensed, recognizing the broken quality in her voice that he had grown to hate. Miles was a dead man for humiliating her like this. 'You see, I ... um ... I really, *really* can't sing. In fact I'd say that it could even be considered a health hazard if I performed in public.'

'Come on, Lou! Don't be such a pussy!' Miles shouted from just in front of the stage, and a ripple of laughter spread through the crowd around him. He then stood and got up on his chair.

'Who here thinks the birthday girl should just bloody sing?' he shouted into the crowd, whipping them up into a frenzy. '*Sing. Sing. Sing. Sing,*' he started chanting, waving his arms for the crowd to join in. Once everyone had followed suit he smiled and turned back to Lou on the stage.

∽

LOU SHIFTED ON HER FEET, HEAT FLOODING HER FACE AS she prepared to make her excuses and get the hell out of there. Just as she was about to speak though, she locked eyes with a chuckling Miles, who had crossed his arms over his chest and raised an eyebrow in challenge.

Well, fuck him and the horse he rode in on, thought Lou. She closed her eyes for a second before slowly opening them and taking a deep breath through her nose, fixing Miles with a chilling glare. His smile faltered for a second in the face of her blatant defiance.

That's right, thought Lou, *squirm away, spawn of Satan; you ain't seen nothin' yet.*

∽

DYLAN WAS HALFWAY TO THE STAGE WHEN HE SAW A LOOK of determination replace the abject fear on Lou's face, then saw her turn away from the mic to talk to the sax player at her side. A slow smile spread across the guy's face and he nodded, before moving to form a huddle with the rest of the band. A few seconds later the first chords of Etta James's 'I Just Wanna Make Love To You' rang out through the bar. Lou's hips began to sway and her eyes closed for a moment, before she yanked the mic out of the stand and started murdering the song with gusto.

'*I don't want you ...*' she started, more shouting than singing really, and bearing little relation to what the band were playing, '*to be no slave ...*'

Then the strutting began, back and forth across the stage until she came to a stop in front of the piano.

'*I don't want you ...*' she continued, wrapping a hand around the back of the pianist's neck and then running it up into his hair. A couple of notes faltered, but to give the guy credit he managed to continue valiantly on.

Despite the terrifying noises she was making, the crowd was going absolutely crazy, ripples of laughter and applause coming from all sides of the bar.

'*... to work all day ...*' She moved on then to the sax player, and Dylan noticed the male laughter stop abruptly as she executed a perfect slut-drop onto her haunches in front of the poor guy, and then slowly worked her way up his body. The women were still cheering her on but most of the men were frozen in place, eyes fixed on the stage, their mouths hanging open. This only intensified as Lou ripped her shirt off when she came to a stand, leaving her in a tiny vest top, which showcased her bright pink bra underneath.

'Holy shit,' Dylan heard a man next to him breathe as Lou made her way back to the front of the stage.

'*... But I want you ...*' she continued, her free hand going into her hair and lifting it up to the top of her head, before releasing it with a flourish and shaking it out around her shoulders, '*... to be true ...*' Her focus now fell on the table in front of the stage, and Dylan saw that she was staring straight at a slack-jawed Miles, who'd foolishly failed to retreat a safe distance.

'*... And I just wanna make love to you.*' She pointed at Miles as she started descending the steps into the audience, never taking her eyes of him.

'*Well, I can tell by the way you walk that walk ...*' She was circling a wide-eyed Miles now. Terror and confusion were warring with blatant arousal across his features.

'... *And I can tell by the way you talk that talk* ...' She crouched down in front of him, put her hands on his knees to spread his legs, then moved in between them to work her way up his body until her free hand had slid up into his hair and her mouth was a hair's breath from his. Miles held perfectly still and looked like he was having trouble breathing.

'... *I can tell by the way you treat your girl* ...' she continued, having to move the mic up between them, but still managing to keep her lips centimetres from his, '... *that I could give you all the loving in the whole wide world.*'

She grabbed his tie and pulled him up with her as she stood.

'*All I wanna do is make your bread* ...' Another perfectly performed slut-drop saw Lou at Miles's feet, and then slowly working her way back up. '... *just to make sure you're well fed* ...'

Once back to standing, she pulled him down towards her as if to kiss him. Miles's lips parted and his eyes completely glazed over, mesmerized by Lou's beautiful face.

'... *I don't want you sad and blue* ...' She pushed him down, and he was so stupefied that the move threw him off balance, falling sharply back into his chair. Her leg then came up to rest on one side of the back of his chair next to his shoulder, stretching the dimensions of her skirt almost to breaking point.

Dylan had unconsciously moved through the crowd towards her and realized that he was now directly behind Miles's chair. She briefly flicked her eyes to his, and then nodded towards Miles, whose eyes were fixed on her leg.

Dylan realized what she wanted just in time as she belted out, '... *I just wanna make love to you.*' And gave Miles's chair a firm push with her foot, causing it to topple over backwards.

Before his head hit the floor Dylan caught the back of the chair. He was going to right it, but at the last minute, when he remembered how the bastard had tried to humiliate Lou, and he tipped it on its side. Miles came crashing out and Lou stood over him for a second, before snatching his pint of beer from the table. '... *Love to you*,' she continued whilst emptying the pint over a spluttering Miles on the ground.

Then, before he could get up, she turned on her heel and strutted back up to the stage, finishing off the song with a huge smile on her face. The crowd erupted with applause. Everyone was up on their feet cheering by the time Lou had calmly dipped down to pick up her shirt and sauntered off the stage.

~

'YOU'RE MY IDOL!' SHRIEKED KATIE, BOUNCING UP AND down on the balls of her feet in front of Lou. Lou looked down into her shining face and felt her heart lurch. Why oh why did she have to be so adorable? Why the hell couldn't Dylan find someone that Lou could justifiably hate?

'You. Are. A. Goddess,' Katie continued to shriek, grabbing hold of both Lou's hands in her excitement. 'I mean, holy guacamole, I would have freaked out all over the place. But no, you were all like BAM! "Take that, Miles, you snivelling weasel." ' Katie's arms were flailing wildly as she mimed punching Miles in the face, something Lou was pretty sure hadn't actually happened.

'Then he was all: "Oh no!" ' For some reason best known to herself Katie was using an extremely high-pitched voice to imitate Miles. ' "I made a huge mistake!" ' She was now cowering down in front of Lou, her hands held up in front of her in mock surrender. ' "Please don't kick me in the nuts while you pour beer all over me." '

Lou couldn't help herself; she gave in and started laughing at Katie's performance, vaguely wondering if the girl ever stopped talking, and if anyone could locate her off switch. Dylan reached down and plucked Katie up off the floor with an arm to her waist, laughing along with everyone else in the group around them.

Well, nearly everyone.

Lou had noticed that Rob's friend (another military guy, called Sam) looked totally nonplussed by Katie's performance, and was regarding her like she was something rather unpleasant that he'd scraped off the sole of his shoe. As Katie was Sarah's best friend, Lou assumed she had been around this guy a fair bit before, and wondered what he could possibly have found so offensive about her. She noticed Katie glancing briefly at him as she was set on her feet by Dylan, and saw that her face paled and her smile slipped slightly as she took in his disapproval, before quickly looking away. Sarah slung her arm round Lou's shoulders.

'You've got to teach me some of those moves, Louey-Lou,' she slurred, leaning heavily into Lou's side. Lou smiled at her briefly, but was distracted again by Katie, who had started chattering to Rob. Although Rob wasn't always the most forthcoming bloke, it was obvious that he had a soft spot for Katie, and was grinning in the face of her verbal diarrhoea: something about the local Women's Institute, and would he mind coming and talking to them about pirates.

Apparently a particularly feisty ninety-year-old had asked if she could come for a 'ride-along' when the team next went out to Somalia.

Lou sighed. It was official: Katie was the nicest person she had ever wanted to punch in the face.

∾

KATIE SETTLED INTO THE CROOK OF DYLAN'S ARM AND felt his breathing even out as he fell asleep. This was the first time she'd stayed over, the first time really in years that Katie had felt comfortable enough with a man to allow that level of intimacy. Not that they'd done anything. She knew she wasn't ready for that. But for some reason, despite Dylan's extensive reputation, she felt safe with him; she instinctively knew that he wouldn't push her. It was almost as if he wasn't really bothered either way, which Katie knew should have set off alarms bells but in fact she found oddly reassuring.

He was so much fun, and a massive contrast to her past experiences with men. She had vowed to herself that no boyfriend of hers would ever again be the dark, brooding type – and Dylan was anything but. In Katie's experience grumpy men made grumpy boyfriends, and grumpy boyfriends were *not* fun. From bitter experience she knew just how not fun they were.

Her mind flashed to Sam. Yes, grumpy and broody and mysterious pretty much summed him up, she thought – and bloody rude. Katie knew that she talked too much, got overexcited and was generally a bit of a goof; but there wasn't really any way to hold it in. Lord knows she tried around Sam. She tried to talk less, to not snort when she laughed, not bounce about too much as she was wont to do; but it was too hard, her personality was just too much to contain.

So she endured his obvious disapproval and remained her normal self whilst around him, which fortunately wasn't much, given his commitments in Somalia with Rob's company. The only slight problem was how desperately attracted she was to him. Despite his foul personality, every physical thing about him made her hairs stand on end: his height, his bulk, his thick dark hair and dark eyes, his strong jawline, the way the muscles of his forearms rippled and bunched even when just passing her the salt at Sarah and Rob's house. Yes, in terms of aesthetics that man was pure perfection.

She huffed and snuggled in closer to Dylan, annoyed that she had allowed herself to think about that prick *again*. What was wrong with her? Here she was in bed with an attractive, laid-back, funny, great guy and all she could think about were the forearm muscles of a man who clearly disliked her.

Right: no more thinking about soldier-boy, she told herself furiously, snuggling into Dylan and kissing his neck for good measure. Dylan sighed in his sleep and pulled her closer, and Katie allowed herself to smile against his chest. *Perfect,* she thought, *this is just perfect, exactly what I need.*

'Mmm, babes,' Dylan muttered, obviously still asleep. Katie hadn't heard him call her 'babes' before, and smiled even wider at the endearment. But his next words wiped the smile straight off her face.

'Lou-Lou,' he breathed, pulling Katie more firmly into his side, '*My* Louey, *my* babes.'

After that bombshell, his breathing evened out again, and when he started lightly snoring, Katie felt it safe to roll away. She stared up at the ceiling for what seemed like hours, running all her encounters with Lou and Dylan through her mind.

Sighing in defeat, she began to make a plan.

Chapter 12

Twp

Lou sucked in a breath through her nose and let it out slowly through her mouth, searching for control over her temper.

'I said that she has had an NSTEMI and as such we can't –'

'A whatty-what?' Mr Kent piped up, frowning across the meeting room.

'A non-ST elevation myocardial infarction,' Lou said slowly, staring at Mr Kent in disbelief as his face remained blank. Had this guy actually gone to medical school? And if so, how the hell has he managed to wipe his brain clean of any knowledge obtained there? There were more than a few chuckles from the other orthopaedic surgeons in the meeting, and fortunately Lou was saved from repeating herself yet again when 'Percy', a.k.a. Luke, chipped in from the back.

'He's had a heart attack, boss,' he shouted, and Mr Kent's face cleared of confusion.

'Ah! A dicky ticker is it?' Mr Kent said. 'Well, I'm sure you chaps and chapesses can sort that out. We'll hold off on the old chop-chop and bang-bang for the moment. You just give us the go ahead when you're ready.' Lou opened her mouth to reply but was cut off. 'Right, I do so enjoy these little chats but must dash. You can tell Percy here anything else you need to.' After clapping 'Percy' so hard on the back that his tea spilt on his trousers, Mr Kent strode out of the meeting room without a second glance. The rest of the room swung their pained eyes back to Lou, silently begging her to cut the rest of the presentations short.

Every two weeks the Elderly Care team attended the fracture meeting to discuss their patients' medical issues, thus encouraging a 'joint approach'. In theory Lou supported this as a plan, but to be honest, most of the time it was like banging your head against a brick wall.

'Okay, look,' she started, crossing her arms over her chest, and then rolling her eyes when she noticed that this had fixated most of the room's attention below her neck.

'Hello?' she called, snapping her fingers. 'Stay focused, boys. Eyes up here.' Some of them had the good grace to look mildly embarrassed, but most just sat there smirking. 'Let's cut the crap. All I want is for you to stop fluid-overloading Mr Jenkins overnight. Leave the fluid balance to me. Just 'cause he's not pissing thirty mils an hour doesn't give you leave to pump him full of normal saline.' After a few moments of staring at her blankly (most were still focused on her chest) Lou sighed, saying: 'Right, okay. Lecture over. Off you go back to your power tools.'

～

'IT'S NOT THAT THEY DON'T CARE, BABES,' DYLAN SAID carefully (he wasn't about to risk their recent truce). 'They've got their skills and you've got yours. Maybe it's just best that we all stick to what we know.'

Lou sighed and ground to a halt outside the entrance to the

ward, turning to him. 'I understand that, Dylan,' she said, laying her hand on his arm and looking up at him. Since 'Lou kicking smug wanker arse night', as it had been christened by Katie (she was still in bewildered awe of Lou after watching her humiliate Miles, who it turned out had thrown a few snide remarks Katie's way previously), Lou had seemed to soften towards Dylan, and their friendship was nearly back to how it was. This, being what Dylan had been working towards for bloody ages, should have made him happy; instead he felt strangely empty.

Somehow, friendship with Lou was no longer enough. To be honest, it hadn't been enough since the night he woke up in her bed. In fact being with Lou and *not* holding her, kissing her, and doing other things to her (things that his imagination had catalogued in meticulous detail) felt almost painful.

His efforts to win back her approval and respect by being in a relationship for a change had backfired big time. Admittedly he was now sure that he'd been wildly off base about what he wanted in a woman before (he now knew now that shy and quiet was not for him), and technically Katie, being bubbly, loud, outrageous and cute as a button, should have fitted the bill perfectly; but the problem remained that she simply wasn't Lou.

'I understand that, I promise,' she continued, dragging him back to the present. 'And that's why we share care; but you guys know the basics, you know you do. Sometimes it's like you're deliberately trying to block it out, and the fact is that your patients aren't just a bunch of bones to be hammered together, they're people with medical conditions and social issues too. There's no getting around that and you know it.'

'URGH,' DYLAN MUTTERED UNDER HIS BREATH AS HE TRIED to pull Alun up into a sitting position. Christ, the guy was heavy.

'Fuccoff!' Alun grunted, pushing Dylan away with surprising strength, considering the state he was in. 'Drink!'

Dylan sighed.

'No wets right now, Alun, okay? Let's just try and work out what's wrong with –'

'Twp bugger,' Alun slurred in between his quick raspy breaths, eyeing Dylan and swatting at him like he was an annoying fly. 'Lou!' he shouted.

Dylan looked up to the ceiling, seeking patience. 'She's on her way, big man, okay?' At least he hoped she was, he'd bleeped her enough times.

Alun snorted behind his oxygen mask. Things were going south quickly, and Dylan was realizing that he had lost control of the situation. He had no other choice.

He turned to the ward sister, who was looking increasingly concerned at the unfolding disaster before her. 'Fast-bleep Miles,' he told her, and saw a look of relief flash across her face. He clenched his jaw. The last thing he wanted was for that smug bastard to see him floundering like this, but he didn't know what else to do short of putting out an arrest call, and seeing as Alun was still very much alive, that would make him look even more of an idiot.

Dylan had started the rehab ward round without Lou. She'd told him she would be late today – some reason he couldn't quite remember. And as soon as he arrived he was dragged over to a gasping Alun. The problem was Dylan didn't have the first clue why Alun was fighting for breath. His temperature wasn't high (if anything it was low) and there were no signs of pneumonia or fluid overload. He hadn't aspirated. His chest was clear.

'I've fast-bleeped him but he's all the way over at the main hospital, could be a while for him to get here,' the ward sister told him as she swept back into the cubicle.

'Lou!' Alun shouted again, and Dylan rolled his eyes.

'Get me some furosemide,' he bit out, desperation lacing his tone. Surely that would sort Alun out.

Clearly relieved that Dylan was finally making some sort of medical decision, the ward sister strode off to the treatment room.

'Twp bugger,' Alun repeated, although not quite as forcefully as before.

'Thanks again, big man, but if you hadn't noticed I am bloody well trying,' Dylan said through clenched teeth, rearranging the oxygen more firmly on Alun's face when he saw the sats dip to the low eighties again.

'Bah!' Alun exclaimed, waving his hand dismissively. 'Uffar gwirion*,' he continued to shout, pointing at Dylan. 'Idiot.'

'Here you go,' clipped the ward sister, shoving the syringe into his hand. He opened the valve on the cannula and was about to inject ...

'What's happening?' Lou's clear voice rang out as she swept back the curtains, and Dylan's eyes closed in relief.

'I was just –'

She grabbed the syringe out of his hand, frowning down at it.

'Furosemide?'

'I thought –' He was cut off as Lou moved him aside, took her stethoscope out and grabbed Alun's obs chart. After listening to his chest, examining his abdomen, and ascertaining that his urine was clear, she cocked her head to the side and pulled back the sheet covering his legs.

'Sepsis,' she muttered, running the back of her hand down Alun's leg. Dylan sucked in a shocked breath, having seen what he had missed. Lou put her hand to Alun's leg and started to bend it at the knee.

'Argghhh!' Alun shouted, leaning forward as much as possible what with being hooked up to the oxygen and i.v.'s.

'Sorry, Alun,' Lou muttered, gently placing his leg back on the bed. She then turned, dropped the syringe of furosemide in the bin and grabbed the drug chart.

'Fluids, i.v. flucloxacillin and clindamycin.' She turned to Dylan. 'We'll need –'

'To aspirate the joint,' he interrupted, scowling down furiously at Alun's knee. The overlying skin was clearly reddened, the joint itself was swollen. It didn't escape Dylan that this was an orthopaedic diagnosis. One that he should have been able to make.

'But ... but he wasn't pyrexial,' Dylan muttered in an attempt to justify his ineptitude. Had he actually given Alun that furosemide, it would have been very bad news for the old bastard, stripping him of much-needed fluid when he was septic and already dehydrated.

'Ever heard of the SIRS criteria, Dylan?' Lou asked once they were in the treatment room, Dylan preparing the tray to aspirate the joint and Lou on the phone waiting to speak to HDU.

'I ... well, I ...'

Lou sighed. 'Patients don't always have to be pyrexial to be septic; *hypo*thermia is a sign of sepsis too.'

'Shit,' Dylan breathed, yanking syringes and needles off the shelves. 'Could be nothing though, doesn't have to be septic arthritis ... Gout?' He knew he was clutching at straws, but admitting that a lack of medical knowledge had led to missing a major *orthopaedic* emergency was galling. Lou frowned at him for a second before her expression cleared.

'Look, don't beat yourself up about it, okay?' she said softly, laying a hand on his arm to halt his jerky movements. He shook her off, in no mood to be placated.

Unfortunately what Dylan didn't notice was the tension around Lou's mouth, the paleness of her face, and the red that rimmed her eyes, before they'd even started this discussion. In fact those things were in evidence before she had even seen Alun, but Dylan had been way too stressed to let it penetrate.

～

'SHARP SCRATCH FOR A SECOND, ALUN,' DYLAN WARNED AS he pushed the needle into the joint space. Lou could practically hear his prayers for clear fluid to come out of the needle. Anything rather than admit that a little medical knowledge might actually help him be a better orthopaedic surgeon.

'How was the feeding frenzy?' Miles slapped Lou on the back, sending her forward onto one foot. Great. The absolute last thing she needed was his smug face mocking her.

'What are you doing here, Miles?' she asked, her voice cold.

'Your boy here fast-bleeped me,' he explained gleefully, turning to Dylan. Dylan's shoulders tensed but he didn't turn away from his task. 'Did you need me to change you? Maybe hold your hand so the nasty medical knowledge didn't try to infiltrate your brain?' He chuckled but Dylan continued to ignore him.

When Lou turned to glance at him, she was surprised when he visibly flinched. In contrast to Dylan, Miles it seemed had not missed the effect that this morning had had on her appearance. Lou basked in a rare moment of awkwardness from Miles, who, at the sight of her obviously tear-stained face, was rendered momentarily at a loss for words. 'Lou ... are you? ... Um ...'

Lou stared at him levelly. If he didn't like the result of his petty vendetta, then he could bugger off and leave her alone. She wasn't about to hide it from him.

'What ... what happened?' he asked, shifting uncomfortably next to her.

'Cut the shit, Miles,' she hissed. 'Don't worry, you got what you wanted.' A look of genuine confusion crossed his face, which only served to deepen Lou's scowl. He was quite an actor. She turned away in disgust, focusing again on the syringe Dylan was holding and noticing with detached fascination that it was rapidly filling with grey-green pus. Dylan's shoulders slumped. Lou knew this was hard for him.

The old Lou, the Lou that had been a doormat for the last ten years would console him; she'd reassure him and try to make him feel better. But after what had happened at her appraisal this morning, that Lou was dead. Her heart was finally behind a wall of ice that wouldn't ever be penetrated.

Not ever.

*UFFAR GWIRION – *SILLY BASTARD*

Chapter 13

Definition of 'hard to get'

'Looks like my argument for us just sticking to hammering nails and playing with our power tools is wearing pretty thin,' Dylan joked as they turned into the main ward. Lou smiled at him but as usual it didn't reach her eyes.

Since the Alun disaster, Lou had made out to everyone else that it was Dylan's save *and* his diagnosis, saying things like: 'Wasn't it lucky that we had an orthopod on the team to catch that one?' and 'It just goes to show how brilliantly the teams can work together.' It was safe to say that Dylan was firmly out of the shit as far as the geris consultants were concerned, and he knew that it was entirely down to Lou. In fact, there were quite a few times Dylan could recall when Lou had extracted not only him but also numerous others from potentially disastrous situations.

Before he could make any more asinine comments in an attempt to lighten the heavy atmosphere, they rounded the corner into Mrs Jones's and Mrs Talbot's bay. Lou slapped down a copy of the *Radio Times* on Mrs Jones's bed-table. It had Kylie on the cover. It was lucky that Kylie didn't seem to have aged for the last twenty years, seeing as Mrs Jones was still stuck firmly in 1987: it meant that the magazines and newspapers Lou bought for her featuring Kylie went down a treat.

Mrs Jones snatched it up, flashing Lou a rare smile. The smile Lou gave her in return *did* reach her eyes, and Dylan felt his jaw clench in frustration. It had been over two weeks since he'd misdiagnosed Alun. And Dylan had finally learnt his lesson. Now he arrived even earlier than Lou on the wards to prepare for the rounds, and was surprised by the volume of work he had been allowing her to do for him.

He was worried about her.

She'd lost weight, and although she still strutted down the corridors there was definitely less bounce in her step. Dylan had been so wrapped up sorting Alun and his septic arthritis out, that he felt like he had missed something crucial that morning. He'd been standing in theatre in the afternoon washing out Alun's knee, when the image of Lou's face from earlier flashed into his mind. He could have sworn she'd been crying (a rare event in itself for Lou), and he wished that he'd paid more attention to what that little weasel Miles had been asking her about.

Something had happened – and now Dylan was at a loss, yet again, as to how to get through to her. Although this time around it didn't seem to be only him she was blocking out. A grim-faced Miles had approached her numerous times over the last two weeks and she was equally distant towards him. Not that she had ever been particularly close to Miles, but she had always at least acknowledged him enough to spar with him, not either blank him or offer him the bland smiles she did now.

'What are you ffwcin doing here?' Both Lou and Dylan turned to see a red-faced fat man barrelling towards them across the ward. Dylan recognized him as Mrs Talbot's son, and was surprised. Since Dylan had chucked him off the ward the last time he had been keeping a low profile. Dylan was not averse to throwing this guy out again, and was about to intercept when Lou laid a hand on his arm. He looked at her, and she shook her head.

'Mr Talbot,' Lou started in a level voice whilst straightening up from leaning over to speak to Mrs Jones. 'I'm still your mother's doctor and I –'

'Had your wrist slapped, didn't you,' Mr Talbot sneered, a triumphant look crossing his face, having obviously noticed Lou holding Dylan back. 'Need to show me some respect now don't you, you superior little ast*.'

Dylan frowned. What was this guy on about? Lou bristled at his side.

'Maybe, Mr Talbot; but that doesn't mean that you don't have to show *me* some respect when you step onto *my* ward.' Mr Talbot took another step towards her, his hands curling into fists at his sides, and Dylan was about to move when he was interrupted.

'For God's sake, Dafydd, will you just bloody *shut up!*' Everyone froze and turned to an enraged Mrs Talbot, her eyes for once seeming completely lucid. 'You were a horrible little boy and now you're a horrible, greedy little man. Leave my doctor alone. I'm not dead yet, you miserable bastard, and I intend to hang on a good while longer just to spite you and keep your grubby hands off my money. Now get out!'

'Mam, I –'

'Get out, get out, *get out!*' she shrieked, rolling up the *Radio Times* she had snatched from Mrs Jones's table and throwing it at his head, with which it connected in a most satisfying way between his eyes. The look he threw Lou before he stormed off was pure venom, a muscle ticking behind his jaw.

Dylan watched his retreating back with a strange sense of

foreboding. Something wasn't right about this guy, and something about the undiluted hatred he displayed when staring at Lou made Dylan feel slightly alarmed.

'What does he mean, "had your wrist slapped"?' Dylan asked once they had calmed down Mrs Talbot and Mrs Jones, both of whom were visibly shaken (Lou had to draft in Frankie with some of her millionaires' shortbread, but the smug look on Mrs Talbot's and Mrs Jones's faces once they were set up with their favourite cake and some tea made Dylan suspect that some of their swooning may have been for effect).

'It seems he's a pretty resourceful guy. He's complained to the CCG, his MP, the GMC. They're worried that he'll go to the press. The public lap up those stories about hospitals mistreating the vulnerable elderly,' Lou replied, shrugging and striding off to the next ward. Fortunately Dylan's legs were significantly longer, even with the stilts-slash-shoes she opted for, so he kept up easily, much to her annoyance.

'What mistreatment?'

'His word against ours ... and he's very vocal.'

'But you shouldn't stand for that, we should –'

She ground to halt outside the pathology lab and swung to Dylan.

'What do you care?'

～

LOU ROLLED HER EYES. SHE KNEW SHE SHOULDN'T HAVE said that. She shouldn't sink to his level – but he was so two-faced and obvious she just couldn't help herself. All this time pretending he knew nothing about what happened two weeks ago was ridiculous. Well, she didn't care any more; she'd made her decision. Not that she had much choice; not that the hospital was giving her much choice.

'Look, Richard's at a meeting; you don't need to be here.' Lou had had enough, there was no point dragging him all over the hospital. 'Tomorrow's your last day anyway. What's the point?'

'Come on, Lou. I've worked up the patients for you. It'll be quicker if I –'

Lou shook her head in confusion. 'I don't get it, Dylan. What? Just because you nearly dried out an already dehydrated and septic Alun, you're on some sort of medical kick?'

Although she wouldn't admit it to Dylan, especially now, he had actually stepped up in the last two weeks. But that didn't change the fact that he had been dumping work on her for the last six months, or what she had found out two weeks ago. Since then she'd been on a run of long days and nights and had barely seen or spoken to anyone. She hadn't even told Frankie what had happened.

Lou was just so used to being the one who looked after her friends, Frankie being no exception, that when she herself needed someone to lean on she found it hard to admit. Being vulnerable was not Louise Sands's forte; her mother had taught her long ago that it was a bad idea. She also knew that Dylan's betrayal and subsequent treatment of her back there in the mess had dented his relationship with Frankie, and much as she hated him at the moment she didn't feel like she could kill that off altogether.

'Lou!' An out-of-breath Miles came jogging down the corridor towards them, looking uncharacteristically flustered. 'God, I'm glad I caught you. I just wanted –'

'Go away, Miles,' Lou said through clenched teeth. 'I'm not in the mood to listen to your bullshit today.' Miles ran his hands through his hair in a gesture of frustration.

'Look, you've got it wrong. I don't know how you –'

'Miles, I think Louise asked you to leave.'

Finally, a decent human being, Lou thought, grateful that Rich had chosen that moment to arrive on the ward. Out of everyone, he had been the most supportive, even giving up his free sessions to talk her through her options now that the foundations of her career had shifted.

'Listen, Dick, I was talking to Lou and –'

'And now you're not.' Rich took Lou's arm and led her away, leaving Dylan and Miles gaping in the doorway.

Now, Lou was not really the kind of woman who appreciated someone leading her away or trying to fight her battles for her, and she felt a twinge of annoyance as they walked to the ward desk; but she shook her head to clear the feeling, reminding herself how kind and patient Rich had been. Both men made a move to follow, but Rich quickly dispatched the ward sister, who was not the sort of lady you argued with if she didn't want you on her territory. Lou managed to beat back yet another twinge of annoyance at that too: taking up precious nursing time to fight her battles wasn't her style either.

Maybe she should talk to Frankie, she thought as she printed the ward list. Maybe relying too heavily on Rich wasn't that great an idea.

～

'HONEY, OPEN THE DOOR.'

'I'm fine, Lou, honestly.' Frankie's sad little voice drifted through the locked bathroom door and Lou felt like her heart was breaking. What on earth had happened now?

'Please, Frankie.' Silence followed, broken only by soft, muffled sobs from behind the door. 'Shall I call Tom? Surely he must –'

Lou was suddenly propelled backwards as the door was flung open. Frankie was surprisingly strong for her size.

'No, no, no, don't call him, not yet.' Frankie's pale face was awash with fear and she gripped Lou's hand like it was some sort of lifeline. Lou narrowed her eyes. She'd told Weasel what she would do to him, or, more specifically, to his manhood, if he hurt her best friend.

Frankie shook her head, having caught Lou's furious expression. 'No, Lou, it's nothing he's done. It's me. I've been stupid and careless and irresponsible and now ... now ...' Her breath hitched and she collapsed onto Lou, drenching her T-shirt with tears.

'Hey, shhh, what's all this?' Lou cuddled her close and moved them both over to the sofa. Once they were sitting, with Frankie wrapped in both Lou's arms, Lou felt something stabbing into her hip. She looked down and gently pulled a white plastic stick out of Frankie's stiff fingers.

'Ah,' she said, understanding dawning as she took in the two blue lines. 'Does Tom know?' she asked, biting her lip. If he did know and he'd left her in this state she was going to have his balls for breakfast.

'Of course not,' Frankie cried in horror. 'I've only just had the courage to take the test. I'm not even that late for my period but ... well ... you know how I've been staying over at his a lot?' Lou nodded against her hair. 'Well, I forgot my wash-bag a couple of times and ... I mean, I told him that it might be ...' Jesus, Lou thought. Frankie, whose cheeks were now traffic-light red, was literally the most prudish person Lou knew.

'You had sex anyway,' she said, putting Frankie out of her misery.

'He said ...' Frankie's breath hitched as a fresh wave of tears threatened, '... he said it would be fine. He said not to worry ...'

Lou had a suspicious mind. She'd seen how Tom had often hassled Frankie out of the flat with only a half-packed bag. She was going to kill him, that sneaky little Weasel.

Despite her anger she managed to keep her voice level when she suggested: 'I think I'd better ring him, Frankie, okay? Ask him to come over. I'll stay if you want.'

'He's going to be so angry,' Frankie whispered, and Lou rolled her eyes in frustration. She suspected that the last thing Weasel would be was angry.

Shifting so that she could pull her phone out, and not bothering to wait for a response from Frankie, Lou put the phone to her ear.

'Weasel? I'm with Frankie. You better get your arse over here or I'll find you and drag you myself.' She paused at the flurry of questions down the line. Tom could no doubt hear Frankie's muffled sobs in the background. 'Just get here, okay?' she said, softening her tone in the face of his obvious concern.

Worryingly it only took ten minutes before Weasel was banging on the door in his typical bossy manner, causing Frankie to nearly leap out of her skin.

'Wait here,' Lou told her as she disengaged from her on the sofa and moved to the door. Her heart seized when she looked back at a despondent Frankie sitting, twisting her fingers together, and she felt a fresh wave of anger.

'Back up,' she barked at Weasel as soon as she opened the door, poking him in the chest to make him reverse out into the corridor. She thought for a minute that he would push past her, but he must have seen the determination in her face, and took a reluctant step back. Lou pulled the door to behind her, and crossed her arms over her chest.

'Frankie's terrified in there,' she told him, her voice low and vibrating with anger.

'What's happened?' Tom tried to push past her again, but was rewarded with a firm poke the same place as last time. 'Ow! Will you stop, you nutter. Honestly I swear you'll break one of my ribs doing that one day.'

'It's no less than you deserve.'

'What does that mean? What have I done now?'

'It's what you didn't do that concerns me, Weasel.'

'What? Look Lou –'

'How about: "Come on, Frankie, let's just get going, you don't need any stuff to stay at mine." Or, "Don't worry about the pill, Frankie; it'll be fine." '

Tom's face lit up and he made another move around Lou. 'Is she ... ?'

Lou threw up her hands, then pushed him back into the corridor. 'Yes, Weasel – that was the plan, wasn't it?'

Tom's elated expression faltered for a moment and he started rubbing the back of his neck with his hand, looking down at his feet and scuffing the floor.

'It's not like I went out of my way to ... to ...'

'Knock her up? Isn't it? So that's why you weren't too worried that she "forgot" her pills, or why you didn't bother to use a condom?'

'It wasn't deliberate, Lou, but ... but ... I guess ...'

Lou had never seen Tom look anything less than supremely arrogant, and his sheepish demeanour went some way to softening her anger.

'You guess that it was kind of what you hoped for.'

Tom shrugged helplessly. 'I wasn't really thinking to be honest, Lou. I just thought that ... well ... if she did happen to ... you know ... it would mean that she ...' He trailed off and Lou narrowed her eyes.

'It would mean that she would be tied to you?'

Tom sighed. 'I wasn't deliberately going out of my way to trap her, Lou. It's just that she's been the very definition of hard to get, and the thought of her slipping through my fingers again is –' He was interrupted by the door opening behind Lou. Frankie stood in the frame. Her eyes were still red-rimmed but her tears had dried and the look of fear on her face from earlier was replaced by a look of wonder.

'You're happy I'm –' she started to say in a hopeful, breathless voice but was cut off as Tom pushed past Lou and snatched her up in a fierce hug.

'Of course I'm bloody happy,' he said, his voice hoarse with emotion as he practically lifted her off her feet.

'You want me to be pregnant? You're not angry?'

Tom pulled back so he could look directly into her eyes. 'I am the happiest I've ever been in my whole sodding life,' he said fiercely. Frankie searched his face, running her fingers from his temple down to his jaw reverently. Once she'd seen whatever she was looking for in him, her expression cleared, and she smiled her most dazzlingly smile. Lou made a frustrated noise in the back of her throat, and both eyes swung to her.

'Frankie,' she said slowly and with what she regarded as infinite patience. 'You do realize that he *wanted* to get you pregnant? That he deliberately –'

'Really?' Frankie breathed, her hand still cupping his face, her smile if anything more dazzling than before. Lou looked at the ceiling in despair.

'Frankie, that is *not cool*. Weasel shouldn't just get away with …' Lou trailed off when the kissing started. It was clear that as far as the two of them were concerned she had ceased to exist. She huffed, but as Tom started shuffling Frankie back into her room and Frankie threw a huge smile at her over her shoulder, looking absolutely ecstatic, Lou couldn't help a small smile. Maybe he was a caveman, but if he could make Frankie smile like that then Lou could let it go. For now.

Lou's smile died as she made her way to her own room and flopped down on the bed. So much for offloading on Frankie. But as Lou had done, time and time again in the past, she put her own worries last on her priority list, swallowed back her emotions and blinked away her tears before they had a chance to fall.

Chapter 14

Stopped expecting too much a long time ago

'LOVE IS PATIENT; LOVE IS KIND; LOVE IS NOT ENVIOUS OR ...' Lou stopped as she felt a sharp tug on the front of her dress and heard the ripple of laughter go through the congregation.

'Louey, cuccol!' cried Finlay, who was standing beside her at the front of the church, his sturdy little legs planted wide and a stubborn expression on his face.

She looked up from his angelic little face to see the chaos he was causing in the second row as Jack and Benji struggled to contain a squirming Thomas, who obviously wanted to join his brother, and Rob tried to squeeze past everyone to retrieve Finlay. Lou smiled and put up her hand to Rob before bending down to scoop up Finlay and settle him on her hip. Happy with his new position, Finlay snuggled into Lou's neck, and she resumed the reading that she luckily had learnt by heart. Things only got slightly tricky during the last paragraph, when Finlay decided that he would cover Lou's mouth with one pudgy little hand and shove the other down the top of her dress; but Lou continued valiantly on despite the general amusement of the crowd and her own laughter threatening to come. Looking down at Frankie's shining expression, she knew it had been worth it.

There had been enough disappointments today for Frankie without Lou adding to them.

True to form, Frankie was not revelling in the whole centre-of-attention thing, and had been a nervous wreck right up until the moment she saw Tom standing at the other end of the aisle. However, when she caught sight of him it was as if the crowd melted away, and she looked almost confident as she walked towards him. In typical arrogant fashion, Tom hadn't been willing to wait at the other end like a normal bloody person. No: as soon as he saw her he broke away from his best man and started striding towards the wedding party. Lou had never seen anything like it. It was as if he thought Frankie would turn tail at any moment. He snatched up her hand and ended up tugging her along after him to the altar, her arm still linked with a bemused Dylan.

This behaviour, whilst being utterly ridiculous, did at least seemed to cut through Frankie's nerves. And Lou had to admit that, although it made her roll her eyes, it brought a tear to them as well.

Up until that point it was safe to say that things had not gone exactly to plan. Frankie had stayed in the flat with Lou the night before. After the shock of the pregnancy, Tom had used Frankie's dazed state to his advantage, and wasted no time moving her into his house with him. To Lou's frustration this was something he had taken into his own hands with little apparent consultation with Frankie. The sneaky weasel had just loaded up his van with more and more of her stuff each time he collected her, until one day Frankie had realized that not even her toothbrush remained in the flat. It was like watching a sleepy, confused kitten get bulldozed by a lion.

Surprisingly, though, Frankie had dug her heels in about the night before the wedding. She was staying with Lou, and nothing he could say would persuade her otherwise. Lou hadn't bothered to find another flat mate since Frankie left. Frankie had insisted on paying for three months' notice, and Lou could afford it on her own – more than afford it in actual fact. Even now that she wasn't earning. She'd never really needed the rent Frankie had insisted on paying her, and she definitely wasn't in the mood to live with anyone else.

They had been woken that morning by an extremely overexcited Sarah, who came crashing into the flat at the ungodly hour of six-thirty. Lou and Frankie were both sleeping in Lou's bed together. The sheets had long since been stripped from Frankie's bed, and neither of them was in the mood to make it after the frantic organizing yesterday. Also Lou could literally feel Frankie's nervous energy like a living force in the flat, and she knew that she wouldn't want to sleep alone.

Lou had made the unwise decision to give Sarah a spare key to the flat, and thus there was nothing stopping her crashing through and leaping all over both of them in Lou's bed. They had both burrowed further under the duvet, only to have it yanked completely off before Sarah grabbed both their faces, squeezing either side of their mouths and giving their heads a shake, shouting, 'Welcome to the family!' and grinning like a madwoman.

'I'm not married yet,' Frankie said as best she could with her lips being smushed into a weird pout by Sarah's surprisingly strong grip.

'And I'm not planning on joining,' Lou put in, her voice matching Frankie's.

'Bah! You –' Sarah released their faces and punctuated her words by grabbing Frankie's hand and pulling her up to sitting '– are practically married. And you –' she repeated the same manoeuvre with Lou, forcing her to sit up and poking her in the chest '– don't think you can get out of joining the Longley family.'

'Thankfully you have no more obnoxious brothers left to make good on that threat,' Lou mumbled, flinging her arm over her eyes and flopping back down on the bed.

'Uh-uh,' Sarah replied, shaking her head and pulling Lou's arm down so she could catch her eye, 'you're already Auntie Louey to my boys. You can't get out of it just because there's no poxy bit of paper calling you a Longley.' Lou groaned.

'You just want me for my babysitting abilities,' she grumbled, squinting up at her.

'I'll have you know there are people clamouring to look after my little angels.'

Lou snorted, knowing just how far from the truth that really was.

'Anyway, get your arses up and at 'em. We've got some serious prep work to do.'

Thus began the hair-and-makeup torture session. Somehow Sarah had managed to convince the famous cross-dressing guy from the MAC counter in town to come to the flat, and even managed to convince him to tone down the 'drama' to a more natural and less drag-queen level. Gabriella had been drafted in for hair at Frankie's request, and did a surprisingly good job despite spending most of the morning crying what she called 'happy tears' and incessantly patting everyone's faces. (Even the MAC counter guy didn't get away without a few face-pats and at least two hugs.)

The fact that Frankie looked so incredibly stunning by the time her hair was pulled back softly from her face with flowers, and the expertise of the MAC guy had made her lashes impossibly long, thus accentuating her high cheekbones, made the hour before they were due to leave for the church all the more heartbreaking.

Lou sensed something was wrong around mid-morning. Frankie kept shooting nervous glances towards the door of the flat, and checking her phone every five minutes even though it wasn't on silent. When her phone did finally ring she nearly lost an eye to a mascara brush as she shot out of her seat to grab it. But when she registered the tune (in typical Weasel fashion Tom had programmed Frankie's phone with 'I Need A Hero' as his own personalized ringtone), an odd look of disappointment flashed across her face before she took a deep breath and answered it. Lou was shocked. It was unprecedented that a phone call from the great man himself caused Frankie to display the barest hint of disappointment. At the start of their relationship it had often provoked fear and apprehension, but that had since morphed into slightly sickening, unbridled glee whenever that obnoxious song started playing.

After a few minutes on the phone to Weasel, her tone not wavering from fake excitement, and a weird, forced smile of her face, Frankie handed the phone to Lou. 'He wants to talk to you,' she said, shrugging slightly at Lou's confused expression but obviously still distracted.

'Weasel?' Lou said into the phone as she watched a beautiful Frankie clad in a towelling dressing gown glide over to the window and stare down at the street.

'What on earth is going on with her?' Tom snapped. 'She's totally checked out. I thought you lot were going to look after her?'

'I know as much as you, Weasel,' Lou whispered into the phone, although she doubted that Frankie would have heard her anyway: she looked a thousand miles away. 'I mean maybe the whole centre-of-attention thing is getting to her.' Lou continued to watch Frankie, whose eyes were still fixed on the street below. She knew Frankie would be worried about today, but she didn't usually react this strongly if it was only worry for herself – unless ... 'Oh bugger.' Lou closed her eyes. How could she have been so stupid? 'Papa Marco ...' She trailed off.

Papa Marco had been over the moon about the wedding, and unfortunately his form of celebrating involved a fair amount of Stella. But he'd promised, he'd *promised* to walk Frankie down the aisle.

'I'm on it.' Weasel's curt reply came through just before he cut off. Lou walked over to the window, put her arm around Frankie's waist and rested her head on her shoulder.

'How's the bean doing?'

Frankie's lips curved slightly in the first semblance of a true smile that Lou had seen from her for the last two hours, and her hand moved to rest over her still-flat lower abdomen.

'He's okay,' she said softly, and Lou gave her a firm squeeze. They stood like that for the next fifteen minutes, with Lou fielding the others' questions until they eventually got the hint and left them to it. That was until the door burst open and Lou smelt the unmistakable aroma of Special Brew and vomit.

Frankie spun around, and before anyone could stop her she ran across the room and threw her arms around a dishevelled Marco, who was being held up between Ash and Dylan. He had a black eye and a small cut under his cheek.

'We found him outside the house,' Dylan said, his voice tight. 'He was asleep in the front garden, hidden behind the azalea bush.'

Marco had been a lot better recently. He was staying in Gio and Gabriella's annex and had even started doing some odd bits in the restaurant; but that had only lasted a few weeks and he'd never stopped drinking completely. Frankie reached up and framed his beat-up face with her hands, her tears making tracks through the previously perfect makeup.

'I was so worried, Papa,' she whispered.

'Francesca,' he slurred, appearing to struggle with the weight of his head and having difficulty focusing on her face. 'Bella Francesca. Sono orgogliosa.'

123

'He was excited for you last night, Frankie,' Ash's quiet voice put in, his eyes on her wet cheeks. 'I think ... I think he just lost control, he didn't –'

Frankie tore her eyes away from Marco and looked at Ash, giving him a shaky smile. 'I'm not angry, Ash. I was just scared. He wanted to be here so much ... he was so excited. When he didn't arrive I was worried that something had happened. I'm just relieved he's okay.'

'I'm so sorry, Ladies,' Dylan whispered, his free hand reaching to squeeze the back of Frankie's neck. Frankie took one of her hands away from Marco's face and rested it on Dylan's chest.

'I stopped expecting too much a long time ago, honey,' she whispered. 'I'm fine, honestly.'

Marco started sagging more, and Lou realized that he had actually fallen asleep standing up.

'Put him in my bed,' she said firmly, ushering them through to her room.

'But Lou –' Frankie started.

'No lip,' Lou said, propelling Frankie towards the now agitated MAC man, who was looking appalled by his ravaged makeup job. 'You get fixed up. We'll sort him and then we can go.'

Even though there was plenty of time, and even though everyone was ready to go early, they were still late to the church. This was because, as they were about to get into the cars, Frankie suddenly turned back.

'One minute,' she said to Lou, shoving her flowers at her and then racing back up to the flat in her heels. When Dylan and Lou made it up there they heard Frankie's voice singing softly in Italian. She was lying on Lou's bed in all her wedding finery, her fingers sifting through a snoring Marco's hair. When she'd finished the song, one that Lou had heard Marco sing to Frankie many a time before, she kissed his forehead and whispered, 'Arrivederci, Papa,' in his ear before slipping off the bed. There were no tears, no anger. In fact she looked happier than she had all morning.

'At least I know he's safe,' she said when she drew up next to Lou and Dylan, surprising them by smiling and linking her arms through both of theirs. As they moved through the flat she looked up at Dylan.

'Dyl, I was wondering if you ...' She trailed off, looking down at the floor for a moment, before squaring her shoulders with determination. 'I mean, would you mind ... I know it might be weird but ... would you walkmedowntheaisle?' Dylan took a moment to decipher the rushed words, but once he had, he wasted no time in snatching Frankie up in a fierce hug, nearly lifting her off her feet.

'Is that a yes?' Frankie wheezed. Dylan set her down and Lou could see his face was flushed and his eyes were wet.

He cleared his throat and blinked a few times. 'You bet you're sweet wedding-g-string-clad arse it is,' he said, smacking said arse, and then putting his arms around both Frankie and Lou. Frankie shot Lou a venomous look (Lou might have lied about the fact that the wedding underwear debate they had had last week was a tad bit loud not to have been overheard), but smiled up at Dylan. Of course, he'd blinked back the emotion and made a joke of it, but they all heard his voice break slightly whilst he did it. Lou could tell what this meant to him, and she was all the more glad she hadn't told Frankie anything that would change that.

125

Chapter 15

'Anger begins with madness and ends with regret'

WHEN LOU HAD THANKFULLY FINISHED THE READING, SHE gave Dylan – who was shaking with laughter – a warning glance before stepping down and walking back to Sarah at the front. Their dresses were long, dark blue and high-necked but almost completely backless (much to Sarah's annoyance, who Lou thought looked amazing, but who claimed that she had an elaborate suspension system underneath. 'Breastfeeding,' she said ominously. 'Just you wait; you can kiss goodbye to those perky bad boys.').

The rest of the ceremony was amazing, even if Tom did embarrass Frankie by giving her a full-on snog at the altar. The vicar's face was red with poorly concealed rage by the end, although Lou didn't know what else he had expected. After he'd told Tom at one of the pre-wedding counselling sessions that he didn't approve of kissing in the church, Tom had informed him that his fiancée was already knocked up, so it was safe to say the congregation would know that ship had sailed a while ago.

The whole thing was so beautiful that Lou experienced nearly an entire hour of forgetting about everything that had happened over the last month. But once she stood to walk back down the aisle, her arm was tucked firmly into Dylan's, and she was reminded yet again why last week's decision was the right one. She could feel his strength and warmth through his morning coat, and the temptation to lean further into him was almost unbearable. She actually breathed a sigh of relief when they made it outside the church and she could finally break away. That was until she collided with Miles during her getaway.

'Omph!' Although Miles was nowhere near as stocky as Dylan, he was still pretty solid, and Lou felt winded for a moment as his hands came up to steady her. 'Sands, you don't have to fling yourself at me to get my attention you know.' Lou shot him a filthy look, still trying to suck air into her lungs.

'What on earth are you doing here?' she wheezed, and then her eyes widened when she saw Rosie approaching his other side and taking his hand.

'He's, um ...' Rosie looked at Lou uncertainly for a moment, then squared her shoulders. '... He's my plus one.'

Granted, Lou had been away for a while – but not that long. How on earth had Miles pulled this off? Rosie was one of her friends, or at least Lou thought she was.

'How nice,' she said to Rosie, and watched as her face drained of colour. Lou pasted on a fake smile and started to move away, but her arm was caught and held by a persistent Miles.

'Where've you been for the last month, Sands?' he asked. Lou searched his face for any sign that he knew something, but it was a carefully controlled mask.

'I had a lot of annual leave stored up,' she replied nonchalantly, shrugging as if that explained an absence of over four weeks.

'Well, you need to ...' Miles broke off, and Lou watched his jaw clench, before glancing at Rosie and continuing in a softer tone. 'We ... we kind of need you. There have been a few incidents, and we seem to be ...' He glanced away, and when he looked back at her Lou was surprised to see that his expression was sincere. 'I don't think anyone, least of all the management, knew what kind of workload you were carrying, Lou. There've been a few locums, but to be honest they would have to employ at least three full-timers to cover everything you were doing.'

Lou's mouth dropped open. She wasn't surprised the department was struggling without her (although, after all that had happened, it did give her a sick sense of satisfaction), but she was shocked that Miles had the balls to admit as much, especially after what he'd done. She started to feel the slow burn of fury prickling under her skin, and ignoring Rosie completely she stepped further into Miles's personal space.

'You should have thought of that before then, shouldn't you,' she hissed. 'This just proves that "your brain's so minute that if a hungry cannibal cracked your head open, there wouldn't be enough to cover a small water biscuit". '

'Series Four,' a familiar male voice said from behind her, and Lou felt a big, warm hand fall on the small of her back.

'Episode?' she said automatically, the game so ingrained that it would have taken an earthquake to stop her asking.

' "Captain Cook",' was Dylan's smug reply.

Miles was looking between them in confusion, and then shook his head. 'What are you two on about? You're both so weird around each other, like you've got some sort of secret language or something.' He turned to Lou. 'And *what* are you on about? What should I have thought about before?'

Lou stared at his bemused face. Her hands curled into fists at her sides and she took a calming breath to stop herself slapping him silly.

'Don't you *dare* pretend you want me in the department,' she said, her voice tight with barely controlled anger, vaguely registering that she still hadn't lost the heat of Dylan's hand on her back. 'You did everything you could to get me out.'

'What are you on about?' Miles semi-shouted, and looking into his furious face Lou felt her control snap for the first time in weeks. So what if he knows? So what if they all find out? Who cares?

'Well, don't worry, you got your way.'

'What way?'

'I failed my RITA, you bastard. Even better result than you hoped for I bet.' Both Miles's and Rosie's mouths dropped open and Lou heard Dylan suck in a shocked breath behind her.

'I ... what ... why?' Miles stuttered, and Lou rolled her eyes in disgust.

'Well, the first thing they brought up was my three-sixty-degree appraisal. Apparently there was a very compelling argument from a "colleague" who didn't think I was up to standard. Hmm ...' Lou tapped her chin in mock contemplation. 'I wonder who that could have been?'

'Lou ... I didn't –'

'But lucky for you there was also a well-timed complaint from a seriously pissed-off relative, who I'm reliably informed has recently gone to the press. I think the headline's going to read: "Unfeeling Doctor has Elderly Lady's House Taken From Her." '

Dylan swore from behind her and Lou stiffened. She was tired of this bullshit pretence and his fake concern. It was time for it all to come out. She turned to face him, dislodging his hand from her back.

'But do you know what really clinched the deal?' she said. Dylan shook his head slowly. 'It was a trainee report that was submitted about me.' Lou paused for a second, and watched with satisfaction as all the colour slowly leached from Dylan's face. 'Now let's see: "poor teaching methods", "uptight and prickly to work with", "unapproachable" – and my own personal favourite: "The worst registrar I have ever had the misfortune to work for." '

'Christ,' Dylan said, tearing both hands through his hair. 'Look, Lou, I was angry … it was just after you'd landed me repeating the stint in Elderly Care. I thought I'd have to miss out on my research project and I … look, I didn't even think I'd sent it. I must have pressed send rather than cancel accidentally. I didn't mean to –'

'What are you talking about now, loser?' Miles interrupted, and they both turned to face him. He was frowning at Dylan, his face flushed red. 'You do know that she saved your sorry arse don't you?' Dylan just stared at Miles in confusion. Lou made to step around him, but he moved with her, blocking her way.

'Hold on a minute, babes,' he said, catching her arm at her elbow, then turning to Miles. 'What do you know about it?'

'Well …' Miles drew out the word, his facial expression resetting to his standard smug now that he felt he had the upper hand. 'I don't know what you *think* happened, but *I* was actually in the meeting between your bosses and mine. There was a big push to have you chucked off the rotation altogether, something about you setting the record for being the laziest, most disinterested trainee they had ever had. Good old Kenty was trying to stick up for you, but you know how difficult he finds forming a cohesive sentence, leave alone outline a decent argument, so it was left to the only friend you had in the room.

'Lou suggested you could stay if you did a few months of geris sessions, and when nobody wanted you on their team she volunteered for that too. Without her you would be out on your ear, mate.'

Lou wrenched at her elbow, but Dylan's hand had tightened around it almost painfully and she couldn't get free. He turned to her.

'Lou, I ...'

She watched in fascination as a vaguely green complexion suffused his pale face and he continued to struggle for words. Dylan was never at a loss for words.

'Is ... is that true?' he asked, trying to move them away from Miles and Rosie down the church path, then cutting Miles a frustrated look when he moved with them.

Lou rolled her eyes. 'What do you think, Dildo?'

To her that was the real question. She had never let him down in the past, never given him any reason to doubt her loyalty as a friend. He released her elbow and ran both his hands through his hair.

'I'm such an idiot.'

Lou could see that he felt bad and her instinct was to comfort him, tell him that everything would be okay. But she would not allow herself to be weak. Louise Sands was never weak. And she had taken enough crap from both of them.

'Well then,' she said breezily, waving her hands between them. 'Now that we've established that you've both ruined my career over petty bullshit that didn't even happen, I think I'll be getting back to Frankie.'

Surprisingly it wasn't Dylan but Miles who sprang forward to block her way this time.

'I don't know what report you think I gave, Lou, but I've never thought of you as a bad colleague, and I wouldn't lie about something like that on an appraisal report.'

Lou's eyebrows shot up, practically into her hairline. Miles hated working with her. Didn't he?

'I know you don't believe me but I actually liked working with you. I really got a kick out of pissing you off.' Lou regarded him for a minute.

'He's telling the truth, Lou,' Rosie said from his side, taking his hand in hers. 'He just enjoys being this arsehole guy. It's all for show really, love him.' Lou looked between them and for a moment her conviction that Miles had written that report slipped; but she noticed that when Miles saw she was wavering, the smugness started creeping into his earnest expression. Maybe he'd convinced Rosie he wasn't a complete prick, but the fact that he wanted to get in Rosie's pants on a regular basis would probably have proved a fairly big incentive. No way was Lou falling for the old 'there's a heart of gold underneath that annoying, manipulative exterior' play.

'Look, maybe he's decent to you, Rosie, but I'm not falling for it.'

She glanced at Dylan, who was still frozen in place on the path with his hands in his hair, and noticed Katie approaching him with a concerned expression on her face. Then, ignoring whatever other crap Miles had started spouting at her, she turned and strode off in search of the wedding party.

'You okay?' Rich fell into step with her as she was striding across the lawn to where the photographer was set up. She slowed her pace, offering him a small smile.

'Fine, absolutely fine,' she said with conviction, and Rich smiled back at her.

'I've talked to a few of the board members and I think they might be able to work around the whole RITA thing so your training's not too delayed,' he said, his eyes lighting with enthusiasm. At least somebody cared about her sputtering career. 'Of course, you won't be getting your CCT on the planned date, but I –'

'Hey, that's so kind of you, Rich,' Lou cut in. 'But ... look, I haven't told anyone yet, so I'd appreciate if you didn't spread it around, but: I've quit.'

Richard stopped abruptly, turning towards her with his brows drawn together. 'Quit? What do you mean you quit?'

Frankie started frantically waving Lou over and she realized that the other bridesmaids and all the ushers were already assembled.

'Oh balls,' Lou muttered. 'Sorry, Rich, have to catch you later.' She threw a glance over her shoulder as she scurried away, and was confused by the absolute fury she saw written across Rich's face before he carefully masked it.

~

IT TOOK A FEW MINUTES FOR DYLAN TO COME BACK TO himself and realize that he couldn't simply stare at his feet forever. He had to concentrate on forcing his hands, which were gripping his hair, to relax, and carefully paste some semblance of a neutral expression on his face. When he glanced at Katie, who still had her small hand resting on his bicep in concern, he knew that he hadn't quite achieved neutral.

'Hey, D, you okay?' she asked, her kind, open face awash with concern.

'Um ...' Dylan looked up and stared over at where the bridesmaids were gathering for the photos with Frankie. Sarah was bouncing up and down in a state of extreme excitement (this seeming to be her default setting throughout the entire service). Frankie was literally shining with happiness, and, at first glance, so was Lou. In fact Dylan was probably the only person there who could see the small lines of tension around her eyes, or notice the way her smile was ever so slightly forced.

He'd seen so little of her in the past six weeks that being in the same room as her that morning had actually felt like a physical relief. But in the last hour all the relief he'd felt had become overshadowed by guilt, and something which felt strangely close to panic. He couldn't actually remember everything he wrote in the feedback form, but what he did know was that by some tragic coincidence the three-sixty-degree assessment request had come into his inbox literally minutes after he'd read the email from Mr Kent confirming that he would have to give up on his research. It was like a red mist came down over his vision, clouding all reason. He'd dashed off the assessment in a fury – but he was sure he hadn't actually sent it, deciding instead at the last minute to confront Lou directly and storming off to seek her out in the mess, further screwing everything up.

What had he done? The thought of losing Lou's friendship for good this time made him so ill that he could feel the bile rise up in his throat.

'Did ... um ... did something happen?' Katie asked. 'You guys all looked pretty intense over here.'

Dylan's shoulders drooped and he let out a long breath. 'I'm a twp bugger,' he muttered, managing a small smile for Katie's benefit

' "Anger begins with madness and ends with regret." '

Dylan sighed and fought back the urge to smack Ash in the mouth; it wasn't his fault that his proverb compulsion was intensely annoying.

'Thanks, mate,' he said through gritted teeth. 'Seems the grapevine didn't spare the horses.'

'Rosie,' Ash explained with a shrug.

Great: half the wedding would know what a prick he was by now; Rosie was not renowned for her discretion.

'I hate to interrupt your self-pity session but we're needed over there,' Ash said, pointing at the wedding party.

'Oh, sorry, Ash,' Dylan said sarcastically. 'Just coming to terms with the fact I've lost my best friend for good this time.'

' "The key to all things is determination," ' Ash replied, slapping him on the back and even cracking a smile, the crazy bastard.

But before he could actually succumb to the urge to punch

Ash in the nose, Katie linked arms with him on his other side and they both propelled him forward towards the photographer.

'Listen to "The Guru",' she said, patting Dylan's arm and causing Ash to roll his eyes. Katie had nicknamed the poor guy within minutes of hearing his first proverb.

'You'll make it right. You could charm the hind legs off a donkey.'

'Right, well, Lou's not a donkey, more a vicious Rottweiler that you don't want to piss off but if you do ...'

They drew to a stop and Katie leaned up into Dylan's personal space and whispered, 'Listen to Ash. Man up. Be determined.'

Chapter 16

You never have

Lou's forced smile, as she posed for yet another bridesmaids' photo, slipped a little as she watched Katie lean into Dylan to whisper in his ear. How watching him be casually intimate with another woman had the power to hurt her now that she truly hated him was beyond her, and a little depressing. Turning her head away sharply, she pretended to notice a wrinkle in Frankie's dress, and reached down to smooth it out, but Frankie caught her hand.

'Everything okay?' she asked, and Lou faked a smile so wide she feared her face would crack under the strain.

'Of course.' With Frankie's disbelieving look, she realized that she would need to be a little more convincing; the last thing she wanted was to overshadow Frankie's day with her own issues.

Framing Frankie's face with her hands, she pulled her forward until their foreheads were touching.

'I love you, you loser,' she whispered. 'And, annoying as Weasel can be, I love this day for you. I love him for you. My best friend in the world finally has what she always deserved and I couldn't be happier.' Frankie's eyes welled, but she blinked the moisture away as she pulled Lou in for a crushing hug.

'Love you too,' Frankie said fiercely.

'Can everyone stop hugging?'

Frankie and Lou started when they heard the whiny voice. Benji was standing in front of them, his sturdy legs planted wide with both his hands resting on his hips in a hilarious recreation of his daddy's exasperated stance, oft directed at Sarah's frequent antics. 'Girls,' he muttered in a disgusted voice, rolling his eyes.

'Sorry, honey,' Lou said, reaching to tousle his hair. When he shrugged her off she leaned forward and gave him a quick hug, pressing her lips to his cheek in a big sloppy kiss.

'Ugh! No soppy stuff, Louey.' He was wiping his cheek but there was no hiding that his lips had curved up in a reluctant smile. When Jack drew up next to them, Lou wasted no time in giving him the same treatment, and was met by the same furious response.

'I'm sorry,' she said, straightening and holding her hands up in front of her in mock surrender. The smile on her face was the first that felt totally natural that day. 'I couldn't resist. You guys make the cutest pageboys.'

Lou and Frankie watched as both boys' faces flushed red.

'We are not pageboys,' Jack told her, practically yelling.

'Uh-oh,' Frankie muttered under her breath.

'We're ushers,' they both shouted together, drawing the attention of the whole churchyard.

'Course you are, boys.' Dylan slapped them both on the back. 'You've been ushering the hell out of everyone all day. Lou's just kidding. Aren't you, Lou?' He shot Lou a warning look, having already endured the horror of the full-on tantrum that had ensued at the mention of the word 'pageboy' this morning.

137

Lou felt her dress being tugged and looked down to see that Finlay had a firm hold of her skirt. He reached out his arms, looking up at her endearingly through his curly fringe. Once she'd given in and lifted him up, he pulled her face to his with his chubby hands.

'Ushers,' he said firmly, likely not having a clue what he meant but echoing his brothers anyway.

Lou pressed her lips together to stop herself laughing, and then buried her face in his soft neck, blowing raspberries till he was giggling uncontrollably. When she finally looked up she caught Dylan's eye. His expression was so intense, and so out of character for him, that she looked away in confusion.

Luckily at that point the photographer took over and they were all assembled into various combinations of family and wedding party. When the boys started wriggling and getting more and more grumpy, Dylan and Tom started flipping them upside-down, shouting, 'Usher me now, you nutters! Usher me!' and when that hilarity wore off Katie started doing the robot from behind the cameraman, then gave him bunny ears, which really brought forth the smiles they were after, causing Lou to clench her teeth. They were the perfect little double act.

∼

'Could the maid of honour and her partner please take to the floor.'

Lou cringed and was about to bolt, but she caught sight of Frankie's terrified face on the dance floor and knew she couldn't do it. A big, broad shadow moved into her line of vision, and she sighed.

'Let's get this over with,' she said, taking his outstretched hand and trying to ignore the familiar thrill that always shot through her when she touched him. She reluctantly looked up into his face, and watched as his jaw clenched.

'Lou, look,' he said, pulling her up out of her seat and onto the dance floor. Tom's parents and Sarah and Rob had all now been forced up there as well, and Frankie was looking relieved. 'I need to –'

'You know what, Dylan?' Lou cut him off. She was tired of everything being about what he needed. 'If you don't just shut up and dance with me I think I'm going to scream.' Dylan opened his mouth to say something more, but snapped it shut when he saw the look in her eyes. She watched again as his jaw tensed so much that she could see the muscle ticking in the side of his face, before he sighed and pulled her stiff body to his.

'Fine, Lou,' he whispered into her hair. 'I just seem to keep buggering everything up when we talk anyway, so maybe this is better.'

And, just for the three minutes left of the slow song Frankie had chosen, Lou allowed herself to relax into him, letting the feel of his big arms closing around her wash away all of her hurt and resentment. *Just these three minutes*, she thought to herself. *I'll give myself three minutes of this, then ...*

'Enough,' she whispered into his chest, feeling hers constrict painfully.

'What?' Dylan asked, drawing slightly away to look down at her as the song came to a close.

'I said enough now,' she told him, cupping his face with one of her hands. 'It's been too long.'

'I don't understand,' he said, his brows drawing together in confusion. Lou made a pathetic attempt at a smile and shook her head.

'I know,' she told him. 'You never have.' Before he could reply or even make an attempt to catch her arm, she had spun away and melted into the now crowded dance floor.

~

'GODDAMN IT.' DYLAN THREW BACK ANOTHER GLASS OF champagne as he scanned the crowd again for her blonde head.

You'd think that with his height it would be a snap to locate one errant bridesmaid, but she'd managed to evade him for the last two hours. He'd hoped that after the interminably long meal and speeches he might finally have a chance to talk to her. That was why he'd made sure to bribe the lead singer of the band to call the maid of honour to the dance floor, and had positioned himself to pounce as soon as the announcement was made. At least that would buy him a few minutes with her – although what he was going to say he didn't know. But, then again, he *was* king of the chat. He could talk and charm his way out of anything.

It was with this supreme confidence that he had pulled her into his arms. Even when she told him she didn't want to talk, he knew that he could get round that. He could get round anything if he put his mind to it. But when his hands had wrapped around her bare back and he'd felt her body relax into his, he'd lost all ability to think, let alone form a coherent sentence.

So now here he was, standing on tiptoes like some weird, huge, Welsh meerkat, having no success locating the one woman he wanted to talk to, whilst fending off hordes of women he didn't.

He felt a light hand on his arm and was about to spin around, ready to give the brush off to another of Sarah and Tom's horny cousins, but then heard Frankie's soft voice.

'Hey, you. Having a good time?'

He turned to her, and felt his breath catch at how beautiful and happy she looked. Pregnancy suited her, and being married seemed to suit her too. If anything she was more stunning with her dark hair slightly mussed and her cheeks bright with excitement after the copious amounts of dancing Tom had been making her do. He wrapped an arm around her shoulders and pulled her into his side, kissing the top of her head.

'Of course, Ladies,' he said, pulling back to smile down at her. 'The wets are free. The women are loose. I'm a happy man.'

She narrowed her eyes at him for a moment; Frankie was perceptive.

'What's going on with you and Lou?' she asked suddenly; but before he could answer he felt a sharp pain in his foot. He looked down and saw a small ball of five-year-old fury staring up at him.

'Benji!' Frankie cried in horror. 'That was *not* kind.'

Benji rolled his eyes at Frankie dismissively. 'We understand each other,' he said, more like a middle-aged mafia boss than a kindergartener. He turned back to Dylan. 'I thought *you* were going to look after *my* Lou.'

'Benji, I –'

'If you're looking after her so well, why is she leaving?'

Dylan stood completely still for a moment. He felt like he'd been hit by a truck.

'Leaving?' he asked, his voice having taken on a hollow quality. 'What are you talking about, runt?'

'She's going away for *ages*,' Benji whined, aiming another well-placed kick at him, and this time connecting with his shin. 'And we can't even visit her because she'll be in stupid –' another kick caused Dylan to grunt and take a step back '– bloody –' another kick '– *Africa*.'

Dylan glanced at Frankie, who shrugged, looking uncomfortable. 'She only just told us all tonight,' she explained. 'I'm sure it won't be for long. Some sort of sabbatical or something.' Dylan could tell Frankie was trying to make light of it, but he could see the sadness in her expression.

'I don't want her to go on a sabbamathmatical,' Benji put in, glaring at Frankie. 'Tell her you need her to stay, Auntie Frankie. Tell her you need help to grow the baby in your tummy.'

Frankie knelt down in front of Benji, wrapping him in a tight hug, and Dylan could hear his loud sniffs as he lost his battle with tears. When he lifted his head from her neck he started furiously wiping his eyes and casting furtive glances at Dylan, obviously not keen to be labelled a crybaby.

'It wouldn't be right for me to tell her she can't go, Benji,' Frankie said softly, smoothing his thick fringe back from his forehead. 'And I've got you, and your uncle, and everyone else to look after me. It's selfish to try to make her stay.'

'I'm bloody cross with you,' Benji said through his sniffs.

'Benji,' Frankie said in warning.

'And I'm bloody, bloody cross with you too.' Dylan just managed to sidestep that small foot again, which seemed to infuriate Benji even more. Luckily Rob swooped in at that point and picked up a struggling, red-faced Benji.

'I'm not bloody tired!' shouted Benji as he was carried with ease through the marquee.

Chapter 17

Knight in shining bloody armour

'You okay?' Lou looked up in surprise to see Rich approaching her where she stood just outside the marquee. She was still smiling after the torrent of bloodies she'd just heard as Rob had carried Benji up to the house. That kid was stubborn.

'Not like you to hide from a good party.'

Lou shrugged. 'I'm not hiding exactly ... more like ... pausing.'

'Well, you pause really well.'

'Uh ... thanks, I think.' She paused well? What?

He was staring down at her chest now, and she was starting to feel a little uncomfortable. She'd let her hair down from its confines when she thought the pins would start drawing blood earlier, and she pushed the heavy mass away from her face now as she straightened from her position leaning against the pillar of the marquee. Rich tracked the movement and stepped closer. He reached up with one hand, picking up a few strands of her hair and rubbing it between his fingers.

'Christ, I knew your hair would be soft, but there's soft and there's fucking soft.' Now that he was closer, Lou could smell the alcohol on his breath and she took a nervous step back.

143

'Um ... Rich, I don't think –'

'I could help you, you know,' he interrupted, moving to block her way. 'I could put a word in for you with the committee.'

'See, I don't need –'

'One word from me and this whole thing could go away.' His voice had dropped lower and she could hear a slight slurring to his words. 'We've been dancing around this for ages and I'm getting a bit fucking sick and tired.' He had moved right into her personal space now, caging her in, his hands resting either side of her shoulders on the marquee. She put her hands to his chest to push him away, but if anything he seemed to take that as some sort of encouragement, moving his face so that his lips were a hair's breadth from hers.

'I don't need your help,' Lou said. 'I mean ... Rich, I told you I quit the rotation. I'm leaving, going to Africa actually. My brother –'

'You what?' All traces of the slurring she'd heard in his voice before were gone, his tone now hard and sharp. 'What were you thinking?'

Lou was starting to feel more than a little intimidated, especially now that he was shouting in her face. She couldn't really understand his fury anyway. What was it to him if she left? Sure, they were friends and he'd been great throughout this whole thing and always supportive at work, but other than that they weren't particularly close.

She shrugged, subtly inching her way down the side of the marquee to get away from him, until he shot out an arm at the side of her head to block her escape. 'I ... um, I wasn't really in the mood to jump through all their hoops to be honest, Rich, having worked my arse off for the last six years and then finding out that none of it counted when it really mattered.'

'You stupid bitch.'

Lou's eyes flew wide, she'd never heard Rich speak to anyone like this before; it was like he'd suddenly transformed into a different person. 'You were supposed to come to *me* after the fucking RITA. I could have sorted it for you. Why do you have to be so bloody-minded all the time? It's like banging my head against a brick wall. What on earth are you doing swanning off to goddamn Africa anyway?'

Lou narrowed her eyes at him. Ignoring the rest of his rant, she focused in on what was, to her, the most relevant part. 'What do you mean by *"supposed to"*, Rich?'

Rich flinched, his angry face suddenly becoming blank and unreadable. Lou's mind started whirling as she put the pieces together.

'Oh my God,' she breathed. 'The report – it wasn't from Miles was it. It was from *you*.'

'I ...' Rich started looking uncomfortable, and shifted from foot to foot where he stood.

Lou shook her head slowly. 'But that doesn't make any sense. Why would you ... ?' She trailed off and looked away for a moment, before her head whipped back round to glare at him. 'You thought that if you were my knight in shining bloody armour that I'd just fall to the ground, legs akimbo, didn't you?'

Rich's face had started flushing an angry shade of red again, other than a white ring around his lips, which were tightened in fury; but Lou was too angry herself to read the warning signs.

'I wouldn't go out with you, so you thought you'd make it impossible for me to say no. Jesus, what sort of loser are you?' she sneered.

It was then that she noticed Rich's growing rage. She tried to dash around him but was too late. Both his large hands clamped around her upper arms, and he started shaking her so hard that her teeth rattled.

Lou wasn't weak, but there were some things that caused

her to disconnect from herself. She hadn't been shaken since she was a child, but the viciousness and regularity of those episodes had been ingrained in her psyche, and the fear of Rich's violence rendered her limp and silent – not a natural state for Lou at all.

'You snooty little bitch,' he roared, continuing to snap her back and forth. 'You think you're so much better than everyone, strutting around the hospital like some sort of doctor-slash-stripper. Not caring who you piss off, not caring who you hurt. So what if I wanted to make you feel a little more human? Maybe make you a little bit grateful for once? Why shouldn't I have a turn with the hospital slut? I can think of –'

One minute Rich had a death-grip on her and the next he was flying through the air. Lou immediately started rubbing her arms and leant heavily against the marquee. She watched in detached fascination as Dylan spun Rich around and punched him in the face.

'Don't you dare touch her,' he roared down at a shocked Rich, who scrambled to a sitting position, pushing himself backwards and holding up a hand to ward Dylan off. Dylan made another lunge at him but was held back by Ash and Tom before he could make it. Obviously feeling a bit safer now that Dylan was being physically restrained, Rich's face turned hostile again.

'What's it to you, Valleys' Boy?' he sneered, pushing himself back up onto his feet. 'You don't want her, do you?'

A heavy silence followed that statement, during which both Lou's and Dylan's faces drained of all colour. Rich started laughing, turning to Lou and looking at her in disgust.

'Don't think I haven't noticed how you're always panting after him. It's pathetic. That hurt little look you're always so quick to mask when he's shagged yet *another* member of the multi-disciplinary team. He's the only bloke who stands half a chance with you, and yet he's pickled his onion with practically all the available women in South Wales *but* you.'

Dylan struggled forward again, and this time Ash and Tom didn't make any move to stop him. He collided with Rich and they both went down on the ground, a flurry of fists and bodies. By the time sanity was restored (only after both Katie and Rosie had appeared on the scene and started shouting for them to be pulled apart), Lou found herself shaking – actually physically shaking, her teeth chattering together and everything.

'Lou? Babes?' She could hear an urgent voice in front of her, but couldn't seem to focus on who was speaking until a large warm hand rested on the side of her face, another on her shoulder. 'Babes, look at me.' She flinched when she realized how close Dylan's face was to hers. He had a nasty-looking bruise blossoming over his cheekbone, and his eyes were a little wild. Her shaking gradually subsided and she started to come back to herself.

∾

'Is she okay?' Miles had emerged from the marquee at some point and was standing next to Dylan.

'Bugger off, Miles, I'm handling this,' Dylan muttered, not taking his eyes off Lou. She might have stopped shaking but he didn't like the fear he could still see written all over her tight features. He was angry with himself. He should have seen to Lou and beaten the crap out of that tosser later. Instead he'd forced her to witness yet more violence after being shaken around like a rag doll. Rich might deserve a kicking but Lou definitely didn't deserve to have to witness it.

He also found the fact that they were now surrounded by concerned parties immensely annoying. If he had his way he would send them all packing and take Lou home himself.

Maybe then they could finally sort out this mess. Maybe then he wouldn't feel this hollow sensation in the pit of his stomach.

'Oh sorry, I didn't realize. You're *handling* it are you?' Miles sneered. The prick had perfected a particularly good sneer. 'I didn't realize that you being engulfed with the red mist and going all *Swansea* on Rich whilst Lou is virtually catatonic was that productive. My mistake.'

Lou's eyes had now cut away from Dylan and sliced to Miles, and Dylan felt that loss like a punch in the stomach. He was losing her again, and he found that he was tired of bloody losing her all the time. All he wanted was *five minutes* alone with her to explain.

'Miles,' she said, her voice steady but much quieter than normal. She put her hands up to Dylan's forearms to pull them away. He found himself tightening his grip before he remembered that she had already been manhandled, so that might not be the best move at the moment. He let his hands drop with extreme reluctance and stepped back.

Lou didn't even spare him a glance; she just stepped around him to Miles.

'I'm sorry,' she said, and he blinked.

'I misjudged you, Miles, and I'm sorry.'

'Oh … right, well …' Miles was shifting uncomfortably in front of her, shoving his hands into his pockets. 'Um …'

Rosie let out a huge sigh and shoved Miles from behind. 'For Christ's sake Miles, stop being such an emotional cripple. Accept the apology.'

'Oh yes, right, well, of course. Don't worry about it.'

Rosie huffed again. 'Now tell her it's understandable as you're such an annoying git most of the time.'

'Okay, well, yes, I suppose I can be a bit … abrupt at times, and that can come across as …'

Rosie, who was clearly done with Miles's lame attempts at

bridge-building, decided to take matters into her own hands. 'It comes across as you being annoying because you are, in fact, being annoying. But that's something you're going to work on, isn't it? Now hug her.' She gave Miles another slightly less subtle shove, and he did manage to give Lou a rather awkward, one-armed hug. After shaking off his embarrassment, however, he was back to his old self.

'Now, what's all this nonsense about you swanning off to work in the colonies? Isn't Wales stuffed full of enough wild natives, disease and depravation for you?'

Dylan rolled his eyes. If he didn't think it would further scar an already traumatized Lou, he would have dished out a second kicking of the day.

'Well, this native thinks you've said enough,' Rosie put in, tugging on his hand.

'I'm not saying that I didn't *like* the wild natives,' he replied, ruffling Rosie's hair, then pulling her in to kiss the top of her head, his mood having lightened considerably. He turned back to Lou. 'Seriously. Stop having this tantrum and get back to work.'

Dylan watched as Lou's face flushed red and her fists clenched at her sides. Usually he would stand well back when he felt her about to blow, but now he could feel himself inching forward. At least this pompous arse had some uses – angering Lou to the point of shaking her out of that awful, frozen expression of fear she had been wearing being one of them.

'Tantrum?' she asked, her voice low and dangerous: another warning sign that Dylan easily picked up on, but one which Miles, unfortunately for him, was completely oblivious to. 'After working like a maniac for that wretched department, I was told I'm not up to scratch, that I've got to repeat the last six months, that I was being referred to the deanery for remedial training. Who was it that was actually training the trainees? Who was doing the bulk of the work? Who was carrying the whole freaking department?'

'Don't you think they know that now, Lou?' Miles blasted back at her. 'After your little disappearing act, don't you think they've realized that? Look, I know you don't want to –'

'You have no idea what I want!' Lou was shrieking now, control long gone. Dylan flinched at the intensity of her voice and he moved toward her again, this time laying a hand on her tense shoulder.

'Babes, calm down.' At his touch and the sound of his voice, she whirled around, throwing his hand off.

'None of you have any idea what I want!' she continued, shrieking, clearly now at breaking point. 'You never have!' This last was said directly to Dylan, her voice lower, and the emotion in it almost painful to hear. Dylan saw the tears shimmer in her eyes for a moment before she turned and ran back into the marquee. By the time he'd pushed through the crowd on the dance floor to get to her, she was gone.

Chapter 18

High Maintenance

I 2 YEARS EARLIER ...

'You need to swap tables with me.' Dylan tore his eyes away from the dark-haired girl opposite him to glance briefly to his side; the blonde was tapping her toe impatiently and scowling at him for some reason. They'd only just started freshers' week and he knew, as beautiful as she was, he couldn't possibly have got around to tapping that, so he had no idea why she was looking annoyed.

He looked back at the dark-haired girl and was rewarded by a brief flicker of direct eye contact before she looked across at the blonde. He felt his heart almost stop and his stomach twist. Big, deep brown eyes framed with thick lashes, olive skin, petite frame; she was the most stunning thing he'd ever seen, and the fact that she would only briefly glance at him made her all the more intriguing.

There was no way he was swapping tables.

He turned fully to face the blonde. 'Sorry, babes, not happening. This body's taken, see.' The blonde, who had been full of attitude a moment ago, seemed to have slipped into a somewhat catatonic state. Her mouth was slightly open and her eyes had glazed over as she stared into his eyes. He really hoped that she wasn't going to pass out, or worse, hurl; the dissection lab wasn't everybody's cup of tea after all.

Her gaze drifted down to his chest and then lower before she stammered, 'Wh-what?'

He smirked. 'This body,' he said, speaking with deliberate slowness and gesturing to the cadaver outstretched on the table in front of them, 'is ours. Get your own.' That seemed to snap her out of her stupor and brought the fire back into her eyes.

'Listen, boyo.' Oh, a Welsh jibe. He decided he liked this one – feisty. Her toe-tapping had resumed, causing him to glance down at her feet, and he had to hold back his laughter. Who the hell wore crazy-high heels to dissect a body for the first time? 'You can have my body. I need to be at this table.'

He looked over to the body she was gesturing to, and then flicked another glance across at the brunette.

'Look, babes, got to be honest with you –'

'Why do Welshmen say that when they're about to be anything but?' she snapped. 'It's simple, you big oaf, just swap with me.' He noticed that she too had flicked a glance over at the brunette, before looking back at him and resuming that damn toe-tapping. Interesting.

'Sorry, babes, no can do. I need a dong, see, not a gwat. Want to be a urologist not a gynaecologist.' Her face had turned a fiery red, and he couldn't tell if it was from embarrassment or anger. Despite this he also noticed that she was pressing her lips together furiously, and he had the feeling that she was holding back laughter.

'Did you just refer to a penis as a dong and a vagina as a gwat? You *do* know that you're a bloody medical student don't you?'

'Gwat, scut, mott, clout, pussy; who cares what I call it? Nothing against them, in fact I think I get along with them

152

pretty well in my spare time, but not interested in dissecting one of them.'

The blonde rolled her eyes. 'How do you know you want to be a urologist so soon? It's only the first week, you moron.'

He shrugged. 'Just do, and I want to make sure I've thoroughly explored the anatomy of this here one-eyed snake before the year is over, so I'm ahead of the game.'

He heard a muffled, very unladylike snort, and saw her struggling not to laugh, and he smiled. Having beaten back the laughter, she was about to speak again when he caught movement out of the corner of his eye. The brunette had shuffled around the end of the table and come up beside the blonde, laying her hand on the blonde's arm.

Now, this chick was definitely not in high heels. In fact she appeared to be the complete opposite of the blonde: wearing a big, oversized jumper despite the warm day, and baggy jeans. She looked like she wanted to sink into the floor and disappear, which for someone of her beauty he found odd.

'Lou,' she said, and Dylan had to strain to make out her soft voice. 'I'll be fine, I promise. Don't make a fuss, you'll get in trouble.' The blonde, who he now knew was called Lou, turned towards her and stepped in close to whisper in her ear.

'Okay,' he saw the brunette mouth, giving Lou a shaky smile.

'Right,' Lou said, stepping away from the brunette and staring at Dylan. 'Large, Welsh, foul-mouthed, rude, Neanderthal guy, this is Frankie. Frankie this is –'

'I'm Dylan,' he put in smoothly, reaching across Lou to shake Frankie's hand. He was startled to notice a flash of fear in her eyes as he closed his big hand around her small one for a moment, before she jerked it away. Hmm ... shy; he liked it.

'She's not all that keen on the whole cutting-up-bodies thing,' Lou said, and he tore his eyes away from Frankie, who was now looking down at her hands as she twisted them together nervously. 'So just be a little bit –'

'She'll be fine with me,' he said confidently. Half an hour of his legendary charm, she'd be eating out of his hand and totally forgetting her squeamishness.

Lou sighed.

'I'm just over there okay,' she said, squeezing Frankie's arm before giving him a hard look and turning to strut back to her table.

Now, there was nothing shy, quiet or shuffling about that girl, he mused, aware of a large percentage of the male eyes in the room fastened onto her backside as she gracefully weaved thorough the dissection tables. Even Mike, who was evidently Lou's dissection partner, looked momentarily stunned when she came to a stop opposite him at their table – and Dylan knew for himself how devoted Mike was to his girlfriend back home. *High maintenance,* Dylan thought as he shook his head and focused back on the down-bent dark head across the table from him. Now, this one was much more his style. He caught her eye and smiled the smile he had perfected in order to melt the knickers off the girls back home.

This should be easy.

∿

'WHAT IS THE MATTER WITH HER?' LOU WATCHED AS Dylan paced up and down in front of her in the corridor outside the dissection room, Frankie having scuttled off as soon as the session had ended.

God he was beautiful.

Everything about him was perfection. His piercing green eyes, his bulky frame, his mouth, which seemed to be perpetually pulled up at the side in a little half smile as if he was always on the verge of finding humour in any situation. He wasn't laughing now though: his mouth was set in an uncharacteristically grim line. He tore his hands thorough his hair, and she distractedly noticed that the sleeves of his jumper were pulled up to his elbows.

Crikey, there was no hope for her. Even just his forearms were virtually reducing her to a puddle of lust.

He stopped pacing and was looking directly at her, his green eyes boring into hers.

'Well?' he asked impatiently. She realized that he'd just been ranting again, and, with the forearm distraction, she hadn't managed to catch a single word.

'Uh ... I'm sorry – what?'

He rolled his eyes. 'I know that you don't really want to lower yourself to speak to me, duchess, but you could at least make some effort to listen to what I've got to say.' She was glad he couldn't read her mind; he had no idea what she wanted. If he did, he would probably run screaming down the corridor.

She'd overheard him talking to one of his rugby mates in the library the other day about her and Frankie. Dylan and his friend Mike had started spending a fair amount of time with Lou and Frankie over the last few weeks. Lou knew it had a lot to do with Dylan's obsession with Frankie, an obsession to which Frankie was completely oblivious. Luckily the boys were both such a good laugh that Lou wasn't really bothered by their motives.

Much.

That day in the library she had been bothered though. That was one of the few days that Lou had actually given in to emotion and allowed herself to cry.

'Those birds that you hang out with, mate,' one of the prop forwards had said to Dylan. Lou was sitting at a computer behind a big bookshelf right next to them but completely hidden

155

from view. 'Care to introduce me, or don't you share? You can't need both for yourself, and your mate is practically a eunuch with how devoted he is to his Mrs back home.'

'Not your type, mate,' she heard Dylan mutter, annoyance lacing his tone.

'Uh, they're fit, they're single; that's definitely my type.'

'Female with a pulse is your type,' another male voice put in. 'In fact I'm not even sure you're *that* fussy. Was that a woman or a sheep you brought home last night? No offence, Dyl. Don't want to insult the way of your people or anything.'

Dylan snorted. 'Ah, more sheep jokes, boys, keep 'em coming; I can't get enough. I must say I'm hoping it was a sheep, then maybe we can go trawling the valleys together of a weekend.' Muted male laughter filled the library for a moment.

'Seriously, mate,' the first guy started again. 'Just a little intro. What's the harm?'

'No you listen to me, *mate*.' Dylan's voice had dropped down an octave and the atmosphere was suddenly thick with tension. 'Stay away from the brunette. She is seriously *not* your type. In fact if any of you rejects so much as breathes on her, I won't be pleased.'

'Christ, don't get your knickers in a twist.' Lou could just make out the prop forward through the books, holding his hands up in surrender. Dylan was facing away from her but she could see his hands where he was gripping his textbook, his knuckles white. 'No brunette. Message received. What about the blonde?'

Lou watched Dylan's hands relax and the tension shift out of his body. 'Have at it, mate; but I've got two words for you: high maintenance.'

'Don't think I'd mind putting in the hard yards maintaining that piece of arse, mate,' the prop forward said.

'Well, good luck to you,' Dylan returned, looking completely relaxed now that they weren't discussing his precious Frankie. 'I like mine heavy on the sweet and light on the ball-breaking-bitch, but each to his own.'

Lou stared at her computer screen, her body frozen solid. Is that how he thought of her? A high-maintenance, ball-breaking bitch? They bantered easily enough, and he sure as hell laughed at her jokes. He'd even snorted a whole load of coke the wrong way in the cafeteria the other lunchtime, he'd been laughing so hard after she had announced her new name for her vagina: Princess Mufflington le Foof.

She felt the tears sliding down her face, but forced herself to remain perfectly still until she was sure they had all left half an hour later.

'Look, Dildo.' With the memory of the library incident fresh in her mind Lou's attitude snapped back into place. 'Maybe not trying to make her throw up would be a start.'

'I was trying to make her laugh or at least get a smile out of her,' he explained.

'Well, you succeeded in turning her stomach and likely scarring her for life. Well done, genius.'

'It was funny,' Dylan said through gritted teeth. 'Everyone else was pissing themselves.'

'Why the hell do you think I wanted to swap tables with you in the first place, you insensitive prick? I told you she was squeamish.'

'Well, I kind of forgot about that,' he mumbled, shoving his hands in his pockets and scuffing the floor with his shoe.

'Yeah, I think I got that today when you reached into the chest cavity, fished out what look like formaldehyde-soaked human tissue, and ate it.'

'It was a ruddy joke!' Dylan blasted, flinging his arms out in frustration before shoving his hands back in his pockets. 'It's not my fault the cafeteria lunch meat looks totally convincing as dead flesh.'

On seeing that little performance, Frankie's face had lost all colour and she'd swayed on the spot for a moment before rushing out of the double doors with her hand over her mouth. Lou had charged after her into the Ladies to find her kneeling in front of one of the toilets, re-experiencing the grim tuna roll she'd forced down at lunch. It didn't help that that particular day had been the day the legs had been taken off, splitting the pelvis in two. Even Lou, who had a cast iron stomach, had balked slightly at various classmates wandering over to the sinks with severed human legs in tow in order to wash them out; and a minor leg-sword fight over the last remaining tap hadn't helped matters either.

'You must have noticed she was looking a bit peaky today,' Lou said in exasperation. 'Are you blind?'

'Some of us bloody love dissection, Lou. I was caught up in the excitement. I mean, we got to use power tools and saws today. How cool is that?'

'I don't know why you want to be a urologist. Orthopaedic surgeon would suit you much better.'

Dylan's eyes lit up. 'Mmm ... maybe you're right. Orthopod – I like the sound of that.' Lou rolled her eyes.

'You'll fit right in.'

Dylan smiled for a moment, then shook his head, his scowl returning. 'Look, just tell me what to do. She's literally said two words to me the whole term, and getting any eye contact is like getting blood out of a stone. I know that all you want is for her to be happy, Lou, and I promise you I can make her happy.'

Lou sighed and looked down at the floor for a moment, an image of Frankie's terrified face on the first day they met, when they were moving into halls, having flashed into her mind. Lou had brought a lot of stuff with her. A lot. One of the reasons she'd brought so much was that she simply had an incredible amount of material possessions; the other reason was that her dad had promised her he would help her move in. At the last minute, however, Lou's mum had managed to convince her dad that he was babying her, and that he should let her go with just Henry the chauffeur. Unfortunately Henry had been briefed by her mother not to help her with her stuff either. He looked uncomfortable driving off and leaving her on the pavement outside her halls surrounded by a great mountain of bags, but Lou knew that he really didn't have a choice: her mother was probably timing his return to the minute.

She noticed Frankie scampering past her, carrying only a couple of medium-sized bags. Lou thought it was a miracle that Frankie didn't collide with anyone, with how down-bent her head was and the amount of hair that was covering her face. Ten minutes later Lou was attempting to move one of the bags (this one being filled only with her cosmetics, of which there were admittedly a fair amount – how she was going to shift the heavier bags she had no idea) when she felt an ultra-light tap on her shoulder. She whipped round and was confronted by a terri-fied-looking Frankie.

'Um ... I ...' Frankie was looking down at her hands, which were twisting in front of her. Lou watched as she took a deep breath and then lifted her head, tucking her hair behind her ears and meeting Lou's gaze with her wide eyes. Lou sucked in a breath; Frankie was so stunning it was almost painful.

'I was wondering if you needed a hand?' Frankie said in a rush, before lowering her eyes back down to her hands. Lou looked at Frankie's petite frame and smiled. Some of Lou's bags were probably double her weight, soaking wet as they were. The fact that this painfully shy girl had worked up the courage to approach her and offered to help, which she clearly found difficult, when dozens of much stronger people had just passed her by, spoke volumes.

'Wow, that would be amazing,' Lou replied with real feeling, earning her a small smile from Frankie.

It took a while to shift all the stuff up to Lou's room, and after some persistence on her part, Lou had managed to get Frankie to say more than two words. By the time they were finished, Lou knew that, behind her barrier of shyness and inexplicable fear, Frankie was not only kind but extremely funny in her own quiet, dry sort of way.

Lou made a point of finding out where Frankie's room was, and the next night she dragged her out to the first fresher event, shamelessly getting her steaming drunk. On their return back to the halls Lou managed to extract the whole bleak story from Frankie of why she was how she was. Lou had been bullied by her mother, but never her peers. When she was at school her forceful personality had been put to use squashing any hint of bullying. Her natural, inbuilt sense of justice just could not stand any form of oppression. She vowed that Frankie was going to bloody well enjoy her uni days, whatever it took.

And if it took giving up something that she desperately wanted, then maybe that was just the price she had to pay.

Lou's head snapped up and she stared straight into those piercing eyes. It wasn't as if she was even giving him up for Frankie, she reasoned. She'd never stood a chance with him in the first place.

'Frankie has what you might call social phobia, so someone like you is particularly intimidating to her.'

'What do you mean "someone like me"?'

'I mean that you are her absolute opposite. You're the most social person on the planet, in more ways than one.' Despite only having spent a few weeks at medical school, there were very few people he didn't know, and even fewer girls he hadn't flirted with.

'You're not exactly a shrinking violet, babes,' he returned. 'And she's okay with you.'

'She trusts me, dipshit. Your size doesn't help either.'

Dylan smirked. 'Can't help my physical prowess, babe,' he said, flexing his biceps. 'Not much I can do to hide these boys, especially in summer. Sun's out, guns out. You know what I mean?'

Lou rolled her eyes and pressed her lips together to stop herself laughing. 'Okay, don't get all roidy on me Swansea boy. I'm just telling you to tone yourself down a bit with her. Go gently. She deserves gentle after the crap she's been through.'

'What's she been through?'

Lou looked at him and took a deep breath. Maybe they weren't her secrets to share, but Dylan was right when he said he would be good for Frankie. And Lou knew that without her help he was unlikely to pierce that armour.

The next day he broke through. And yes, he was good for her – but not in the way he thought he wanted.

Chapter 19

A bit late to present the history

Lou stared at the sharps bin leaning up against the side of the corridor, contemplating her options. Since arriving at the hospital in Malawi six months ago she had encountered countless similar dilemmas. The sharps bin in front of her was overflowing, needles and syringes spilling out onto the floor. She winced as she saw a family with a curious toddler walking down the corridor, and used her body to shield the container from the child's inquisitive gaze. Turning back to it again after they'd passed, she bit her lip and then jumped a mile high, clutching her chest, when Jimbo's loud voice cut through her thoughts.

'Don't even think about it,' he barked at her.

Lou rolled her eyes. 'I'm not stu –'

'Let the guys with some protective gear come to sort it Lou.'

'But what if someone –'

'Don't you think they know not to touch dirty needles around here, sis? Give them some credit.'

'But what if a child ... ?'

Jimbo sighed; he knew from bitter experience just how stubborn his sister could be.

'Wait here, I'll get some stuff.'

Fifteen minutes later Lou grinned up at her brother and handed him back the thick protective gloves. Two full sharps bins sat side by side in front of her.

'Come on, freak, let's get some food,' Jimbo grumbled.

'Ooh! Can you take me to the market?' she asked. 'There was a sort of skewery kebab type thing that caught my eye last time.'

'No way,' Jimbo replied, his skin developing a green tinge with the mention of unidentified meat. 'Last time you forced me to eat there I was sick for days.'

'God, how are we related? You're such a weakling.'

He raised his eyebrows. 'Weak am I?' he asked in a dangerous voice. 'Care to take that back?' Lou slipped out from under his arm and took a step backwards, holding up both arms to ward him off.

'Now Jim – oomph!' Jimbo surged forward, grabbed her into a headlock and slapped her repeatedly on the forehead.

'Take it back,' he said, completely unfazed by her wild struggles. His arm was like iron around her neck and as always she was no match for his strength. He started to walk down the corridor with her still under his arm.

'Okay, I take it back, you big bully,' she spluttered, her voice muffled against his side.

'I take it back. You are big and strong and my Lord and Master for all time.'

Lou was silent for a moment until Jimbo used his free hand to tickle her side, years of know-how allowing him to zero in on her weak spots. 'Okay ... I take it back ... big, strong ... Lord and Master,' she choked out between her giggles, and was finally released. Her face was red as she straightened up, hair flying everywhere.

'Are you ever going to grow up!' she snapped, punching him in the shoulder and trying hard to suppress her smile. In truth this playful version of her brother was far preferable to the forlorn, serious one he'd been when she'd arrived. His decision to take his boyfriend of two years home to meet their parents had been a disastrous one: Jimbo, having never been on the receiving end of their mother's wrath growing up (something she had reserved mainly for Lou and also something that Lou strove to protect her younger brother from at all costs), did not anticipate her venomous reaction. Somehow their mother had managed to not only insult Jimbo's other half but also undermine the entire relationship; she was simply that good at manipulation.

After a couple more weeks of Jimbo struggling to rebuild his relationship, it came to an abrupt end and left him devastated. She knew he'd loved him: his devotion had been written all over him when she saw them together. But it had all gone horribly wrong, and a broken-hearted Jimbo had decided to cut his losses and quit his high-paying job in the city in favour of working for an African charity. It wasn't like he needed the money; they both had trust funds from their grandfather, who had founded the luxury car business their dad inherited. The trust funds were so large that their fortunes far outstripped their parents' (something which Lou suspected may have contributed to her mother's resentment of her). After starting work, he'd quickly agreed to live in Malawi for a year to oversee the allocation of funding, leaving behind the heartbreak and any contact with their parents.

As it turned out, he didn't just oversee where the money was spent; he dug wells, helped in the construction of birth centres – in fact he would volunteer for any manual labour going. When Lou asked about it, he had shrugged, saying, 'Spent a hundred a month on gym membership in London;

out here I can get more buff than ever and it's all for free. And anyway I might be straight-buff, but I'm gay-fat: we have higher standards'. With his sandy blond hair, clear blue eyes, tall frame and the deep tan he was sporting, she could appreciate, even though he was her brother, the loss to the sisterhood.

'What brings you down here anyway?' she asked, once she had straightened her clothes and smoothed her hair.

'Can't I just want lunch with my sister whom I love and adore?' Lou raised her eyebrows and waited.

'Okay, you need to help me decide about allocation of funding within the hospital. I've got to break it down to specifics and produce a report.' He gave her the puppy-dog eyes, which he'd been using successfully to get his way since he was three and she was five.

'Okay, I'll help,' she relented. 'I'm not writing it for you though.' He stepped up the big pleading eyes, and even added in quivering bottom lip. 'Stop that,' she snapped. 'The last one took ages.' They drew to a halt outside the medical ward. 'Look, I've got to do a quick ward round, then we can have lunch, okay?'

'Sure, sis,' he replied happily, switching out of his pout now that he knew she'd cave. 'I'll go grab something.' He shook his head when he saw her about to speak. 'But *not* unknown, Giardia-ridden food from the market. Meet you back here?'

'Fine,' she snapped

'Fine.'

She left him smiling after her as she flounced off onto the ward, finding the others gathered round one of the rickety beds.

'What's the history?' the consultant asked Milo, who was a first year qualified doctor on the ward. Milo puffed up his chest and looked down at his notes. Lou instead looked at the motionless figure on the bed.

'Twenty-two, HIV positive with PCP, came in with short-
ness of –'

'Um, Milo honey,' Lou interrupted softly, laying her hand
on his arm. 'I think it's a bit late to present the history.'

'What? No, look, I –'

She stepped forward and laid two fingers on the carotid
pulse, before fishing her pen torch from her pocket and shining
a light into the fixed, dilated pupils. After a minute she moved
to pull the curtains around the bed, closed the body's eyelids
and pulled the sheet up to cover her face.

'Jesus, when the hell were the last obs done?' Milo's face,
which had paled as Lou had covered the body, now went an
alarming shade of red. He was a relatively new volunteer, and
so the shock value of the poor care these patients received had
yet to fully sink in. He snatched up the chart and his face got
even redder, something that Lou wouldn't have thought physically possible. 'The fluid I wrote up last night hasn't even
been given.' He made to storm off in the direction of the
deserted nurses' station, but Lou stopped him with her hand
on his arm.

'There's hardly any staff, Milo. If the patient really needs
i.v. fluids then you've got to put them up yourself.' He sagged
where he stood for a moment, before drawing back the curtains
and going out into the rest of the ward. All around them lay
emaciated bodies, some with hacking coughs, some shaking with
fevers, all with the same desolate absence of hope in their eyes.

They did what they could as they went round the rest, but
as always the feeling that their efforts were just a drop in the
ocean of the patients' pain and suffering was prevalent.

∽

'I'll do it,' Lou snapped at Jimbo as she sat down opposite him in the canteen, frowning at the sad cheese sandwich he'd presented her with.

'What now?'

'The report, I'll do it.'

'Wow Lou, that would be great –'

'Not just for general medicine, for the whole hospital,' she interrupted, her mouth set in a firm line. Then pushing her cheese sandwich aside, she pulled a pen out of her hair and started frantically writing on the back of one of the envelopes Jimbo had stashed in his clipboard.

'Okay, we'll start with the nursing staff.'

'I thought you were going home in a month?' Jimbo asked.

'I'm doing this goddamn report Jimbo,' she said, her eyes lifting to his. 'Something's got to change. The least these people should be able to expect is to have minimal suffering as they die. I'm not leaving until I know where the funding's going.'

'What about Frankie? What about Dyl –'

'Don't you dare,' Lou interrupted, and Jimbo sighed, knowing exactly what she meant. Ever since she arrived six months ago he hadn't been allowed to mention that name. Ever. He had looked over her shoulder a fair few times when she was on the computer, and he knew she deleted Dylan's emails unread. Somehow the persistent bastard had even managed to find out how to send post so that it would actually get to her, which was in itself a minor miracle. But those letters were also left unopened, and usually chucked in the bin before she even got back to the flat. 'Anyway I'll meet Lucy soon enough. Frankie's got Tom and everyone around. Who do these people have?'

'Ugh, I should never have asked you to come,' Jimbo muttered into his plate.

'What on earth do you mean?' Lou asked, frowning at him.

'I mean that this whole thing is like a red rag to a bull with you. You've always hated injustice, always wanted to save everyone, and now I've brought you to Africa where the whole bloody continent needs saving. It'll take a nuclear explosion to prize you away.

'Loser,' Lou said, shaking her head but smiling as she continued to frantically pour all her ideas out onto the paper.

Chapter 20

Done

As it turned out it wasn't a nuclear explosion that drove Lou home six months later, but a nasty bout of malaria. It was so severe she was left weak and pretty much reliant on a terrified Jimbo for two weeks, who was not in any way used to his courageous big sister needing his help for anything. In the throes of some of her worst fevers she'd said the banned name too many times to count, sometimes sobbing and begging him to come to her. If she remembered this she certainly never let on to Jimbo, and he wasn't about to mention it once she'd come back to herself.

When she could manage the flight she went back to the UK. She was still weak, but could manage to fend for herself. Jimbo had rung Frankie and told her Lou was coming and what flight she was on. This was after Lou had told him specially not to bother anyone – she did not think Frankie needed the extra stress of picking her up from the airport with a six-month-old baby in tow, and she knew that once Frankie got a look at her in her current state there was no way she would let her go home alone.

~

LUCY SQUIRMED IN FRANKIE'S ARMS AS FRANKIE STOOD ON tiptoes, straining to see a blonde head among the arrivals.

'Let me take her,' Dylan said, snatching Lucy from her and nervously bouncing her on his hip. Lucy, who was used to having everyone in her vicinity's undivided attention, was less than impressed with this state of affairs, and communicated this with a high-pitched shriek and tiny, saliva-soaked fist in his face.

'Okay, trouble.' Dylan smiled down at her pouting face, and then dipped his head into her soft neck to blow a huge raspberry. When she was suitably placated, he went back to staring at the arrivals gate, his tall frame making it much easier for him to see than it was for Frankie.

'Relax, okay,' he heard Frankie say. When he felt her small hand on his forearm he realized that his whole body was tensed almost to the point of pain. 'It's been over a year. Even Lou can't hold a grudge for that long.'

Dylan turned away from the arrivals gate briefly, raising an eyebrow at Frankie before continuing his intense surveillance of the people streaming through the gate.

'You'll win her over you know,' she said, and he nodded distractedly. In truth he wasn't so sure. A year was a long time not to respond to a single email, leave alone the letters he'd written.

He sighed. Over the last year, out of desperation and a pathetic need to know how Lou was doing, he'd told Frankie everything that had happened. Understandably Frankie had been furious, but she'd gradually softened towards him when she could see how truly miserable he was in the weeks after Lou's departure, and how hurt he was when she ignored all his attempts to contact her.

~

WHAT REALLY TIPPED THE SCALES FOR FRANKIE WAS THE fact that Dylan was quite obviously in love with her friend. The clues were everywhere: his weight loss, the long moments he spent staring into space, his complete lack of interest in the opposite sex for over a year – but most of all it was the subtle loss of his sparkle. Big personalities like Dylan always sparkled. Whatever the situation, whatever the company, they always shone through. Irrepressible, that was the word to describe Dylan. But, since the loss of Lou, that formerly irrepressible light had dimmed. It was as if he just didn't work properly without her, and Frankie realized that although Lou and Dylan had never been a couple, they also had never really been apart. They had bounced their humour off each other for over ten years. Dylan seemed completely lost on his own.

And that wasn't all.

Frankie had started to remember things, things about Lou's behaviour over the years. Clues which she'd only just linked together recently: the way Lou would watch Dylan; the look on her face after he took yet another girl home; the way she took care of him – helping him through his exams, feeding him when he was hung-over, making him honey and lemon when he was sick because she knew that was what his mum used to do for him back home. So she knew why Lou was so furious with Dylan that she hadn't spoken to him in over a year. She knew why Lou had been so hurt by what he did.

Lucy squeaked again, having realized Dylan's attention had been diverted. Just as he bent to blow a quick kiss in her neck, the crowd in front of Frankie parted.

'Oh my God,' Frankie breathed as she caught her first glimpse of Lou coming through the gate. Dylan's head immediately snapped up.

'What the –'

The screams of both girls drowned him out as Lou pushed her way through the throng of bodies and launched herself into Frankie's arms.

'You're skin and bones,' Frankie sobbed into Lou's hair. The shock of seeing her glorious Lou with sunken in cheekbones and dark circles under her makeup-free eyes was too much. Lou looked as though a sharp gust of wind could snap her in two.

'Where's … ?' Lou's smile died when she caught sight of Dylan, but her eyes lit again when they fell on the gorgeous, dark-haired beauty in his arms.

'Wow, you're even cuter in the flesh,' Lou cooed, reaching for her. Lucy went to her easily, being well used to her face with the amount of skyping the girls had done over the last year. 'Oh, and you're so much more smudgy in the flesh,' she said, cuddling her close and nuzzling her neck. She only acknowledged Dylan's presence after she had done a full baby inspection, right down to counting her little toes.

'Hi, babes,' he said softly, not daring to move towards her, as if she was an easily spooked gazelle in the wild. Lou stared at him for a long moment. Just as the silence was on the verge of becoming uncomfortable, she took a deep breath, stepped into his space and gave him an awkward, half-hearted, one-armed hug, which Dylan returned as best he could around the baby still squirming in Lou's arms.

'Missed you, babes,' he muttered, and she pulled away, giving him a forced smile.

'Good to see you, Dylan. Congratulations by the way.'

Dylan blinked. He hadn't thought Lou would have bothered to find out about him at all over the last year. His career had been the only thing stopping him from going insane without her, which, ironically, after everything he'd done to ruin her career, did his CV no end of good. He'd finished a different research project that had turned out to be far superior to the original he had to give up to Percy, and had flown to conferences all over the place to present the results. Last month he'd been interviewed for the consultant hip job at Cardiff, and, to his shock, beaten all the competition to the post. So now he was a consultant, at the pinnacle of his career. He should have been over the moon, but he'd never felt more miserable in his life.

'Right, well, let's get going shall we?' Frankie said bracingly into the uncomfortable silence. Dylan pushed Lou's trolley through the terminal whilst the girls walked in front, Lou still holding Lucy and both chattering happily. When they got out to the car park Frankie frowned at her ticket.

'I'll just nip and pay for this,' she said. 'Won't be a minute.' She walked off in search of the ticket office and Dylan didn't waste what he saw as a golden opportunity.

'Are you okay?' he asked Lou, who was cooing at Lucy and avoiding any eye contact with him.

'I'm fine,' she said, still not taking her eyes off Lucy, and for the first time since Lucy was born Dylan started to feel annoyed with the cute little bundle of joy. Jealous of a baby. Pathetic.

'Are you better? I mean, should you have even been travelling now? You look –'

'I'm well aware of how I look thanks, Dylan,' Lou said through her teeth. She might seem hostile, but at least she had deigned to grant him direct eye contact.

'Listen, Lou, I –'

'No,' she cut him off. 'You listen to me. I know we share friends. I know we have to be around each other, so I'm prepared to call a truce. But don't mistake me, Dylan, we might share friends but you and I *are not*. We'll be polite and put up with each other for other people's benefit, but that's it. I'm done.'

Chapter 21

I'm not giving up on you yet

'WELCOME BACK, DR SANDS.' LOU LOOKED UP FROM THE ward desk into the sharp eyes of Dr Hudson. The old bag hadn't changed a bit, her grey helmet of hair still firmly in place along with her severe expression.

'Yes, well, for now anyway,' Lou muttered, gathering all the notes together and dumping her list on top. 'I'm locuming, filling in for Miles these next two weeks whilst he's on holiday.'

'But you will be coming back onto the rotation?' Although loosely phrased as a question, Lou got the impression that it was more of an order. She found this confusing, having never thought that Dr Hudson enjoyed working with her in the slightest. In fact she'd always made Lou feel that she was bordering on incompetence.

'Let's get going shall we?' Lou said, instead of elaborating on her plans. In truth she only planned to be staying a few weeks. Once she got her strength back she wanted to go back out to Malawi. The project she'd started with Jimbo was only halfway complete, and there was nothing holding her here, not any more.

Dr Hudson looked like she wanted to say something more,

but when her eyes met Lou's determined expression she seemed to bite back her words.

'Right, now you listen yer, you old ast*.' Lou and Dr Hudson jumped as a large, red-faced man came barrelling towards them down the corridor.

'Oh dear,' Lou heard Dr Hudson mutter under her breath, not seeming in the least bit fazed. There was something familiar about the angry man, Lou was sure she recognized him, especially whilst he was shouting.

'Got to be honest with you,' he kept shouting, after stopping just in front of Dr Hudson, 'this is a bloody shambles. I want another assessment. All this money for ffwcin nursing care is bleeding us dry.'

'Mr Talbot, do please refrain from using foul language on the ward. We have had this discussion before, but as usual it seems to have had very little effect on your behaviour. I'm afraid you are under the mistaken impression that I can influence the allocation of funding for "continuing health care" for your mother. Unfortunately I have no such power. She simply does not meet the criteria. I would also like to point out, as I have many times previously, that it is not yourself she is "bleeding dry". It's her money, not yours, not yet.'

Mr Talbot's face was becoming steadily redder as Dr Hudson's speech went on, and Lou was relieved when the hospital security arrived.

'Come on now, mate, we've been down this road before haven't we,' one of the two large, middle-aged security guards said to Mr Talbot, putting a hand on his back.

'Fuck off, *mate*. Me and Dr Stick-up-her-arse are having a chat and I'm not leaving till it's sorted.' Lou moved from around the ward desk and came to Dr Hudson's other side.

'Maybe we should just start the round,' she muttered to Dr

Hudson, who looked as though she was gearing up for another lecture.

'You!' the red-faced man suddenly shouted, staring directly at Lou. 'I know you. You're the little ast* that started all this. I thought they'd got rid of you.'

It was then that it all clicked into place in Lou's head: this was Mrs Talbot's angry son, the one Dylan had practically ejected from the ward the last time he had shouted at Lou. The man who'd made the board so nervous at her RITA by kicking up such a stink.

'Pleasure to see you again also, Mr Talbot,' Lou said breezily, actually taking hold of Dr Hudson's arm now to lead her away. 'If you'll excuse us we do need to see to the other patients now.'

'You'll pay for this! You just wait!' he yelled after them as they moved away down the corridor. Lou glanced back to see that the two security guards were restraining him, although despite their size they looked to be having some difficulty holding him back.

'Well, as you can see, it turns out that Mr Talbot is not altogether mentally stable,' Dr Hudson said as they turned into the first patient bay. 'A fact that I could have told the hospital administration over eighteen months ago had they bothered to listen to me.'

Dr Hudson stopped in her tracks and turned to face Lou. 'You do realize that none of those complaints hold any water any more don't you? I believe there were also some other assessments of yours that had been, shall we say ... withdrawn.' She searched Lou's face for a reaction, but Lou made sure to keep her expression carefully blank. 'You know if you wanted to –'

'Mrs Talbot!' Lou cried, happy to see the familiar face of one of her favourite patients, and relieved to be able to escape the discussion Dr Hudson was clearly intent on having with her. 'What are you doing back in here?'

'Ah, Myfanwy, at last,' Mrs Talbot blustered. 'Where on earth have you been? You better not have been out with that Davey character, mother will roast us both alive if she finds out.'

Lou sighed and sat on the edge of Mrs Talbot's bed, laying her hand over the papery wrinkled one. 'Don't worry, Olwen,' she said softly. 'I think the chances of your mum finding anything out now are pretty slim.'

Mrs Talbot's face clouded with confusion for a moment, before she shook her head slightly as if to clear it. 'Right, well, make yourself useful, cariad, and get me a cup of ...' She trailed off as her eyes moved to the still-steaming cup right in front of her on the tray table over her bed. 'Oh ... I ...' Confusion washed over her features, and her eyes came back to Lou then swept across the patient bay, her shocked expression at her surroundings difficult to witness. Suddenly she gripped Lou's hand so tightly Lou almost winced; she was stronger than she looked.

'What is this place?' Mrs Talbot asked, fear now threading through the voice that only a moment ago had been full of attitude.

Lou glanced up at Dr Hudson, who had opened the obs chart up, and then squeezed Mrs Talbot's hand gently. 'You're in hospital, Olwen. You're safe. You're staying here whilst the doctors make you better, remember?'

The fear and confusion in Mrs Talbot's eyes dimmed but did not fade completely as she nodded and released her tight grip on Lou's hand. Lou opened up the notes and started reading. Mrs Talbot had been readmitted two weeks ago with a suspected urinary tract infection and horrific bedsores. Apparently the carers that social services had arranged for her had not been allowed to access the property for two weeks prior to that.

Finally, knowing that she could do little for herself and not trusting the odious son, a particularly brave carer had demanded to be allowed inside or she would call the police. The state Olwen had been in when they finally got to her broke Lou's heart to read: covered in urine and faeces, dehydrated and delirious. Lou felt her blood boil as she took in all the sad details of wilful neglect.

'You look much, much better today, Mrs Talbot,' Dr Hudson said bracingly from the end of the bed. 'And the lab have grown that bug in your urine and shown that you're on the right antibiotics, so –'

'Am I to stay yer?' Mrs Talbot asked, her eyes darting nervously around. 'I'm not sure I want to ...' The pitch of her voice was rising in distress and Lou tore her eyes away from the horror-story of her notes, breathing a sigh of relief when she spied the ancient telly with inbuilt VCR player. Reaching up, she took the only tape that was balanced on the top and slotted it into the machine. As soon as the *Neighbours* theme tune started, Mrs Talbot visibly relaxed, her eyes glued to the screen. Her time spent watching this particular episode with Mrs Jones whilst they were next to each other in the patient bay had made Mrs Talbot another Kylie and Jason superfan. And Lou remembered that Mrs Jones's niece had left the old VCR tape and player with Mrs Talbot before Mrs Jones was discharged, saying that they had made a DVD copy for Mrs Jones to use in the home.

'I think it may be prudent to get back to my patients now, Dr Sands,' Dr Hudson said, resting a hand on Lou's shoulder and using an unusually gentle tone of voice.

'Oh, isn't she ... ?'

'Transferred to Dr Morris's care,' Dr Hudson replied. 'Lots of complaints from her adoring son, but it was more the harassment of myself and my team that led to the switch.' Lou opened her mouth to speak but was cut off. 'Right, well, it's not all doom and gloom around here; I know for a fact that there's a patient coming to clinic this afternoon who'll cheer you up no end.'

~

'Mr Davies.' Lou bit back a smile as she took in Alun's grumpy face, and then started beaming when she saw him get up from the chair unaided, and walk across the room with only a stick to steady him. She couldn't help herself, even though the waiting room was full, and even though she knew he wouldn't welcome it: she flung her arms around him when he drew near.

'You did it!' she semi-shouted, pulling back a little but keeping her hands on his upper arms to keep him steady. 'I knew you could. I knew it. You're a miracle.'

'Bugger off,' Alun mumbled, and Lou gave another delighted little squeal.

'And your speech! It's amazing. It must be so nice to be fully understood when you're swearing at people.' She just caught a brief twitch of his lips before he masked it with his standard thunderous expression.

'Crikey, I hope we all get that treatment,' Lou heard another patient say to the woman next to him. 'Reckon a hug from that blonde would fix me right up.'

'Barry!' the woman exclaimed in disgust, hitting him with her handbag for good measure. As they made their way into her room, Lou was shocked to see Alun turn to the man briefly and wink before going in.

Lou was riding high for the rest of the afternoon, but she should have known that, with her luck lately, it wouldn't last.

Susie Tate

Towards the end of the clinic she went to retrieve more notes, unsurprised that the remaining set were the most colossal. As she hefted them up into her arms she heard footsteps behind her, and turned to be confronted by Richard Morris. Lou was exhausted. She wasn't yet at full strength after the malaria, and it had been a long day. A confrontation with this particular slimeball wasn't exactly on her to-do list.

'Dr Sands,' Rich said, the formality surprising Lou. 'It's good to see you back,' he continued with this outright lie. His expression seemed to communicate that it was anything but. Lou sighed.

'Yeah, right,' she deadpanned, then stepped to the side to get past him. He seemed to anticipate this, and moved with her, blocking her only exit.

'I want us to clear up any misunderstandings, Dr Sands,' he continued; then his voice dropped down a level as he stepped into her personal space. 'I hope you know that I can make things very difficult for you here.' Lou, who had been avoiding his gaze, jerked her eyes to his, her blood boiling with fury.

'Oh, you mean like getting me chucked off the rotation? Well, I'm not on it and have no wish to be. You mean stopping the hospital offering me locums? Even your pathetic little efforts couldn't stop that; they're so desperate for locums that they'd probably even give Shipman's CV the once-over.

'Even if you could stop me getting work, do you think I care? Have you any idea how rich I am, you snivelling little scumbag? I could buy and sell you. Christ, I could buy and sell this whole hospital if I wanted.'

She shook her head in disgust at his shocked expression. 'Do your homework, dickwad, you can't touch me.' Just then she saw movement over Rich's shoulder, and was surprised to see both Miles and Dr Hudson standing behind him. Miles's mouth was hanging open, his eyes wide, and Dr Hudson had her arms crossed across her chest, a small smile playing on her lips.

'Why you smug little bi –' Whatever Rich was about to say was cut off as Miles's heavy hand landed on his shoulder and spun him round. He'd obviously overcome his shock at Lou's outburst, and was done listening to any more venom from Rich.

'I think the lady asked you to move out the way, mate,' Miles said in a low, dangerous voice.

'I'm not your mate; I'm your consultant and you can't –'

'Not for much longer, *mate*,' Miles said, and Rich's face seemed to lose some of its colour. 'Yeah, that's right. I got the job yesterday. Say hi to your new colleague come September.'

'Not exactly writing the book on how to make friends and influence people are you, Dr Morris?' Dr Hudson put in, and Rich, who was now looking decidedly sick, gave Lou one last furious glance before charging out of the alcove, avoiding both Miles's and Dr Hudson's stares.

With Rich gone, Miles started to look uncomfortable, and Lou realized that this was the first time she'd seen him since she'd been back. In fact, now she thought about it, it was weird that he hadn't come over with Rosie earlier in the week. They were still together; he'd even proposed a couple of months ago. Rosie had seemed to be glowing with happiness, but when Lou asked where Miles was she had been dismissive and mumbled something about a golf tournament. Lou knew for a fact that Miles didn't play sport of any kind.

'Hey,' Lou said, trying to catch his eye. 'Congratulations by the way.' Miles looked up at that, and she smiled tentatively. She was then flabbergasted as he rushed forward and engulfed her in a heartfelt hug, notes and all.

'Missed you,' he mumbled into her hair. Lou wasn't quite sure how to react to this affectionate, caring version of Miles, and was relieved when he went on to mutter, 'Glad you've finished scrambling about in the colonies, loser,' before releasing her, but not without grabbing the heavy set of notes out of her hands and sweeping off to the waiting room to call in the next patient.

'He's grown up a fair bit,' Dr Hudson put in to the stunned silence that followed. 'You swanning off for over a year did that for him, I think. He had to shoulder more of the workload, decided to man-up finally. By the time of the interview he was far and away the best candidate.'

'That's ... that's great,' Lou said, forcing a smile. She was surprised by the surge of disappointment she was feeling at the fact that she herself would never now become a consultant. She'd thought that she'd put all that behind her.

'You know that Prof will be retiring next year, I suppose?' Dr Hudson said, watching Lou carefully for her reaction. Prof's stroke-consultant job met the exact criteria of what Lou wanted, and after seeing the improvement in Alun today she found that she was no longer that keen to give up on her dream. She shook her head.

'I –'

'Just listen to me a minute, Louise.' Lou stopped abruptly what she was going to say. Dr Hudson had never used her first name before. 'I know what you're doing in Africa is important, and I know you don't need the money, but you're so close to getting your CCT.'

'I'm not even in the rotation any more,' Lou protested.

'Fiddlesticks,' Dr Hudson scoffed. 'One word from me, another review of the evidence, and you'd be back in like a shot and you know it.' When Lou shook her head again Dr Hudson moved forward and placed both her hands over her upper arms. 'Don't underestimate the importance of being an NHS consultant,' she said fervently. 'I know it's not only Africa you want to change. I know your plans for the improvement of stroke care in this country. To effect change you've got to have the clout behind you. Don't just do the easy thing, the short-sighted thing. *Your* country needs you too.' With that Dr Hudson released Lou's arms and stepped back but still held eye contact, her eyes lit with determination. 'I'm not giving up on you yet, Louise Sands.'

Chapter 22

Gifted

'I'M BLOODY COMING TOO!' BENJI'S FEET WERE PLANTED firmly apart, his little fists clenched at his sides, his face red and set with determination. Lou was mostly successful at swallowing the giggle that was bubbling up, but she still emitted a strangled, choked sound, causing Sarah to give her a warning look. Benji's penchant for that particular word was still going strong.

Lou tucked her face into Finlay's neck and gave an inelegant snort against his soft skin, causing him to shriek in delight and wriggle on her lap. It seemed that absence had only made the heart grow fonder with these boys, and since Lou had arrived for tea at Sarah's house Finlay had glued himself to her like a limpet. Jack being the oldest at nearly eight had been slightly more aloof, but a now six-year-old Benji had been her little shadow since she arrived.

They'd skyped frequently throughout the year but not since Lou had contracted malaria. From the look on Benji's face and the way he hadn't left her side (almost like a miniature bodyguard), it was obvious that he had noticed the change in her appearance. Lou wasn't too surprised: he was a perceptive child and had obviously inherited a strong protective streak from his father.

'Why don't I just take him?' Lou asked. 'He can come back with Tom.' Lou was about to go into the hospital for the night shift, and Tom would be just finishing a long day.

Sarah took one look at her son's determined face, and sighed. She had her niece Lucy firmly planted on her hip, was making tea with the other hand, and, at five months pregnant, she was already looking pretty large. She didn't look like she even had the energy to finish boiling the kettle, leave alone take on her son in a shouting match. It wasn't as though Sarah had decided to get pregnant this time – in fact she'd been on the pill and booked in to be fitted with a coil – but somehow Rob's 'toxic evil mega-sperm', as she called them to anyone who would listen, had breached that barrier, and now she was well and truly up the duff for the fifth time.

Frankie, who was sitting at the table with Baby Thomas (now more Toddler Thomas, but until the arrival of the next addition his baby title would stick), started to get up, but Katie was closer and unencumbered by a large toddler. She moved to Sarah and reached for Lucy, who went to her with heart-breaking ease.

Okay, so it was impossible not to like Katie. She was quite simply adorable. But it was difficult not to have some less than generous thoughts about someone who went out with the man you'd been in love with for over ten years, and who'd practically become your replacement whilst you'd been away. The fact that Lucy knew Katie better and went to her more willingly actually hurt Lou, which was ridiculous. Lou felt like the lowest form of life, but she couldn't help hating Katie just a little. Finlay gurgled from under her chin, and she smiled; at least someone was loyal (although that might have had something to do with the Maltesers she slipped him earlier).

Benji took one look at his mother and smiled at Lou. 'Come on then, slow Jo,' he said, tugging at her hand, and then transferring his efforts to removing a disgruntled Finlay.

'Fu ... fooey,' Lou said, glancing at her watch and nearly dropping an increasingly unhappy Finlay. 'I'm going to be late.' She stood, and deposited Finlay in his chair with a big sloppy kiss on his cheek.

'Thanks for dinner, honey,' she said, hugging Sarah tightly and then moving to Frankie to do the same, Baby Thomas and all. That was when it got awkward. Without even thinking about it she kissed Lucy on the cheek, and then whirled towards the door, grabbing her bag on the way. Such was her panic that she missed the brief, hurt expression that flashed across Katie's face as she was leaving.

'Argh!' Lou was just putting the key in the ignition when she heard the click of the seatbelt next to her and shot half a mile in the air. Benji had somehow managed to get his booster seat, put it firmly on the passenger seat of her car and secure himself safely on it before Lou even had a chance to turn the key.

'Benji, I –'

'I'm coming,' he cut her off. 'It'll take ages to remove me from the car, I promise you,' he said ominously. Lou sighed, leaned forward and hit her head against the steering wheel.

'Fine, small stuff.'

'I'm not small,' Benji said, clearly affronted.

'You're smaller than me.'

'So? I'm not done growing.'

'Okay, get back to me when you're at least as tall as Katie: she's tiny.' Lou smiled to herself. Yeah, bitch, take the love of my life, steal my friends, steal the affection of my friends' kids. Whatever. You're still a midget.

∼

BENJI SAT IN HIS SEAT AND FUMED. HE WAS *NOT* SHORT. IN fact he was the fifth tallest in his whole class, which was pretty bloody tall. And he didn't like the way Lou called Auntie Katie 'tiny'. It didn't sound like the teasing, cutesie way Mummy and Daddy sometimes did it. It sounded mean, and Benji knew Louey was not mean. Lou could make him laugh till he weed himself, but she never did it by being mean about people. Then again, there were lots of things that had changed about his Louey. She didn't look the same: too skinny. Before, she had been like a superhero or something, all action and energy and Lego Ninjago dance moves.

Although she was still funny, Benji could tell the difference. He could tell when people were happy or sad. Just like when he knew his teacher was sad and had sneaked away from the carpet when everyone else was glued to *The Lion King* at the end of their Africa topic the other day. He'd gone to the back of the classroom where Miss Chadwick was sitting. The lights were dimmed so he couldn't see her face, but when he hugged her he could feel the wet on his hair, and her chest shake as she drew in breath.

Benji had asked her what was wrong, and she had pulled back slightly to look in his face and whispered, 'I'm being silly, Benji, honey. Nothing for you to worry about.' Benji had just stared at her, and luckily Miss Chadwick knew him well enough to know he wouldn't give up.

'It's just a ... friend, a best friend, and he ... well, he doesn't want to be my best friend anymore. Do you understand?'

Benji did understand. He understood loads more than Miss Chadwick would probably be comfortable with him under-standing. He understood that the way Miss Chadwick wanted to be best friends with that man was how Mummy and Daddy

187

were best friends, and he knew that that was the same way that Lou wanted to be best friends with Dylan. Benji was observant. He watched people, and he'd watched the way Lou watched Dylan, and he knew. Well, Dylan might not want to, but Benji had decided that when he got bigger *he* was going to be Lou's best friend, and she wasn't going to be sad ever again.

Lou pulled into a space in the underground car park next to the hospital. Benji knew she had turned to face him, but he was still grumpy, so he crossed his arms over his chest and stared out of the window.

'Hey,' she said softly. Benji felt her lean forward, and before he knew it she'd blown a big wet raspberry on his neck.

'Urgh! Louey, gross,' he shouted, shrugging up his shoulder and wiping the spit away. Lou used the opportunity to put her hand to the back of his neck and pull him forward so that their foreheads were touching.

'Sorry I called you short stuff,' she said softly, and he shrugged. 'You're a Goliath among six-year-olds, bigger than the Incredible Hulk at your age, okay?'

'Okay,' he replied just as softly, but as she was pulling away he added, 'You can't say mean stuff about Auntie Katie either.' He saw Lou's face close down, and hurried on. 'She's nice and funny like you.'

'I know she is, sweetie. I didn't mean it that way.'

'And you've got to hug and kiss her too. Auntie Katie hugs and kisses more than anyone. I should know, cause she's been doing it to me all my life, and it's annoying. But she get's sad when you hug everyone and not her. It breaks her feelings.'

'*Hurts* her feelings, honey,' Lou corrected. 'You hurt your feelings and you break your heart.

'That too,' he said.

'You see more than we give you credit for don't you, sweets.'

'I see everything; I'm "gifted". '

Lou burst out laughing and pulled him in for a hug. 'And so modest,' she said through her laughter, kissing the top of his head. 'Right, we'd better go.'

Benji *did not* like underground car parks. They were dark and smelly and spooky. Although he would never admit to being scared, he did make sure he stuck real close to Louey as they walked to the lifts. Two cars pulled in as they rounded the corner. One went into a space with a yellow wheelchair on it and the other swung really fast into a space opposite. Benji watched as a large man got out of the fast car. When the man caught sight of Benji and Lou, he froze, and then stared at the back of Lou's head with a funny expression on his face. Benji did not like the look of this man. Even from this distance, and even only at a brief glance, Benji could tell that he was mean; and the way he was staring at Lou was weird.

Benji wasn't lying: he really did see everything. And he could see that man was dangerous and that for some reason he *did not* like his Louey. He tore his eyes away from the man, grabbed Louey's hand and started dragging her to the stairs.

'Benji, it's five floors up,' Lou protested, pulling back on her hand. 'We're taking the lift. I've go to be on my feet all night you know.' Benji looked back at the man, who had started walking towards them, and shook his head vigorously. Somehow he knew for absolute certain that they should not stand still. They should not wait for a lift.

'Let's just bloody go,' said Benji through gritted teeth – but Lou was pulling him towards the lifts.

'Benji!' she cried as they struggled to a standstill and she managed to press the button. 'What on earth are you ... ?' Benji stopped struggling as he felt the man getting nearer. He instead turned in her arms to face the large approaching figure, putting himself in front of Lou but not having the size to shield her.

'Doc,' the man said, his voice low; and Benji, who noticed

everything, definitely noticed the darkness in it. He felt Louey stiffen behind him, and tried to puff himself up as much as possible. Unfortunately there's only so far a six-year-old can expand, and the man didn't even spare Benji a glance.

It was then Benji noticed that the man was swaying slightly and his eyes looked all red and squinty. The smell coming from him was strong. Benji knew that smell 'cause it was how Papa Marco smelt when he wasn't feeling very well and was acting all funny. Strangely this made Benji feel a bit better. When Papa Marco smelt like that it usually meant he was either going to be sick or go to sleep very soon, so hopefully this man would too. Lou turned them both away from the man without saying a word, and Benji could feel her hands shaking on his shoulders.

'Nothing to say, you snooty little bitch?' the large man spat out, and Benji stiffened as he started prowling towards them. He caught a flash of something silver just before Louey roughly pushed him behind her. She had her shaky hands up in front of her now, and was speaking very slowly. 'Just let the boy go and then we can talk. Maybe I can look into the case again for you. With my recommendation we could –'

'Oh, so now Dr High-and-fucking-Mighty wants to get me my funding. Now she wants to help me keep my fucking house.' His voice was all slurry and funny. Benji had heard the f-word before, but only a couple of times: once when Mummy has stubbed her toe and once when Uncle Tom was cross before Auntie Frankie would be his best friend. Both times he had extorted a bag of sweets out of the situation to keep his silence, but at neither of those times had the words sounded so vicious and scary. 'Get going, you little shit.' Benji saw that he had moved even closer and was peering around Louey at Benji.

'Run, Benji,' Lou said in that slow voice.

'No.'

'Run, *now*,' she said firmly, and pushed him away. Benji

skirted the man quickly, then looked back to see his large frame was now blocking Louey's exit. He was walking slowly towards her, and she was going backwards with her shaky hands still up in front of her. She caught Benji's eye and saw that he'd stopped running. 'Bloody run, Benji!' she screamed. 'Get help.' Her scream seemed to spur the man into action, and Benji stood, horrified as he made a lunge towards Lou.

'Omph!' Lou's back hit the concrete wall behind her and Benji saw that flash of silver again. Lou caught his eyes over the man's shoulder. He could see hers were saturated with pain and shock. 'Go,' she tried to shout, but was cut off as the man lunged into her again.

I'm not bloody leaving, Benji thought – and then an idea flashed into his brain. He crept forward until he was right behind the man. Feeling for his marbles in his pocket, he pulled them out, then swung them forwards between the man's legs. There were at least fifty marbles in there and the bag was pretty heavy. Benji had accidently-on-purpose punched Jack in the willy last week for being a tattletale, and it took Jack almost an hour to get better, so he knew that fifty marbles would be even better. And he was right.

'Fuck!' screamed the man, dropping the silver thing, which was now covered in red, and falling to his knees on the ground. He swung round to Benji and made a lunge for him. 'Why you little –'

Thwack. The man was cut off by a hard blow to the side of his head from a long stick. Benji looked up to see a very, very old man (perhaps the oldest man he'd ever seen in his entire life) standing over the now completely still large man, and wielding a wooden cane. The effort of clobbering the man round the head was enough to make the old man stagger slightly, but he righted himself once his stick was back on the ground and he could lean heavily on it. After a brief rest he raised his stick again and brought it down on the unconscious man's skull twice more. There was blood seeping from under the man's head now. Benji didn't think that he was getting up any time soon.

'Alun ...' Benji could hear Louey say from the ground; her voice sounded strangled and cracked. Benji looked down and sucked in a large breath. There was a big pool of red around Lou as well, and she was holding her stomach, her fingers soaked in it. He ran over to Louey and dropped down to his knees in the red stuff, his hands grabbing hers.

'You know where to go to get help, boy?' the old man asked from behind him, and Benji nodded, not taking his eyes off Louey's, which were beginning to drift closed. 'Now, you've been a brave boy.' Benji started crying at the old man's words but furiously wiped the tears away, in the process getting the red stuff all over his face. The old man dropped to his knees beside Benji, moved Benji's and Louey's hands, and pressed his coat over Lou's tummy, holding it there firmly. 'You've just got to be brave a bit longer. Can you do that, soldier?'

Benji nodded, tears streaming down his determined little face. Then he turned and ran.

Chapter 23

Still his

'It's not me! Get off! Get off! You're not bloody listening!'

Dylan froze in the corridor outside A&E. He knew that shout.

'I'm not hurt. It's Louey. You've got to help her!' Dylan spun on his heel and ran into resus. He was confronted by a mass of people attempting to contain a small mass of flailing limbs, blonde hair and ...

'Oh my God,' he breathed. From what he could see there wasn't much of the little boy that wasn't covered in blood.

'Benji, mate. It's me. It's Dylan.' Dylan fought through the throng of people, including the haggard-looking paeds consultant, until he made it to Benji. When he got there, Benji took one look at him, stopped fighting, and threw himself into his arms. The boy was sticky all over from the blood, and the sickly-sweet smell hung in the air around them. Even his face was covered, his tears having made tracks through it on his cheeks. Dylan started checking him over but stopped when Benji grabbed his face between his two small hands and pulled it to his bloody one.

'It's not me,' he said firmly. 'It's Louey. You listen to me now. She's hurt. Level E in the car park.' Dylan shot to his feet and his eyes cut to the A&E consultant.

'Trolley. Now,' he barked, and everyone jumped into action.

~

Lou squinted up into Alun's face and tried to focus. He was pushing down on her stomach with something, and his other hand was stabbing randomly at her mobile phone.

'Piece of junk,' she heard him mutter as his eyes cut to hers.

'Don't you go to sleep now, doc,' he said. She tried to smile, but by the look on Alun's face it was more like a grimace. 'You stay with Alun. You hear me? You didn't get a twp bugger like me to carry on living just so that I could watch you die on this filthy goddamn floor.'

The pain in her stomach had started to fade and Alun's gruff voice was strangely soothing. She could feel herself start to drift; everything was getting fuzzy around the edges and his voice was sounding further and further away ...

~

She was being jostled, each small bump causing a jolt of pain through her midsection. Her eyelids flickered, then quickly closed in response to the bright lights above.

'Lou? Babes, you're fine, you're fine.' She heard the familiar voice next to her, and felt her hand being squeezed in a strong, warm grip. Everything else was cold, so cold; all except for her hand, like it was the only thing anchoring her to the world. She tried to blink but her eyelids were so heavy. Whatever she was lying on was jostled again and she felt another jolt of discomfort.

The pain seemed to rouse her enough for her to open her eyelids a crack, and she realized that she was moving at speed down a brightly lit corridor. She turned her head and saw Dylan running beside the trolley with her hand gripped in his. He looked terrified, his green eyes standing out starkly in his pale face. She tried to speak but felt that heaviness pulling her under again ...

~

'I'M HERE, BABES. I'M HERE AND YOU'RE GOING TO BE FINE. You'll be fine. I promise. I promise. I promise,' she heard him chant from beside her, his words trying to reassure but his voice aching with desperation and fear. She managed to squeeze his hand, and her eyes flickered open again. Dylan's face was hovering inches from hers, and on seeing her eyes open, his free hand moved to cup her jaw. She felt a sharp pain in her other arm and could hear a bustle of activity around them. Scissors were cutting through material and her clothes were being peeled back. She vaguely wondered if her bra and knickers matched, but beyond that her sense of unreality was stopping her from becoming too concerned.

Focusing on the face hovering above hers, she let herself take in the features she'd seen so little of over the last year. Despite everything that was happening around the two of them, she almost felt a surge of relief to be this close to him again, and allowed the longing and love she usually kept under rigid control to come to the fore. Tears were glistening in his eyes now, and she wanted to reach out to him, but couldn't move her other arm.

'S'okay,' she whispered, slipping away again, but wanting to stem that awful pain in his eyes before she did. 'I'll be okay.' Her eyelids fluttered closed but she just managed another whisper, barely audible above the chaos of resus: 'I miss you,' she got out before the dark descended again.

⁓

FRANKIE SLIPPED HER ARM AROUND DYLAN'S STIFF shoulders as she sat on the plastic chair beside him. She tried to push a styrofoam cup of the minging brew the hospital coffee machine produced into his hand, but he pushed it away. Every muscle in his body was held in a state of extreme tension, and had been for the two hours they had been sitting in the waiting room. He was leaning forward, his elbows resting on his thighs and his face buried in his hands. As soon as Frankie had arrived she knew he was at breaking point. Rosie and Ash had filled her in on all the details; all Dylan had been capable of was repeating, 'She'll be okay; she said she'd be okay. She promised,' over and over until it sounded almost like a prayer. His face was streaked with tears but it was like he'd gone beyond crying at this point, only retaining a wild, frantic look in his eyes.

Upon registering Dylan's loss of control, Frankie managed to tamp down her own panic and be the strong one in the situation. She knew that people underestimated her, but just because she was shy it didn't mean she was weak. Her childhood spent with parents descending into alcoholism, the eventual death of her mother, and the ongoing problems she had with Papa had given her the ability to deal with the kind of grief and loss that was foreign to most people. Lou had been strong for Frankie since they met, had dragged her out of herself and given her a life she never thought would be within her reach. It was *her* turn to be strong now.

The door to the waiting room opened and Frankie shot to her feet as the ITU consultant, Dr Cassandra Tobin, came in. Her eyes swept through the room and came to settle on Frankie.

Dylan had also risen to his feet and was holding himself perfectly still.

'Right, well ... this is an unusual situation seeing as you're not actually Louise's family, but –'

'Yes we are,' Frankie cut her off. 'We're her family. We've been her family for the last twelve years.' She took Dylan's hand in hers and squeezed.

'It seems that Dr Sands would agree with that; you are both listed as next of kin and emergency contacts on her medical records. No mention of her parents or her brother.' Frankie's eyes flashed as the mention of Lou's parents, but she continued in as calm a voice as she could muster.

'As I said, we're her family. She wanted *us* to make decisions for her, not her parents.'

Dr Tobin nodded, then glanced at the rest of the room. It was packed with Lou's friends and colleagues, a clogging atmosphere of fear in the air.

'Would you both like to come through,' she said, and Frankie nodded quickly, pulling on Dylan's hand to move him forward towards the door. Dr Tobin led them into ITU and Frankie's breath caught in her throat at the sight of beautiful, vibrant Louey lying completely lifeless on the hospital bed. A ventilating tube was in her mouth; blood was hanging from the drip stand and going into a wide-bore cannula on her arm; the monitors' steady beeping and the whirring of the ventilator filling the air. Dylan had frozen next to her in shock, and when she tried to move forwards she realized that he was as good as welded to the spot.

'Hey,' she said, reaching up to his shocked face to pull it down so he was looking at her. 'She needs us now, honey. We need to walk over to her and talk to her so she knows we're here and that we're not scared.' Dylan's eyes flicked away, taking in

Lou on the bed again, and when they returned to Frankie's, they were swimming with unshed tears.

'She looks ... I can't ...' He trailed off as one of the tears escaped and fell down his cheek onto Frankie's hand. Frankie knew exactly what he was trying to say. The Lou on that bed didn't look like their Lou at all; her face was devoid of all the usual animation, her body limp and hooked up to machines. Lou was always larger than life, a force of nature, and seeing her so still and lifeless was horrifying.

'I know. But you can and you will,' she said firmly, and then turned to Dr Tobin. 'Is she ... ? I mean, how long will she be ... ?

'They removed her spleen in the emergency laparotomy,' Dr Tobin told her. 'Luckily the other stab wound didn't hit anything vital. She's lost a lot of blood. We've induced a coma for at least the next twenty-four hours, but after that she should be on the mend. I'd anticipate an ITU stay of about two days.'

'Thank you, Cassie,' Frankie said, then started tugging on Dylan's hand again. He unfroze and allowed himself to be pulled forward towards Lou.

When they reached her bedside Frankie bent down, grabbed Lou's hand and started talking in her ear. 'Hey, Louey,' she said in a low, calm voice. 'You had us all worried you know, always the drama queen. You're going to be just fine now. They're keeping you asleep for a bit so you can get all that energy back and start giving everyone gyp. Ash's in the waiting room and – I don't know if he's in shock or something, but not a single proverb in two hours; can you imagine? It's weird.'

Frankie glanced up at Dylan and saw that he was standing on the other side of the bed, but about a foot away from it. His eyes were fixed on something at the other end of the unit, and the expression on his face was so fierce that instinctively Frankie let go of Lou's hand and made to move around the bed towards him.

'Dyl –'

'You've got to be shitting me,' Dylan forced out through his clenched teeth. Frankie followed the direction of his gaze, and saw a large man with what looked like severe head and facial injuries lying on a bed on the other side of the unit. One look back at Dylan's face and she realized who the patient was. She rushed to Dylan and laid both her hands on his chest to hold him back, but he started moving forward as if she wasn't even there.

'Why the fuck is this arsehole in here?' he bellowed, and the whole unit turned to see what was going on.

'Dylan, calm down.' Frankie grunted in the fruitless effort to hold him back.

'I'm going to fucking kill him.' Dylan's voice was cold; he meant what he said. The last few hours had pushed him over the edge. As he got closer to the bed Frankie looked over her shoulder and saw what must have been the patient's wife stand up from the plastic chair she was sitting in, her pinched face pale and locked on an advancing Dylan.

'Cassie,' Frankie shouted. 'Send the boys in from the waiting room and call security. Get him out of here now.'

Dylan kept walking to draw alongside the bed, completely ignoring Frankie's attempts to hold him back. When he was level with the bloody-faced man, he drew his arm back and Frankie screamed. Just as his fist was about to connect with the man's face, three sets of much stronger arms managed to push him back. Despite their size, Tom, Ash and Miles still had great difficulty pulling Dylan away. Miles received a vicious punch to the jaw and the others didn't fare much better as Dylan struggled wildly to get to his target. When they finally managed to drag him out of the unit he started banging on the locked door to get back in, and Frankie decided that she was done.

'Dylan,' she clipped, and he stopped pounding for a

moment, likely taken aback by her tone: Frankie was not the type of person to clip anything. 'How will this help, braining the guy responsible whilst he lies defenseless in ITU?'

'It'll make me feel a fuck of a lot better,' Dylan said to the door, his voice still cold.

'Well, boo-hoo,' Frankie shouted. 'Poor little Dylan is cross and having a tantrum, so he wastes time beating up somebody who is not worth going to prison for. Ruining your life. Maybe even ruining the chances of having that piece of filth properly punished for what he did. Don't you think I want to hurt him too? But I want him to be punished the right way. I don't know what prison is like but I would imagine that for someone who's stabbed a woman, a doctor, it's pretty blinking uncomfortable.'

Dylan had stopped pounding on the door mid-Frankie's tirade and was now facing her. She moved forward and grabbed both his hands in hers. His were still balled up, but she worked her small fingers inside the fists and he allowed her to slowly uncurl them.

'She *needs* us, Dylan,' she said, more softly now. 'We're her family and she needs you here, not locked up.' She watched as the anger slowly faded from Dylan's eyes, the green again beginning to swim with wet.

'He hurt her,' he whispered. 'He hurt my Lou. They've unzipped her whole stomach. They've taken bloody organs out of her for Christ's sake.' Frankie moved forward and hugged him round the middle. There was a second's pause before the tension drained from his body. He crushed her to him fiercely, as if trying to absorb her strength.

'Look,' she said after finally pulling back. 'Have a break ...' He started shaking his head but Frankie cut him off before he could respond. 'She needs her things around her. You'll know what she'll want. Tom will drive you back to her flat and you can pack a bag for her.' Dylan nodded. He needed to get himself together. There was no way he could go back into the unit like this, and by the time she was awake he needed to be in complete control.

Lou had put him down as her next of kin. He didn't care what had happened over the last year, the fact that his name was on that form meant that she was still his Lou and he was going to make goddamn sure that everyone, most especially her, knew it.

Chapter 24

We'll talk about that later

'SHOULDN'T WE BE GETTING ONE OF THE GIRLS TO DO THIS?'
Tom asked as he watched Dylan rifle through Lou's underwear
drawer and shove a handful into the hot-pink wheelie bag he
had out on the bed.

Dylan shrugged. 'It's not anything I haven't seen before,
mate. You know what Lou's like: this stuff is her daywear
around the flat, summer or winter.'

'Still, I think I'll just ...' Tom started backing away from the
pile of brightly coloured silk and lace now sprawled across Lou's
bed. Dylan knew it would be entirely fruitless to search for
more appropriate, possibly cotton-based, underwear. Just like he
knew that there was a raggedy old grey bit of cloth under her
pillow that she'd had since childhood. The same one that she
had stuffed up her sleeve and taken to every test and exam she'd
ever done. He knew all these things because he *knew* Lou,
inside and out. He didn't give a monkey's if him rooting through
her stuff was a tad inappropriate; he was the one who would
know absolutely what she wanted to have in hospital with her.

The sense of numbness and unreality still had him firmly in

its grip as he started digging into the pile of clean clothes on the bottom of her wardrobe, looking for some sleepwear that was vaguely decent for a hospital stay. After realizing that nothing Lou had was decent, and grabbing all the tiny sets of what passed in Lou's eyes for pyjamas he could, he stood suddenly and banged his head on the shelf above him. Something fell on his head, and then what seemed like hundreds of photos, bits of paper and random objects rained down on him. He blinked when he saw his own smiling face staring up at him from the floor.

As he took in the rest of the chaos he realized that it wasn't just one image of him amongst hundreds of others of their friends: *all the photos were of him.* Sometimes he was alone in the picture and sometimes he was with other people, but he was always the focus. It was weird seeing himself in so many different poses: happy, pissed off and giving the camera a one-finger salute; drunk, half naked on the beach (he noted with some satisfaction that that photograph was particularly dog-eared). There were bits of paper too with his handwriting all over them, sometimes combined with Lou's. He recognized them as some of the notes he'd passed her in lectures at uni, and more recently in the Grand Round teaching at the hospital. Looking back on it, he'd sent more notes to Lou than anyone else. There was something about being the one to make her do what he called her 'blowfish face' – the face she made when she was desperately trying to hold in a laugh (because let's face it, his notes, which were often accompanied by liberal illustrations, were bloody funny) – that gave him a feeling of huge achievement.

He lifted up a creased piece of A4 notepaper, and was taken back in time to a biochemistry lecture ten years ago. He'd drawn a caricature of Professor Thomas in dominatrix gear spanking a cheeky-looking mitochondria (this had been sparked off by the Prof saying how some intracellular organisms could be naughty in certain circumstances). He could remember Lou's snort like it was yesterday as it filled the lecture theatre, rapidly followed by the loud sounds of her choking on her bottled water. Her face had been bright red, her eyes watering, and still she was so incredibly beautiful that it almost hurt to look at her.

Dylan grabbed the shoebox to start replacing all the photos, and noticed something small rattling at the bottom. He reached in a pulled out a small pink and white shell. After staring at it for a second and turning it over and over in his palm, he finally put it back in the box and sat down heavily, leaning against the side of the wardrobe. He spent a couple of minutes staring into space as the numbness of the last few hours started to lift. A slow smile spread across his face before he got up to sort out the mess. He needed to get back to Lou.

∾

Lou cracked her eyes open and turned her head to the side. She blinked as she took in an unshaven, sleeping Dylan swamping the hospital chair next to her. Her hand went to her neck against the burning in her throat when she swallowed. There was a glass of water on her side table, and she made the mistake of trying to sit up to reach it. White-hot pain ripped through her midsection and she gasped, lying back down on the bed with both hands clutching her stomach. She saw movement out of the corner of her eye, and when she turned to the side Dylan's green eyes were staring back at her, his face splitting into a huge, and what looked like a relieved, smile.

'Hey, sleepyhead,' he rasped, his voice heavy with sleep.

All Lou could do was stare up at him in shock. What on

earth was he doing here? Her shock deepened as he reached down to tuck a chunk of her hair behind her ear, completely ignoring her attempt to flinch away from his touch. Unfortunately her stomach didn't seem to like any sudden movement, and even that small flinch caused another shot of pain. She watched Dylan's smile vanish as he noticed the tightening of her features. He frowned as he looked down at her hands, now clutching at the sheets over her abdomen. Before she knew it, he'd nabbed her remote and pressed the call bell. A harassed-looking nurse Lou recognized popped her head round the door.

'Oh hi, you're awake,' she said cheerfully, looking at Lou. 'What do you need?'

'She's in pain,' Dylan answered for her, and Lou narrowed her eyes at him. 'If you wouldn't mind getting some morphine for her – and I'd like to speak to the anaesthetist on call.' Dylan's voice was set to his most amiable charm-the-knickers-off-the-nurses-to-get-what-I-want, and was accompanied by his trademark ultra-charming smile.

'Right ... okay. I've just got to finish the drug round so I'll be there in about –'

'She's in pain *now*,' Dylan clipped, and Lou's head whipped round to him in shock. His face was stony. Smiley, amiable Dylan, a thing of the past. 'She needs morphine *now*, and I want to speak to anaesthetics *now*. Or do I have to call the ward sister?' Lou's mouth dropped open; Dylan never spoke to any of the nurses like that. He never spoke to anyone like that. The nurse's face had paled as she backed out of the room.

'No problem, no problem,' she said hastily, abandoning the drugs trolley behind her in her rush to get to the treatment room.

'Dylan,' Lou said in a hoarse whisper, unable to get anything else out through her burning throat. 'What are you ... ?'

His eyes snapped back to hers and he smiled again. 'Do you remember talking to the surgeons on ITU, babes?'

She frowned and concentrated. She remembered bright lights, pain, Frankie's voice asking questions, Dylan's voice telling her she was okay, his big warm hand engulfing hers.

'You were pretty out of it,' Dylan explained, after taking in her confused expression. 'Do you remember what happened?'

Lou nodded slowly and shivered when she thought of the knife going in like a punch to her stomach, and the horror of the blood surrounding her. Her eyes flew to Dylan's again in a panic.

'Benji,' she whispered frantically. 'Is he okay?'

'He's fine,' Dylan said, gently pushing her back down into the bed to stop her straining her stomach more than she already had. 'Benji's tough as old boots, so is Alun. The same cannot be said of that evil twpsyn* that attacked you. I doubt he'll live down being beaten up by a five-year-old and a frail eighty-five-year-old recovering from a stroke in a hurry.

'What happened to him?' Lou felt a jolt of fear as she remembered Mr Talbot's furious face and wild eyes when he shoved her back into the wall.

'He's still on ITU,' Dylan told her. 'Alun smashed his skull in pretty good. They had to drain a small subdural haematoma and it's early days, but unfortunately they think he'll recover.'

Lou squeezed her eyes shut and tried to control her breathing. Her fear was in no way rational but she knew she'd prefer it if he were dead.

'Even if he recovers, he's still totally screwed, babes,' Dylan said, as if weirdly being able to read her mind. 'Not just for stabbing a doctor nearly to death, but also for the amount of class-A drugs he had on him when he was brought in. Not to mention the amount of drugs and money at his house when it was raided yesterday. Seems that was why he wasn't letting social services in to see Mrs Talbot, in case they saw anything they shouldn't, which would have been likely since most of the rooms were being used to grow cannabis and the rest had a large amount of heroine and cocaine strewn all over the place.

'The selfish prick didn't want to have to move his "business" elsewhere; that's why he made such a fuss about "continuing health care" funding for his mum. He needed her out but he didn't want her to have to sell her house to pay for a nursing home, seeing as it was supplying half of Cardiff's druggies with their regular fixes.

'You don't have to worry about him now, Lou. I promise.'

Lou looked away from him and nodded, just as the nurse rushed back into the room.

'Okay, morphine,' she chirped, checking the syringe and reaching for Lou's cannula.

'But I didn't –' Lou was cut off by another jolt of pain so severe that she could feel all the blood drain out of her face and a wave of dizziness come over her. Dylan cupped her jaw with his hands and smoothed her cheekbones with his thumbs, his eyes searching her face. The shock of having his face so near to hers, and the concern in his eyes, distracted her from the pain. Before she realized what was happening, the nurse had administered the morphine and was backing out of the room.

'Hey there,' Lou heard from the doorway, and turned to see Cassie smiling across the room at her. 'It's so great to see you awake. How are you feeling?'

'She's in pain,' Dylan replied for her, his terse tone causing Cassie to stutter slightly in her walk over to Lou's bedside. Lou scowled at Dylan; she was getting really pissed off with this whole answering-for-her thing. Although she had to admit, now the pain was rescinding, that the morphine might have been a good idea.

'Oh dear,' Cassie muttered, eyeing this new, angry Dylan warily. 'Well, we could –'

'She needs a PCA, Cassie,' Dylan practically growled. 'She should have had one set up before she came to properly.'

'Now, I'm not sure that –'

'She's in *pain*,' Dylan repeated, and with the strain in his voice it almost seemed as if Lou's pain was causing *him* physical pain. 'I want it sorted.'

'Okay,' Cassie said slowly, and Lou got the strange impression that this wasn't the first time she'd had to deal with a less than reasonable Dylan. Had he been this ridiculous the whole time she'd been unconscious? And for God's sake, why? 'But I think now that she's more awake we can try oral analgesia as a first port of –'

'No.' Dylan's hand sliced through the air to emphasize his point, and Lou stared at him in fascination. What on earth had gotten into him? 'She needs a fucking PCA. I'm not going to have her –'

'Stand down, crazy man,' Lou managed in her weird raspy whisper. 'I can speak for my bloody self.' She swallowed and then blinked for a little longer than was normal. In addition to the blessed absence of pain, a warm fuzziness was now enveloping her and she could feel herself start to drift.

'Hey, gorgeous, stay with me a little longer, yeah?' Dylan's face was back to being inches from hers, his hands cupping her jaw again. 'Come on, you've got to stay awake. Who's going to fight with me and call me a prick if you go to sleep again?'

'Prick,' Lou whispered, a small smile tugging at her lips; but she couldn't fight the fuzziness any longer and her eyes drifted shut. Just as she was about to lose herself in sleep again, she managed to whisper, 'What are you doing here?'

'Looking after you; you're my best friend,' he whispered back, his mouth close to her ear.

'Why are you being weird?' she asked, her voice fading even more.

There was a long pause before he whispered back, 'We'll talk about that later.' Lou could hear the smile in his voice, and frowned, but was sucked into the void before she could reply.

*TWPSYN — *IDIOT*

Chapter 25

Oh, the Welshman's here

'I won't poke her in the tummy; I'm not stupid.' Lou could hear a familiar high-pitched voice cut into her dream and start dragging her back to full consciousness. 'I'll just poke her in the cheek or something.'

'Benji,' Lou heard Frankie whisper in a warning tone. 'No poking, full stop. We're going to wait until she wakes up by herself, and you promised Mummy that you wouldn't make any noise if you came.'

Lou could hear feet scuffing on the floor as Benji muttered, 'She's been asleep bloody ages.'

'She's recovering.'

'Recovering is dead *boring*. All she's doing is lying in bed. I haven't even got to see where she was stitched up.'

'You're not here just to look at where she's been stitched up, Benji.'

'Auntie Frankie, if you think that you can bring me to see Lou after she had her tummy unzipped and not let me see it, you're bonkers. I'm a six-year-old boy, for crying out loud.'

'Stop saying "bloody", and stop saying "for crying out loud". Your uncle was wrong to give you all the gory details.'

'What's wrong with "for crying out loud"? There's no bad words in it.'

'It's just ... not really the kind of thing a normal –'

'Well, I'm not normal; I'm special.' Benji's proud voice filled the room as Lou heard Frankie sigh in frustration.

'Yes, honey, I know you're special, Mummy and Daddy know you're special, your brothers know you're special, your teachers know you're special, your friends know you're special, even the blinking lady in the hospital gift shop knows you're special,' Lou heard Frankie whisper-shout at Benji, and her lips twitched as she imagined him regaling everyone in his path with his heroic story. 'But like Mummy said, however special you are, you still *can't say the b-word.*'

Lou took pity on Frankie, who was clearly losing this round with Benji, and made a concerted effort to open her eyes.

'Hey, slugger,' she croaked, and Benji's eyes widened, his little face paling.

'Hey,' he replied, his voice lacking his usual confidence. 'Why's your voice funny?'

She cleared her throat, but her larynx was too ravaged for it to make much difference. 'Don't worry about my voice, honey. It'll get better.' Benji's face was still pale; he didn't look reassured in the slightest. He bit his lip and glanced up at Frankie, who smiled encouragingly.

'You've been sleeping *a lot,*' he said accusingly, some of his usual confidence returning.

'Sorry about that,' she said as she reached up her hand to ruffle his hair, then moved it down to the back of his neck. She put some light pressure on, and once his face was near enough to hers she risked the surge of abdominal pain she knew she would experience as she lifted her head up to kiss his cheek. 'Thank you, honey,' she whispered in his ear, and when she pulled back she saw that his eyes were wet. Lou waited as he sniffled and wiped his nose on his sleeve. He allowed Frankie to give him a quick squeeze from the side, but did not allow any actual tears to fall.

'Do you know how brave you are?' Lou asked.

'Yes, of course,' he replied, puffing out his little chest and causing Lou to risk another surge of pain as she laughed. Turned out that laughing was a bad idea, however, and she couldn't keep the agony from wiping the smile off her face and causing her brows to pinch. She looked down, finding the button for the PCA, which she had of course been given after Dylan's ridiculous, overprotective crazy-man display. She had to admit that over the last forty-eight hours she had been begrudgingly grateful to him for being so pushy: the pain was pretty bad.

He'd visited a few times since that first confusing awakening, and had been just as weird as before, trying to make all sorts of decisions for her, nosing around in her medical charts, rivalling the Spanish Inquisition whenever anyone involved in her care made the mistake of dropping in. He seemed to have a fair amount of time on his hands for a newly appointed consultant, and the really weird thing was that people were sharing all sorts of medical information with him about her as if he were her family.

Even though his visits were frequent, she had the distinct impression that if it wasn't for Frankie policing her visitors, and the fact the ward stuck strictly to visiting hours and only allowed two people in at a time, he would be welded to the chair next to her bed. Yesterday the nurse had to practically physically eject him from the room at the end of visiting hours, with him fussing around over her fluid balance and scar healing. She drew the line when it was her bowels that were up for discussion, making her voice as threatening as it could be in its weakened state to get her point across.

Once Benji had relaxed and was used to her voice, he livened up, and started asking increasingly gory questions, wanting to go into detail about exactly which organs Lou was missing now, and then about exactly what a spleen looked like. Lou was pretty exhausted by the time he left, but relieved that he did not seem in the least bit scarred himself by the experience. Indeed, he had proudly told Lou that he'd acted out the entire car-park scenario for his whole school, coming in for a special mention and a standing ovation in assembly. (Acting out a gruesome assault probably wasn't what the teachers had anticipated would happen when they called Benji up on stage, but they should have known that with Benji anything was possible.)

~

'SWEETHEART,' LOU'S FATHER SAID, MOVING FORWARD TO give her a tentative hug where she was sitting up in bed. His eyes looked suspiciously wet as he pulled back and scanned her frail body.

'Daddy,' she whispered, her husky voice even more broken with her attempt to hold back tears.

'Why on earth aren't you in a private hospital, Louise?' Lou's mother sneered as she eyed the drab side-room, startling Lou out of her moment of connection with her dad. 'God knows *you* can afford it. Is this some sort of socialist protest thing, darling?'

Lucy, one of the nurses who Lou particularly liked, chose that moment to come into her side-room.

'I can't imagine why anyone would choose to stay in this dump, looked after by these ... people.' Lou flushed with embarrassment as she saw her mother cast a disdainful look at Lucy, who was in the process of taking down Lou's empty i.v. fluid bag. Ever the professional, Lucy just smiled at Lou, gave her a small wink, and whisked the bag and its paraphernalia away.

'Your fluid intake is much better now, Lou,' Lucy told her. 'I think we can do without the i.v.'s, okay?'

'Shouldn't a *doctor* be making those decisions?' Lou's mother put in. 'Someone qualified to do so?'

'Mum,' Lou hissed. 'She's a *qualified* nurse. It doesn't take a doctor to see how much fluid I'm drinking and pissing.'

'Louise Sands! I will not have you using foul language in front of your father and me. I don't care how vulgar you are around your so-called friends ...' Lou rubbed her temples as her mother's shrill voice drilled into her brain, putting down her friends, her lifestyle, her lack of care about her own safety. 'And worst of all, to put a child in danger, Louise. I don't know how you could have possibly thought –'

'Mum ...' Lou cut her off, having to strain her painful throat to make herself heard over her mother's piercing voice. She was too weak to deal with this attack, and as usual her dad was just standing on the sidelines. She knew her mother was just trying to get to her, but by choosing to focus on the danger Benji had been in she'd scored a direct hit. 'Please don't –'

'Hi there,' Dylan cut her off as he burst into the room, looking between Lou and her family. To anyone else he would look relaxed, like he was just there for a casual visit, but Lou knew him better; she could see the muscle twitching in his jaw, and the barely leashed fury in his eyes as he glared at her mother.

'Lovely to see you again, Mr Sands,' he said, moving forward to shake her dad's hand. 'Mrs Sands,' he added, pointedly not offering his hand in her direction.

∿

214

DYLAN HAD HEARD THAT BITCH'S CRUEL WORDS FROM where he was waiting at the ward desk, and he didn't care if Lou was only allowed two visitors at a time, he wasn't going to sit there and leave her to fend for herself when she couldn't even speak or move without pain. He was glad that he'd charmed Lucy and a number of other nurses on the ward to call him if Lou's parents arrived. Lou might not think she needed him but that would change soon enough, and he wasn't going to let them upset her in the meantime.

'Oh, the *Welshman*'s here,' Mrs Sands sneered. 'Lou, darling, have you finally managed to get your claws into –'

'Yes, Mrs Sands, I'm here and my name's Dylan in case you've forgotten, although at your age dementia is a real threat you know.' Dylan was not about to listen to Mrs Sands attempt to embarrass her daughter again. He knew now, after seeing the contents of that shoebox, what she was on about with this. And he definitely knew that Lou had never fancied Wet-pants Ewan. It was something Lou and he would discuss when the time was right, not when she was lying in pain in a hospital bed being ripped into by this harpy.

'Michael,' Mrs Sands spluttered. 'Are you going to let him speak to me like that?'

'Well, I ...'

Dylan watched as Mr Sands looked from his wife and back to him, and then at his daughter in the bed.

'I can't believe this,' Mrs Sands spat out, hands on her hips. 'No wonder your brother won't even bother to come home from whatever Godforsaken corner of the globe he's hiding in to see you; probably doesn't want to put up with your vulgar ways and the horrific company you keep.'

Dylan was about to burst out laughing at how ridiculous she sounded, but his amusement quickly morphed into anger when he caught sight of Lou, slumped back in the bed, eyes closed and looking utterly defeated.

'I begged him to stay out there, Mum,' she whispered. 'He's got to keep the project going or it'll dissolve, there's so much corruption and –'

'Waste of time, waste of money,' Mrs Sands said dismissively. 'I don't know what you two were thinking. There is a reason that those countries have never civilized, you know: the people out there won't ever change, they're just violent savages, and if you think –'

'How dare you.' Dylan had been holding onto his temper by a thread since she mentioned Jimbo not coming home for Lou, but putting down Lou's achievements of the last year was too much. 'Do you even know what she's accomplished out there? How many lives she's saved? She's built an entire wing of a hospital and staffed it with her money and her blood sweat and tears. Do you think that was easy? Of course you wouldn't understand why she did it because you are nothing like her. She's the most compassionate, strongest person with the biggest heart I've ever met in my life. How a monster like you could possibly have produced someone like her is a miracle. And then for her to remain the person she is in the face of her miserable, abusive childhood is an even bigger miracle. You make me sick.' He turned to Mr Sands. 'You both make me sick. Jesus, man-up and tell her where to get off already, you pathetic loser.'

Dylan's tirade was met by a stunned silence. Lou was staring up at him in complete confusion. How did he know the details of what she had done with Jimbo in Africa? She hadn't even told Frankie about the funding for the hospital. Jimbo had initially thought it was a mad idea, but as it started to take shape, and it became clear that the charity he worked for would not approve the project, he'd decided to match Lou's donation.

Between them they had achieved what many thought would be impossible.

In her typical style Mrs Sands ignored most of the uncomfortable information in Dylan's speech, and focused instead on what she considered the only important aspect.

'That money was not left in trust to you for you to squander on pointless charity projects, Louise. If your grandfather was alive today he would –'

'He would have been very proud.' Mr Sands was standing very still, his arms straight down by his sides, and his hands balled into fists. 'He was *my* father, Evelyn. I think I know better than you what he wanted that trust fund used for. He spent a lot of time in Africa, and he would be very proud of what Lou's done.'

'I ... I ... Richard, you can't –' Mrs Sands stuttered.

'Abusive?' he cut her off, no longer looking at his wife but down at his daughter, that one word sounding strangled and almost like it had cost him a piece of his soul to voice.

'Daddy,' Lou whispered, tears swimming in her eyes. 'I –'

'She beat you.' Mr Sands voice was flat. It was a statement, not a question, almost as though he was coming to a realization that, deep in his subconscious, he had already known. 'How was I so blind?'

'I have no idea,' Dylan said, and they all turned to him. 'I knew in the first hour of meeting her what a vicious bitch your wife was. What I also know is that you've both outstayed your welcome and you'll be leaving now.' Dylan's massive arms were crossed over his broad chest, and his face was set in stone. He had no idea how Lou had coped with this sick excuse for a family for so long, but she was not doing it on her own from now on.

Chapter 26

Wrestling a rabid badger

'SO WHEN ARE YOU BACK TO WORK, SANDS?' MILES SAID AS he strolled about her room, picking up Get Well cards at random and shamelessly reading all the messages, most of which made him roll his eyes and mutter, 'Over-sentimental drivel'.

'Miles,' Rosie snapped, stopping him in his tracks, 'she's only just leaving hospital today, you lunatic. She won't be able to come back for ages.'

'Pussy,' Miles muttered under his breath. And then, 'Ow!' he exclaimed after receiving a swift kick to his shin. 'Are you insane, woman? Stop physically assaulting me. Don't you think Lou's seen enough violence recently?' Rosie's face paled.

'Oh God, sorry, Lou,' she whispered.

Lou shook her head at Rosie, taking in Miles's smug expression. 'I don't consider physically reprimanding Miles to be violence, Rosie. After all, you can't train a puppy without a few bops to the nose.'

'He's learning but I sometimes despair at how thoughtless he is. There's no filter between brain and mouth,' Rosie replied.

' "Never attribute to malice that which can be adequately explained by stupidity," ' Ash put in.

'Hey!' Miles objected. 'I am standing right here you know.'

'How come they let you all in?' Lou asked, completely ignoring Miles. 'The ward sister is normally a Nazi about the whole two-at-a-time thing.'

'Oh she *knows* Miles,' Rosie explained. 'I'm more like a dog for the disabled when it comes to him, and therefore don't count as an extra person.'

Lou laughed along with everyone apart from Miles, and was thankful that she could now do this without the tearing pain in her abdomen.

'What's his disability?' she asked through her laughter.

'Oh, he has a very serious condition,' Rosie replied, her attempt at a sombre expression slightly marred by the fact her eyes were dancing. 'It's called Arsehole Syndrome. It's really quite limiting; it gives him this compulsion to be as objectionable as possible to everyone he comes across. Dreadful morbidity and mortality figures I'm afraid. You see, it won't be long before he pisses off the wrong person.'

'Again, I am standing right here, you bastards.'

'Have patience, my annoying friend.' Ash clapped Miles on the back, causing him to go forward a step. ' "Respect comes like a turtle and goes away like a gazelle." '

'I'm annoying? At least I don't speak in riddles.' Miles's face was turning an alarming shade of purple whilst the rest of the room could barely suppress their laughter. Just as Lou thought he might really lose it, the door to her room opened. Glancing at her watch, she realized Frankie must have arrived to take her home. She turned away to get out of bed on the other side so she could start gathering some of her things.

Three days ago, just after her PCA had just been taken down, Yanna, a Filipino nurse on the ward, had bustled into her room and declared that she was there to 'sort her out'. Lou wasn't entirely sure she liked the sound of that, but her objections were ignored as she was encouraged up and out of the bed. Yanna walked her to the bathroom, with Lou stumbling like she was a newborn colt, and then was horrified when the nurse came in with her. The next ten minutes were a blur. Before she knew it, and with ruthless efficiency, she was sitting up in bed, washed from head to foot, and in her own pyjamas and dressing gown. It was amazing to be clean again and in actual clothes. She felt a weird mixture of better than she had since she'd been admitted, and vaguely like she had been assaulted. She'd tried to stammer her thanks, but Yanna had waved away any gratitude.

'Is my job, no need to thank me. I only glad your young man brought a dressing gown. You give everyone heart attack with these ones,' she said, pointing at Lou's cleavage showing above her tiny camisole. 'Need more material, lady.' Lou flushed, and smiled at Yanna. She knew it was pointless to argue that an imminent hospital stay wasn't exactly the scenario she had purchased her nightwear for, and that the set she was currently wearing was in fact her most demure.

Since then, and with the fabulous Yanna's help (despite her increasingly horrified reactions to Lou's choice of pyjamas), Lou had gone from strength to strength. But she was still a bit unsteady, she still had a fair amount of pain, and, even with Yanna's warnings, she still wasn't taking things as slowly as she should. So when she hurried to get out of bed she experienced a massive head-rush and felt her vision narrow, her hand gripping onto the side table to steady herself. Just as she was about to go down, she felt strong hands wrap around her upper arms, and was manoeuvered back onto the bed. When her vision cleared she saw Dylan's gorgeous face hovering above hers.

'Babes,' he breathed. 'Take it easy okay? I don't want you passing out on me before I've even got you off the ward.'

'But ... but Frankie's coming in to get me. She –'

'Well, here's the thing, see,' Dylan said, leaning back from her and avoiding her eyes as his scanned her room for her bag. 'Frankie's only just started back at work and –'

'But she's not at work today. It's Saturday and she's not on call.'

'She might not be, but Tom is,' Dylan said, still avoiding her eyes as he pushed past Ash to get to her bag in the corner. 'Katie and Sarah were too busy to take Lucy, so ...' He trailed off as he started hefting her bag across to her small side-table and, to her horror, started emptying her toiletries (including her freaking tampons) into her bag, then zipping it up.

'That's fine; if she can't take me then I'm sure somebody else would do it.' She looked towards the others, but weirdly they all seemed to be avoiding her gaze as well.

'I guess I cou –' Miles was cut off by what looked like another kick in the shin from Rosie, and Lou noticed Dylan shooting him a filthy look. What on earth was going on? Even Ash was looking distinctly shady.

'I have to leave now, Louise,' he said, moving forward and bending to kiss her cheek. When he straightened, he went on to say, 'I'm sorry but "What is written on the brow will inevitably be seen by the eye", so you will understand in time.'

'What are you on about?' she semi-shouted as far as her still-hoarse voice could manage. 'Hey!' she continued as she noticed that they were all now shooting her apologetic looks and edging towards the door.

'Bye, sweetie,' Rosie said, giving her a small wave but still avoiding direct eye contact. Miles looked mildly confused as she ushered him out.

'Thanks for nothing, guys!' Lou shouted after them, then glared at Dylan, who looked remarkably unconcerned by her reaction.

'I think we're done,' he told her, after sweeping a whole mess of her stuff off the top of her dresser into her bag with a complete disregard to what any of it actually was. 'Oh, I almost forgot.' He dropped the bag heavily on the floor and grabbed a small pile of stuff he had left on the chair. 'Turns out you don't own any loose casual-wear – not that I'm particularly surprised.' He smirked at her and threw a ratty T-shirt and tracksuit bottoms into her lap, which she immediately recognized as his.

'What's this?' she asked.

'It's a T-shirt and some tracky-bums,' he said slowly, as if she was mentally deficient.

She glared at him. 'What is it doing on my bed?'

'Put it on.'

Lou made a disgusted face and threw the clothes back in Dylan's face. 'No way. I'll wear some of my own clothes.'

'Okay, babes,' Dylan said, still smirking. 'Your most casual outfit is your gym kit. Fancy trying to get that lot on over your dressings?'

Lou bit her lip. The thought of trying to force her beaten body into the sparse amount of spandex her gym outfit consisted of was frankly terrifying. The irony was that there was a time she would have killed to wear Dylan's T-shirt. She used to watch his one-night stands proudly strut about in just his T-shirts, whilst fighting that awful churning jealously that felt as though it was eating her from the inside out.

She was still clutching the T-shirt, biting her lip, when Yanna breezed into the room. 'Ah, good: you here,' she said as she bustled in, smiling brightly at Dylan and then turning to Lou. 'Your nice young man here to take you now.'

'I am not going anywhere with him,' Lou spat out, collapsing back into the bed and pressing the heels of her hands into her eye sockets.

'Now, now,' Yanna chided, moving forward and pulling Lou's arms down from her face. 'You are crazy girl. Lovely, big, beautiful boy say he want to take you home, you go with him.'

Lou growled in frustration as Yanna gently manoeuvered her to the edge of the bed. 'Ah!' she exclaimed as she snatched up the T-shirt. 'I prayed for more modest clothes for you. Praise the Lord my prayers answered and you not walking out looking like slut.'

Yanna started tugging off Lou's robe, but Lou squeaked in protest. 'I'm not getting changed with him in here,' she said, crossing her arms over her chest.

'Good for you,' Yanna said, then started shooing Dylan out of the room. 'No boobies and foo-foos till after wedding-ring on that finger.'

Once Lou was dressed in Dylan's clothes, a delighted Yanna called Dylan back in, and, to Lou's complete shock, he produced her favourite pair of slippers, then bent down to put them on her feet, which were hanging off the side of the bed. Once shod, she gingerly climbed off the bed and Dylan moved in front of her.

'Crikey, Lou, I always forget how short you are without those stilts you a cavort about in,' he said softly, then tucked her hair behind her ears, bent down to her upturned face and, very briefly, touched his lips to hers.

Lou blinked. What on earth was going on? After that she was so completely dazed that she barely noticed as he led her out of the ward and past the ecstatic nurses at the ward desk (all of whom were totally besotted with Dylan and had wasted no opportunity to let her know how lucky they thought she was, repeatedly. The fact that he was not her boyfriend, and, to be quite honest, after all the crap he'd pulled, not even much of a friend, seemed to be irrelevant). She knew she had to keep moving to help her recovery, but that didn't mean that each step wasn't a struggle. By the time they reached the front entrance her mouth was tight with pain, and her face had paled.

Dylan turned to her, took one look at her face and muttered,

'Shit. I knew I should have got a wheelchair. It's okay, babes, the car is just over by there.'

'Of course it is.' Lou could feel her lips trying to tip up in a small smile when she saw Dylan's car parked haphazardly just outside the main entrance. She had never before been so grateful for his arrogant, and frankly ridiculous, penchant for obnoxious parking. He moved to his car, ripped the ticket off the windshield, threw it in the gutter (his standard method of dealing with such things) and held open the door for her. She couldn't help the wince of pain she made as she slid into the passenger seat, and noticed Dylan's grip on her elbow tightened significantly when he heard it. Glancing up at him before he closed the door, she could see his eyes flashing with anger and that muscle ticking in his jaw again. After he'd stowed her bag and got into the driver's seat he was silent for a moment, his knuckles turning white where they gripped the steering wheel.

'Um ... are you okay?' Lou asked, after the silence had gone on for a little longer than was comfortable.

'If they didn't have enough evidence to bury that prick alive, I swear I would find a way to make him pay,' Dylan said through gritted teeth.

'What's brought this on?' Lou asked, her anger at Dylan essentially kidnapping her from the hospital forgotten in her bemusement.

'What's brought it on? What do you think's brought it on? How about watching you shuffle through the hospital corridor, pain etched on your face? When the only type of walking I've ever seen you do before is full-on strutting. How about you cringing just from getting into the sodding car? How about me not having to wrestle you out of that place to get you to come home with me because all the fight has been knocked out of you?'

'You wanted me to fight you?' she asked.

'Getting a normal, fully charged Louise Sands out of that hospital and into my car would have been like wrestling a rabid badger, the way you feel about me at the moment.'

'And you would have preferred that?'

'It would have been a pain in my arse, babes, but I would have welcomed it just to see a glimpse of your crazy, stubborn, irrepressible, lunatic self.'

Lou sighed and closed her eyes, sinking back into her chair. All her energy was concentrated on the pain in her abdomen and she didn't have the reserve to deal with a weird-acting Dylan. 'You're the lunatic.'

'Maybe,' he muttered, starting the car.

Just before he pulled out of the space, he reached across, opened Lou's palm and put two painkillers into it and a bottle of water into her other hand. The movement caused him to lean nearly all the way across her, and she opened her eyes when she felt how close he was.

'We'll get you back to being an annoying pain in my arse, babes,' he whispered. Then before she could say anything, he brushed his lips against hers *again* and pulled back into the driver's seat.

Lou glared across at him, her mouth set in a thin line. He wouldn't be helping her get back to anything. She thought about throwing the water in his face but as the car jolted over a speed bump she decided to take the bloody tablets. He might have won this round, but if he thought a couple of stab wounds would transform her into a complete pushover, he had another thing coming.

She was still plotting her escape as the tablets started kicking in and the motion of the car started lulling her into unconsciousness. She would just shut her eyes for a moment ...

Chapter 27

Kidnapped

LOU WOKE UP SLOWLY, FEELING MORE COMFORTABLE THAN she had in days. Opening her eyes, she blinked at the view in front of her. She was staring at a column of tanned male throat and unshaven jawline. Looking down, she realized that she was in her own bed, with her head tucked into what could only be Dylan's throat. Her body was lying mostly on top of his, with her thigh thrown over him, and her arm draped across his stomach. Thankfully he was still fully dressed and she was still in his T-shirt and tracky-bums, but the reminder of the last time they had woken up like this hit her like a sledgehammer, the remembered pain nearly equalling that of her recent surgery.

She pulled away from him and felt unbidden tears sliding down her cheeks. Why was she so weak? Why couldn't she just forget the past and move on? And what the bloody hell was she doing in bed with this man again?

'Hey, babes,' she heard his sleep-laden voice mumble from the other side of the bed. 'Whatcha doin?' He stretched and Lou tried to ignore the ripple of his chest muscles moving under his T-shirt. When he sat up and focused fully on her and her tear-streaked face, his jaw clenched and his tone lost all of its sleepy laziness.

'Babes, why didn't you wake me up if you were in pain?' he clipped, jumping out of the bed and stalking over to her night-stand. Before she knew it, an assortment of pills and a glass of water were thrust into her hands, and Dylan was standing in front of her expectantly, like some sort of psychiatric nurse waiting for a recalcitrant patient to take their meds. Despite the fact he had completely misinterpreted her distress, now that she was focused on it again she could feel the ache start to build in her stomach, so she took the tablets with no fuss other than frowning up at him.

'How did I get up into my bedroom?' she asked after he'd taken her water away.

'I carried you. You were completely outers. Didn't make a peep the whole way.'

'You carried me? Up two flights of stairs?'

'Yeah, well, you *are* essentially a midget, so it wasn't that hard,' he replied, sitting on the edge of the bed and smirking at her.

'Dylan, I'm five-foot-six. You're just not used to seeing me without heels. Not all of us are overgrown apes like you. Now, firstly, what are you doing here? Secondly, how did you get into my apartment? Thirdly, where is the nurse from the agency I hired? And fourthly, and most importantly, what the bloody hell do you think you're doing lying in bed with me?'

'Right, okay,' Dylan began, then held up one finger, 'I brought you home,' second finger, 'I have a key, remember?' third finger, 'I *may* have fired them,' fourth finger, 'I like sleeping with you; you make these weird noises in the back of your throat, kind of like a cat when it's trying to cough up a fur ball. It's cute.'

Lou could feel her face getting redder and redder as the

anger swept through her. Luckily her voice was starting to get stronger and the painkillers were starting to kick in. 'I didn't ask you to take me home; you essentially kidnapped me. What do you mean you fired the nursing agency? I need some help for the next week or so, you idiot.'

'I know you need help, Lou, and I've decided that I'm the one that's going to help you.'

'What!' Lou shouted.

'Easy, babes,' he said, totally unaffected in the face of her anger. 'Don't get excited, it's not a good –'

'There's a reason I need a nurse, you numpty. I need help with *stuff*, not just the odd sandwich made.'

'Oh I know you need help with *stuff*, that's why my mum's pitching in too.'

Lou blinked. 'Bronwen's coming?' she whispered. The mention of his mother had taken the wind out of her sails anger-wise. Lou loved Dylan's mum.

10 YEARS EARLIER...

'Send a prayer up to the Lord, lock up your daughters; the prodigal son has returned!' shouted Dylan as he strode through the pub doors with Mike, Lou and Frankie in tow. Frankie shrank back at the noise and commotion that followed Dylan's announcement, and Dylan moved to wrap his arm around her protectively. The welcome he received was a mixture of back claps, profane insults and shots of spirits.

'Let me through, you crazy bastards.' He heard his dad's gruff voice and the crowd parted to allow him to reach his son. He grabbed the back of Dylan's neck and gave it a squeeze before pulling him in for a tight hug. 'Proud of you, son,' he said in Dylan's ear, his voice thick with emotion. He drew back and studied Frankie, who was still tucked into Dylan's side. Dylan's father was a big man and had a big personality. Tall and broad like Dylan, with a well-weathered face, salt-and-pepper hair and a large tattoo of a Welsh dragon over his biceps, he was as physically intimidating as a pub landlord needed to be, but he had a gentle nature, which was evident in the way he approached Frankie.

'You must be Frankie,' he guessed, softening his tone and earning a small smile from her – unfortunately her shyness had yet again overtaken her and she was unable to actually voice a greeting. As always, Lou was there to rescue the situation. Dylan's father might not have been what she was used to, but Lou being Lou, she was not in the least intimidated.

'Mr Griffiths,' she semi-shouted over the noise around them in her ultra-posh, crisp accent, leaping forward to press a kiss to his cheek and distracting him from Frankie's fearful regard, 'fabulous to meet you. May I say you're so much more attractive than your son.' Her eyes were twinkling as she winked up at him, and Dylan's dad looked very much like he had fallen in love on the spot.

Dylan had to admit that when he had suggested they all go and stay at his family's pub for the Easter break he hadn't expected Lou to enjoy it quite as much as she did. It didn't seem to matter how English or how upper class she was, his entire family and, it seemed, everyone in his town absolutely adored her.

His mam, who had visited Dylan frequently over the preceding year and was well aware of how much Lou was looking after him, was already a huge fan of hers, and it didn't take his father or even his sister long to fall well and truly under her spell. His sister had been sixteen at the time and very into hero-worshipping her big brother. Much to Dylan's disgust Lou attempted to put a stop to that 'rubbish' as she called it, asking instead about Bethan's hopes and dreams. Having a beautiful, intelligent woman take seriously her plan to own her own beauty salon in the future was a turning point for Bethan, who, being the less academic sibling, had always felt like a bit of failure up until that point.

So after those few days at home, Dylan's parents not only credited Lou with their son's successful start to medical school, but also their daughter's new-found confidence. For his part, Dylan had never seen Lou as happy. She was in her element in the pub atmosphere, joking and setting up a darts championship with the regulars, winning them over despite the difference in their backgrounds, and effortlessly drawing a shy Frankie and an amused Mike into the fun.

At the time Dylan didn't fully understand the tears in Lou's eyes as she was enveloped in the hugs from each member of his family before they left. He understood a little more when he learned about her own cold upbringing; but it was only after another ten years had passed that he could truly comprehend what she was yearning for, and by that stage he was more than determined to see that she got it.

Present day...

'Yup, there's no need for you to pay for a nurse, when Mam can do it just as well.'

'I can afford it, Dylan.' Lou sighed and rested back on the bed. 'I can more than afford it. You know that.'

'Right, yes, I do know that,' he said, and, unusually for easy-going Dylan, his voice was laced with steel. 'What I also know is that I'll not let you be looked after by ffwcin strangers who don't know what you like to eat, what DVDs you want to watch, what magazines you read, that you always have to have a box of Bendick's mints in the house and you try to hide it but you feel physically violent towards anyone who eats the gold ones, that you like your feet rubbed but not your toes, that you still have a blanky under your pillow and you don't like it to be washed very often (rank, by the way, but each to their own). You might have enough money to hire an entire fleet of nurses, cooks, cleaners, whatever, but you are going to be looked after by people who care about you.'

'Dylan, we've barely spoken for over a year.'

'That was your decision, Lou, not mine.'

'I –'

'And I understand why you did it. I was a complete prat; I know that. But you've had your time to be pissed off with me. It was a long freaking time as well, but that's over now.'

'You don't get to tell me when it's over, Dylan Griffiths,' Lou said, crossing her arms across her chest. 'It's up to me whether I forgive you or not.'

'That's fine,' Dylan shrugged. 'You decide when to forgive me, but in the meantime I'm not going anywhere.'

Lou was so frustrated she actually growled. 'You are the most irritating, stubborn, annoying ... Ugh ... how do you even still have a key? I made you give me back yours before I left for Africa.'

'I ... well, I ...' Dylan shifted uncomfortably for a minute, then stared straight at her, totally unashamed as he said, 'I made a copy.'

With that, Lou's temper, which had been hanging on by a thread, snapped. She grabbed the closest thing to her and threw it at his head. Seeing as the closest thing had been a pillow, this action didn't have quite the impact she was hoping for as it hit Dylan in the chest with a soft thump. Looking at his smirking face, Lou could feel the red mist descending. How dare he push her around and think he knew what's best for her? She snatched up the water glass from her bedside table and hurled it at Dylan's face. He ducked and the glass smashed on the wall behind him.

They looked at each other in stunned silence for a moment before Dylan's face broke into a huge grin. He stalked towards her saying, 'Knew she was still in there. Knew that a bit of pain and major surgery couldn't take all the fight out of you.'

Lou was too shocked by her own behaviour to speak. What was she thinking? She could have seriously hurt him. So when Dylan bent and kissed her on the lips for the third time that day, she was too distracted to do anything but kiss him back.

'Hello there? Kids?' they heard shouted from the living room, causing Lou to come to her senses and pull back from him. His hands were framing her face and hers were buried in his hair as she stared into his green eyes, watching as they flashed with irritation, and then closed slowly before he rested his forehead on hers.

'Dylan Griffiths, get out here and help me with this shopping.' There was a lot of rustling, followed by an alarming amount of crashing coming from Lou's kitchen.

'Perfect bloody timing, Mam,' Dylan muttered as he reluctantly moved back from Lou, but not before kissing her briefly once more, then smiling at her stunned expression.

Lou lay back into the bed and listened to Dylan and his mother banging about, putting what sounded like a colossal amount of food away whilst bantering affectionately back and forth. She sighed. With Bronwen in the mix it was unlikely that she was going to be able to revert to the nursing agency plan in a hurry.

She'd come up with it in hospital after realizing she was going to need a fair amount of help to get through the first couple of weeks at home. Most people would have family to care for them, but with Jimbo in Africa and her mother a complete non-starter in the caring stakes, she was out of options. Frankie and Sarah were at first adamant that they could look after her, but they had their own children to think of, and Lou didn't want to impose. Anyway, after the first day of arguing with her, they both seemed to back off completely, and with the benefit of hindsight Lou could see that that had been more than a little suspicious. The question was why they would be happy to let Dylan look after her, given the way they knew she felt about him since last year? It didn't make any sense.

Gingerly pushing herself up onto her feet, she made it to the mirror and barely recognized the pale, haunted face staring back at her. Grabbing a hairband from her dresser, she tied the blonde, tangled mass up into a messy knot, wincing as the move pulled on her scars. She reached for her makeup bag but her hand froze; no amount of makeup was going to do her any good at the moment.

'Hey, Mother Teresa,' she called from across the living room, having decided that now was as good a time as any for a showdown with Bronwen. Bronwen whipped around to see Lou standing in the doorway of her room, and smiled.

'Beautiful Lou,' she said, moving across the living room to get to her, the tiny bells on her skirt jingling as she went. Bronwen was one of the most eccentric, kind and extremely *Welsh* people Lou had ever met. She had dark hair and sparkling green eyes like her son, but that was where the similarities ended. Bronwen had a petite, well-rounded figure and she dressed like some sort of crazy Welsh gypsy, in long flowing skirts and an overabundance of scarves. As she drew up in front of Lou her expression changed from excitement to shock, then settled on concern.

'Oh, cariad,' she muttered, searching Lou's face and no doubt taking in the dark circles under her eyes and her sunken cheeks. Lou watched in fascination as Bronwen's expressive eyes filled with tears as she reached up to tuck a stray strand of blonde hair behind her ear. The sight of Bronwen's uncensored reaction was enough to tip Lou over the edge and she felt her nose sting with the effort of holding back the emotion. Bronwen reached out and pulled Lou in for a tight hug. Maternal affection had been in short supply in Lou's life, and the feeling of being engulfed in Bronwen's softness was almost too much. Lou's body bucked with a sob as she held on for dear life. 'Ah, cariad, you give it all to Bronwen now. There's nothing a good cwtch can't solve.'

Lou looked over Browen's shoulder as she cried. She saw a box of Bendicks mints on the counter, along with diet cherry Cokes and all her favourite magazines. She tried to fight it but she knew the warm feeling in the pit of her stomach was spreading, and despite everything, she did not have the strength to fight any more. There was no way she could resist this, and for the moment she was going to give in. For once in her life she was going to let herself be taken care of.

Chapter 28

Slutens

D<small>YLAN LISTENED AS</small> L<small>OU MADE ANOTHER OF THOSE WEIRD,</small> hairball noises in the back of her throat. She lay sprawled across the bed and him, completely unguarded and uninhibited. This was why he always made sure to wake a good hour before he knew she would: it was the only opportunity he had to catch her with her guard down, and definitely the only opportunity to feel her soft body pressed against his.

She'd gone back to wearing her skimpy pyjama sets, which he took as a good sign. Then again, he had been enjoying seeing her in his T-shirts; it had felt like he was a step closer to her actually belonging to him. Sheets of her thick, shining, wavy hair were spread loose down her back and over his arm at her waist, her long eyelashes casting shadows over her cheeks, which already had a much healthier glow. Her graceful jaw jutted out as she ground her teeth, still making the weird noises in the back of her throat, and Dylan didn't think he'd ever seen anything so beautiful. She was starting to stir, and after a few minutes she flopped away from him in the bed, her arms going above her head as she lay on her back. The movement exposed the lower half of her abdomen, and Dylan's jaw clenched as he saw the vivid red line down the centre from the laparotomy, and the smaller, inch-long scar next to it from one of the stab wounds. He'd become used to the sight of her scars by now, having slept in bed with her for the last two weeks. Even though the laparotomy scar was the longest, running the entire length of her stomach down the midline, he found that he actually loved it; it represented the saving of her life, and for that reason he hoped it never faded. In contrast, the smaller scars from the stab wounds he absolutely hated, and had to tamp down the familiar anger he felt every time he caught sight of them.

That evil son of a bitch was recovering on the ward now. There was still some minor brain damage from the beating he took, but the bastard was having rehab. *Rehab.* As if he deserved to be rehabilitated after what he'd done. If it wasn't for the fact that the evidence against him was so compelling that he was guaranteed a lengthy prison stay, Dylan would consider finishing the job that Alun had started.

She shifted again and Dylan carefully moved forward, burying his face in her neck and thick hair, and inhaling deeply. He knew from experience that he only had a few more minutes until she was fully awake and back on her guard, and he wanted to make the most of what time he had left.

It was two weeks since he'd brought her back to the flat and essentially moved himself and his mum in with her. After that first argument when she had hilariously thrown the glass at him, she had been surprisingly compliant with the situation. Dylan suspected it had something to do with his mum's arrival. He wasn't above playing dirty to get what he wanted, and he knew that she wouldn't say no to Bronwen. At this point he was fully prepared to use every weapon he had to wear her down. There was no way a bloody stranger was looking after his Lou.

When Frankie had told him that plan, it felt like it was he that had the knife plunged into his gut. Of course Frankie and Sarah weren't going to let her use the agency, but Dylan decided that it was time to make sure everyone knew where he stood when it came to Lou. Frankie was sceptical, but when Dylan took her aside and told her what he'd found in Lou's wardrobe, she reluctantly gave in, after promising to put *him* in the hospital if he hurt her again. He had never heard Frankie threaten anyone with violence before, and despite her size and angelic appearance, the gleam in her eye and the stony expression she wore as she issued it made her sound surprisingly menacing.

He had managed to get two weeks off work, and even though everyone had agreed to back off and let him look after her, that did not mean they trusted him. The flat was like Charing Cross with the amount of visitors Lou had every day (thankfully none of whom included her actual family), and Dylan had had to lay down the law on more than one occasion when he could see Lou was flagging.

But however tired she was, Lou never allowed him to turn away the children, especially Benji, who was one of the most frequent visitors. Despite all his bravado, it seemed that Benji was having a few problems since the attack. When he was over at the flat he stayed close to Lou the entire time, shadowing her movements in a way that was almost disturbing. When Dylan asked Sarah about it, she'd told him that Benji had been having nightmares so extreme that he would wake the entire house with his screaming. The only uninterrupted nights he had were after he'd seen Lou in the day; hence the frequent visits that included not only Benji but also his three brothers and, often, Lucy thrown into the mix. In Dylan's opinion this was not restful, but Lou seemed to almost draw strength from cuddling the toddlers or talking to the boys, almost as though their sheer life force was healing her.

The fact that she had been letting Dylan sleep in her bed, and in her sleep had proceeded to wrap herself around his body, had been encouraging. She had also seemed to accept his sustained assault of regular and casual affection, which he had embarked on since she left hospital. He reasoned that the sooner she got used to it, the better. He wasn't going anywhere, and eventually he was going to wear her down. But over the last couple of days the colour had slowly been coming back to Lou's face, and along with that, he could see her building up her strength to pull away from him.

The year he'd spent without her had been the worst of his life, and seeing her hurt had definitely been one of his worst experiences. She could push him away all she wanted – he was staying put. Ever since he'd found that box in her wardrobe, he'd been convinced that he could win her over; but recently that conviction had been wavering. He could feel her slipping through his fingers, and, other than at night when she wrapped herself around him in sleep, he felt like he was losing the little ground he had gained.

He felt her shift again, and pulled back from her neck to see her beautiful, sky-blue eyes staring up at him. As on every morning, when she woke up a look of pure wonder passed across her face before she masked it and withdrew behind her shield again. Yes, he thought to himself, definitely making progress.

'You two keen on a cooked breakfast?' he heard from behind the bedroom door, then closed his eyes in frustration as it was pushed open and his mam peered around it. 'It's your first day back today, isn't it, cariad? Need to make sure you're on top form for saving lives and all that.'

His mam had actually moved out a week ago, when Lou had

stopped needing any help with showers and the like. She had told them that, now Lou could do everything for herself in the bathroom, she wanted to give them some time alone together before Dylan had to go back to work. Lou had rolled her eyes and told her that she could take Dylan with her, but to Lou's obvious exasperation his mam just laughed her off, as she had done all Lou's attempts to put her straight about the nature of their relationship over the last two weeks.

His mam might have moved out, but that didn't mean she wasn't still making full use of the key Dylan had foolishly given her, along with his dad and sister.

'Mam,' Dylan said through gritted teeth, 'I've told you not to just burst in here this early. It's weird and it freaks me out.'

'Pah! Fiddlesticks. You've never been a shy boy and it's not the first time I've seen you in bed with a girlfriend. And at least this girlfriend I actually love like a daughter; not like some of the slwtens* you've presented me with.'

'Mam!'

'Okay, okay,' she said, holding her hands up in mock surrender. 'I'll go, but I'll come back in if you're not out here in five minutes for your breakfast. Your father might skip the odd breakfast, but he only serves drinks and fixes what needs fixing around the pub. You fix *human beings* and you can't do that on an empty stomach.'

～

LOU THOUGHT IT WAS CUTE THAT DYLAN'S MUM ALWAYS made it sound like he was single-handedly keeping the NHS afloat, and the lives of the Welsh people firmly in the Saved category, whenever she talked about his career. It was the antithesis of how her parents referred to her work, and she found it refreshing. She knew that, although Dylan hated it, and his face would always cloud with irritation when she did it, he would never say anything to make her stop. He adored his mum, as well he should, and Lou knew there was a lot he would tolerate from her before he called her out. She pressed her lips together to stop herself laughing, and Dylan's irritated green eyes narrowed at her as she tried to contain her amusement. She finally snorted a giggle after she heard the door click behind his mum. At the sound of her suppressed laughter Dylan's face cleared of irritation and his eyes dropped to her mouth.

'Christ, you're beautiful,' he breathed.

Lou sucked in a shocked breath and started pushing on his shoulders in an attempt to dislodge him.

'Get off,' she huffed. When he didn't move she glared at him and said, 'You're hurting me.' He wasn't, but she needed to work out what the hell was happening, and she couldn't do that with his body pressed against hers. He moved off her immediately, as if he had been given an electric shock, his face awash with concern. Needing more space between them and also feeling at a disadvantage lying in bed with him, she flung her feet over the side of the bed and stood on shaky legs.

'Why are you doing this?' she whispered, and he frowned at her.

'Doing what?'

'This,' she said gesturing between the two of them. 'All of it: staying here, looking after me, moving in, moving your mother in, kissing me, treating me like I'm actually important to you. Why are you doing it?'

She'd been thinking over the last week. Thinking about why he was suddenly showing her the kind of interest she had craved from him for so long. As the fug of pain and weakness had cleared, her brain had finally shifted into gear, and she had come to the only possible conclusion.

Guilt.

Guilt was the driving force behind everything he was doing for her. He knew he'd had a hand in ruining her career, he had acted like a complete bastard, and now he was feeling bad. He'd seen her get hurt and wanted to do the right thing.

'You've always been important to me, Lou,' he said, sitting up in bed so that the duvet fell to his waist and the glorious planes of his broad chest came into view, momentarily distracting her. He must have noticed her eyes flicking down from his to check him out, because he gave her a smug grin. It was a mistake. You should not grin like that at a woman as close to the edge as Lou was in that moment. Lou focused again on his face, losing her temper.

'Oh yes,' she snarled, her voice low and thick with emotion, 'so important to you that you shagged every – what did your mother call them? Ah, yes ... sltwens* ... in sight at uni, right under my nose. That you even used me as some sort of wing-woman in your sick games to accumulate yet more women to shag.

'That you copied my notes, let me nurse you through your hangovers, defend you to the professors whose lectures you couldn't bother to turn up for, drag you through the course-work you were too lazy to complete on your own, had me ring you every morning in our clinical years to remind you to get your sorry arse out of bed and into the hospital for ward rounds. Never saying thank you, never really thinking about why ...' She broke off and looked down at her shaking hands, her pride preventing her from voicing anything to boost his already colossal ego. 'I went toe to toe with my whole depart-ment and yours to save your bacon, and all I got in return was ugly words hurled at me in front of everyone.' Her voice dropped to a whisper. 'You know about my family and you used that against me. I trusted you and you went out of your way to hurt me. So don't you fucking tell me that I've always been important to you.'

'Lou, I –' Dylan's face was the palest she'd ever seen it, desperation and what looked almost like fear written across it.

'Get out.'

*SLTWENS — *SLUTS*

Chapter 29

It never even began

He walked towards her, and Lou hardened herself to the anguish in his eyes. Cupping her face in his big hands, he leaned his forehead down against hers.

'Please,' he pleaded, pain lacing his voice. 'Please let me show you what you mean to me. I'll prove it. I'll spend the rest of my life proving it to you if you'll just let me.' She put both her hands against his chest and pushed him away, stepping back from him.

'Why now?' she asked. 'Why all this interest in me now? I've spent over ten years watching you chase, sleep with, charm, pay attention to every woman you met other than me, so why now?'

'Look, babes,' he gritted out, his jaw clenching in frustration. 'Can we just forget about the other women. It's not as if you've lived like a nun for the last decade yourself.'

Lou let out a hollow laugh and Dylan's brow furrowed in confusion. 'Do you know how many men I've slept with in the last twelve years, Dylan?'

Dylan shook his head. 'No, no, I really don't, Lou. You see, it doesn't matter to me. *I'm* not judging *you* on stuff like that.'

Lou laughed again, and the sound was so heartbreakingly sad that Dylan actually winced. 'You think you have all the answers don't you? You probably think I slept with half your ridiculous friends on the rugby team. Am I right?'

'Let's not rehash the past, Lou, it's not –'

'Am I right?' Lou shouted, close to losing it.

Dylan held up his hands. 'It doesn't matter now,' he said in a voice that was meant to be placating, but only seemed to fire Lou up more.

'I've slept with two people in my life, Dylan.' Dylan's mouth dropped open.

'But I –'

'Yes – yes, I know the rumours. To be honest I never cared that much about what stupid boys wanted to make up when it came to my love life. It started with Terry Aldershot and just spiralled from there.'

'I don't get it.'

'Have you heard from Terry since uni, Dylan?'

'Yes, I saw him at the Old Boys' match a couple of months ago – but what's that got to do with any –'

'Anything about Terry surprise you in the last few years?'

'Well, aside from coming out after we left uni, there's not much ...' Dylan trailed off and stared at Lou.

'You didn't sleep with him,' he said. 'But why would you ... ?'

'He asked me to do him a favour. All you lot were racking up the notches on the bedposts, and he never got any action unless it was down at the Vauxhall Tavern. He was my partner in our physiology project in the first year. We spent a lot of time together. One day I told him about Jimbo and how he couldn't tell our parents he was gay, and after I'd finished Terry burst into tears. He said there was no way he could come out and still live the life he wanted, still be a part of the rugby club.'

'Of course he could have –'

'Really?' Lou raised her eyebrows. 'It wouldn't have been a problem? You showered together for goodness sake. You even shared that insanely huge bath together at the club. Are you saying that no one would have had a problem with Terry?'

Dylan shifted uncomfortably in front of her and said nothing. He knew as well as Lou did that there were a lot of pricks in the rugby club.

'He reminded me of Jimbo: so lost, so scared. I told him I'd buy him some time until he was ready to come out, and I told everyone else we had a wild night together and that he was insatiable. It had to last him a while in the lad stakes, so I had to make the details pretty impressive.

'Little did I know that just that one story would make everyone think I was some king of nympho. The other boys jumped on the bandwagon and made up their own "Sands's wild night of freaky sex stories". Some of them I may have snogged then turned down, but most I'd never even touched. I didn't care enough to correct them. It wasn't as though I was a virgin or anything; I lost my virginity to my boyfriend at school before he left for uni, sort of as a goodbye.

'So the ridiculous thing is that I have this huge reputation for being wild in bed, and I've only had one night of awkward fumbling when I was seventeen with a boy who never breathed a word to anyone, and the other guy I've slept with doesn't even bloody remember it, let alone spread rumours about it.'

Dylan frowned and rubbed his forehead, before his head snapped up and his eyes locked with hers. 'Jesus Christ,' he breathed, taking a step towards her. Lou took a step back but came up against the door. Dylan kept coming until he was caging her in with his hands either side of her face. 'I dream of you. I've been dreaming of you for eighteen months. But they're not dreams are they? They're memories. Memories of something that really happened.' He groaned, and leaned into her even more, his eyes filled with so much pain that she almost flinched. 'Shit, I dream we're lost in each other. I dream about you telling me that you –'

'Shut up,' she hissed. 'Whatever you think you remember, it's bullshit. We might have slept together but I was just as trashed as you. Just because I don't have convenient, morning-after memory loss, doesn't mean I wasn't drunk enough to say and do things I didn't mean.' She tried to keep her voice from shaking as she saw the cogs turning in Dylan's head, and something working behind his eyes.

'You care about me, Lou. Don't deny it. Don't make it sound like that night didn't mean anything.'

'I'm not the one that couldn't even remember it.' Dylan flinched like she'd struck him, but that wasn't going to stop her. 'I'm not the one who thanked God that it didn't even happen. Who said what a mistake it would have been to even go there. So don't you dare tell me it meant something.'

'Lou, please.' The desperation was back in his voice and in his expression as he continued to crowd her against the door. 'I'm an idiot, a selfish, self-centred piece of shit, but I'm yours. I've been yours for years but I was just too stupid to realize it.'

Lou snorted. 'You've never been mine, Dylan, and neither would I have wanted you to be, you loser.'

'Babes, you and I both know that's a lie,' he said softly.

'Ugh! You conceited, arrogant pig. One drunken mistake on my part and you assumed that I'm some pathetic –'

'Stop saying it was a mistake,' Dylan gritted out, shaking her gently by her shoulders. 'Look, I know I've messed up, Lou, but I'm not the only one who's been at fault. Why the bloody hell didn't you tell me how you felt about me years ago?'

'What are you talking about?' Lou's voice had lost some of its strength in her shock.

'I know you never had a thing for Wet-pants Ewan. I know who your poisonous mother was talking about that night at the pub.'

'You're delusional.'

Dylan took a deep breath. He was slowly losing control of his temper. Yes he had behaved badly, but if he'd had even the slightest inkling of how Lou felt about him, maybe he wouldn't have wasted years searching elsewhere for something that was right under his nose the whole time. He was done with arguing this particular point with her. It was time for the truth. Unfortunately, as he pushed away from the door, he was too angry to see the vulnerability in Lou's eyes. Maybe if he had, he wouldn't have done what he did.

He strode across the room to her walk-in wardrobe. Lou started following him, but froze when she saw what he was pulling down from the top shelf. Backing up again, she eyed the shoebox like it was an unexploded bomb, fists clenched by her sides, and watched in horror as he emptied the contents onto the bed. Photographs of Dylan, and stupid little notes from him, were strewn over her duvet; but Dylan pushed all that aside and picked up a pink and white shell from underneath. He moved around the bed to stand directly in front of Lou and brought one of her fists up in front of her. Once he'd uncurled her fingers, he placed the shell inside and held her hand with both of his.

'Don't tell me it meant nothing. Don't dismiss what happened between us. I *know* it meant something. I know I means something to you.'

Lou ripped her hand away from his and took a few jerky steps back. Dylan started to follow her, but froze when he saw the look in her eyes. Humiliation and resentment washed over her. For him to know the extent of her obsession was almost unbearable.

'You bastard,' she forced out, her throat closing as tears

welled in her eyes. 'How do you think it makes me feel that you know this about me? That you know how pathetic and stupid I've been?'

Dylan, having realized that anything he might have wanted to achieve by revealing the box was backfiring on him big time, started looking a little panicked. 'Babes, I –'

'Just shut up! Shut up!' she shouted, feeling on the edge of hysteria. 'How dare you ask me why I didn't tell you I was in love with you?' Dylan's body tensed at her words and his eyes went wide, but she was beyond paying any attention. 'From the moment we met you were obsessed with my best friend. You never showed even the slightest bit of interest in me. Do you think I have so little pride that I would beg you to choose me and not Frankie? I thought at first there was no way you two wouldn't be a couple once you got past her barriers. I thought you were so bloody wonderful that I couldn't even comprehend someone turning you down, and I loved Frankie enough to want that for her. But of course Frankie is Frankie; unpredictable as ever, she had her sights set elsewhere. She didn't even notice how you watched her, how you went out of your way for her, how protective you were of her. But believe me *I* noticed. I noticed and it broke my heart over and over again.' Lou was crying in earnest now, but when Dylan took a step towards her she held up her hand again to ward him off. 'Even after you gave up on her, you still would never have touched *me* with a barge pole.'

'Lou that's not true, I –'

'I heard you in the library. What was it you said to the boys? "High-maintenance, ball-breaking bitch." I think that was it. What? You think I'm so low-maintenance now, you're willing to give me a go?'

'No,' Dylan said warily. 'I don't think you're low-main-tenance.'

'Well then! What's the point of all this bullshit? Don't piss on my Louboutins and tell me it's raining. I'm not buying any more of this crap. Guilt trip is over, okay? All is forgiven. You can stop this ridiculous charade now.'

She threw the shell at him and he caught it in midair.

'This isn't about guilt, Lou,' Dylan said, tucking the shell carefully in his pocket and then running his hands through his hair in frustration.

'Then why?' Lou asked, her voice now small, having lost its previous fire. 'After all these years, why now?'

'Cause I'm twp, okay? Because I thought I knew what I wanted but I was wrong. The only time I've been even halfway on the right course is when I gave you that shell. Do you remember what we promised?'

Lou, who had every moment of that night on the beach burned into her brain and had been holding onto the thin hope it gave her for years, rolled her eyes. 'Of course I remember, dipshit. Why do you think I've kept it like an obsessive stalker for eight years.'

They had been on their elective together in South Africa. Frankie and Mike had long since gone to bed, but Lou and Dylan were lying out under the stars. The beach was covered in tiny pink and white shells. They'd just finished talking about one of Dylan's recent conquests that went pear-shaped, and how Dylan didn't think she was 'The One' anyway. Lou had teased that he had a snowball's chance in hell of finding 'The One', and that the way he was going he'd end up old and alone until some money-grabbing niece or nephew (his sister might not settle down, but the way she was going she was unlikely to avoid an unplanned pregnancy or two) shoved him into a home. They made a pact to marry if they were both still single when they got to forty, and Dylan had picked up one of the shells and tried to shove it on Lou's ring finger as a pre-engagement ring.

'Right, well. There you go. I think that was my subconscious trying to break free or something, trying to get me what I actually wanted.'

Lou stared at him for a minute. She wanted to believe him, but after years of his indifference it was too hard. After she slept with him, she knew for a fact that the old saying 'Better to have loved and lost than to never love at all' was bullshit. The pain of actually having Dylan, then losing him a few short hours later, had been unbearable. She was tired of not being worthy of people's love. She was tired of giving and never getting anything in return.

All those years wasted trying to please a mother who would always hate her, all the years since trying to catch a man's attention who would never notice her. She deserved to meet someone and for them to instantly know, just like she knew with Dylan, that she was the one for them. She was tired of coming in second place.

'I'm sorry but I can't do this,' she said. 'I want you to leave.'

'No, Lou, just listen. I –'

'No, you listen. I'm tired. I'm in pain. I don't have any more strength to fight with you, and I want you to leave.' Lou knew it was an underhand tactic to use her pain as an excuse, but she also knew that it was about the only thing that would get him out at this point. If he thought he was causing her pain, there was no way he'd stay. She breathed a sigh of relief as she saw him backing off, his hands raised in a gesture of surrender.

'This isn't over,' he said softly as she heard him open the door.

Once he was out in the living area, she could hear the rumble of low voices and realized that his mother was still there. She knew that Bronwen was trying to be discreet, but she was not by nature a discreet woman, or a quiet one. There were a few loud thwacks, which Lou was pretty sure were caused by

Bronwen hitting Dylan upside his head, and a lot of whisper-shouted insults, most of which referred to him being a 'twp bugger'. Then there was what sounded like a scuffle – but thankfully Dylan must have convinced her to leave.

'It never even began,' Lou whispered into her tear-soaked pillow as she heard her front door close firmly behind them.

Chapter 30

I just do

LOU TOOK A DEEP BREATH AND LEANED HEAVILY AGAINST the kitchen counter. It was the first time in a very long week that she'd seen Dylan. And even though they had had what seemed like hundreds of people separating them in Tom and Frankie's living room, the way he had been watching her made the others melt away.

She'd had to escape to the blessed peace of the kitchen just to be able to breathe again. The phone calls and texts had finally dried up two days ago, and although listening to and reading them had been painful, it didn't compare to the pain of their absence. She told herself it was for the best; at least she knew how easily he would give up on her. Typical Dylan: things got tough and he ... buggered off.

Mary Longley's commanding voice was vibrating through the walls. It seemed that as far as the christening of the long-awaited first Longley granddaughter went, Mary was very much in charge of the proceedings. Hence this planning evening, getting all the family and godparents up to speed with chris-tening etiquette. At first Frankie had threatened to call off the whole thing in the wake of the attack. She was adamant that if

Lou couldn't stand up as a godmother for Lucy, the whole thing should be cancelled – and the Longleys, along with everything else, were finding that nowadays, when Frankie wasn't having something, it simply was not to be had. Her quota of backbone seemed to have increased exponentially in the last month. Lou knew that Frankie had been one of the strongest at the hospital after it all happened. She'd told Lou that as far as she was concerned it was her turn to be the tough one, her turn to be the strong friend that Lou could lean on.

Since then, although still on the quiet side, Frankie had been regularly demonstrating a stubborn streak a mile wide. Fortunately Lou's pain, although still there to some extent, was much better controlled. She hadn't needed any help over the last week (shopping might have been difficult but Bronwen had left enough food to feed an army, and the suspiciously fresh carton of milk she found in the fridge this morning had her suspecting that Bronwen might still be making use of her key), and she could cope with standing up at the front of a church for half an hour or so.

She heard the door open behind her, and was surprised to see a nervous Katie standing in the doorway.

'Hey there,' Katie said with a small wave, and Lou instantly felt a stab of regret. Try as she might, she just couldn't tamp down the burning jealousy when it came to this girl. Katie was the only one who had lasted longer than a few nights with Dylan since Lou had known him, and even though they weren't together now, Lou had seen them talking more than once with their heads bent close, engrossed in one another enough to make her doubt that there wasn't still something there. Only tonight she'd seen Dylan whisper something to her, and Katie move to give him a tight hug. He was, she knew, an affectionate guy, and maybe she should have just shrugged it off, but instead she'd found herself scowling across at Katie

until she'd caught her eye. Bizarrely, instead of looking sufficiently guilty for mauling her man (okay, so he wasn't technically Lou's, and it was less a mauling than a casual gesture, but
whatever), she'd looked pleased, and had even dared to smile
happily back a Lou, which only served to piss Lou off and
confuse her simultaneously. Was Katie gloating? That didn't
seem particularly likely given her personality and the fact that
she would have no way of knowing how Lou felt about Dylan
anyway.

'Hey,' Lou said in return, forcing a smile.

'I just wanted to ...' Katie trailed off and looked away from
Lou for a second, tucking her hair behind her ears before she
looked back up at her. 'I hope you don't mind but ...'

Lou clicked her tongue; patience was not one of her virtues.
'Sometime this year would be great, I really should be getting
back,' she snapped, then instantly regretted it, seeing Katie
wince.

'Right ... um ... the thing is ...'

'Katie ...' Lou said in warning, and watched as Katie squared
her shoulders and met her eyes with new determination.

'Why won't you just give him a chance?' she blurted out,
and Lou's mouth dropped open in shock.

'What are you talking about?'

'Dylan. Look, I know you like him; I've known for bloody
ages that you like him. Why won't you give him a chance?'

'Look,' Lou started, her tone laced with ice, 'I've no idea
why you're asking me about Dylan. As far as I'm concerned you
two only broke up about five minutes ago so you can't exactly –'
She was cut off as Katie let out a bark of laughter.

'What? You think Dylan and I were together? We went out
on a few dates, but after that night in the club we've only ever
been friends. And ... well ... you mustn't be cross but he needed
someone to talk to, and he didn't want to tell Frankie or any of

the others because ... well ... the main thing he wanted to talk about was you.'

Lou blinked. 'Me?'

'Well, yeah ...' Katie looked confused. 'I kind of thought Dylan had told you how he felt ... I mean he's told everyone else now, so –'

'He's told everyone else what?'

'That he's in love with you and how he knows you feel the same, etc., etc.' Lou stared at Katie, for once lost for words. 'I mean, he's been bending my ear about you for over a year now, so I guess it was only a matter of time before he spilt the beans to everyone else. I don't know if you've noticed but he *does* have a big mouth.'

Lou narrowed her eyes at Katie.

'If he was sooo into me, why did he start going out with you in first place?'

Katie shrugged. 'I asked him the same thing. He said at the time he just wanted to at least be your friend again and that you always seemed to hate his um ... exploits. He thought you might respect him more if he was in a real relationship, and he picked me mostly because I can quote *Blackadder*.'

'Lou's eyebrows shot up into her hairline. 'He told you that?'

'Yeah.' Katie shrugged, a small smile on her lips. 'Real charmer isn't he?'

'Who's a charmer?' Both girls jumped and turned to see a glowering Dylan filling the doorway. Katie laughed, totally unaffected by his glower.

'I'll leave you kids to it,' she threw over her shoulder as she skipped past Dylan at the doorway.

'So apparently I'm to give you space to get your head straight,' Dylan bit out. 'Well, space doesn't seem to be working, so I think from now on I'm going to be doing things my way.'

'I don't want to talk to you, Dylan,' Lou told him. She was

trying to process everything Katie had told her and what it all meant. She needed more time.

'No,' he agreed. 'To be honest that doesn't seem to work for us either.' Before she knew it he had stalked across the kitchen, taken her face in his large hands and was kissing her. It wasn't like the kisses he'd been giving her the two weeks previous. It wasn't soft and gentle and sweet; it was demanding and filled with need. Lou stiffened for a moment, but her pent up feelings wouldn't let her hesitate for long. She buried her hands in his hair, slanted her head to the side and kissed him back. Just as they had eighteen months ago, things got out of control quickly, and before long he'd lifted her up onto the kitchen counter to get better access to her mouth.

'Ahem.' Dylan sprang back from Lou, leaving her perched on the counter, and whipped round to see Benji standing right next to them, a smug expression on his face and his arms crossed over his chest.

'Benji, mate. I um ... didn't see you there. Lou and I were just ...'

'You were kissing,' Benji said accusingly.

'I ... uh ... well, we ...'

'It's fine.' Benji shrugged. 'You can take over from here,' he offered magnanimously. 'Annabel Evans at school wants to be my girlfriend anyway, so I won't have time to look after Lou as well. Mummy and Auntie Frankie will be surprised though. I think I'll just ...'

'Alright, Vito Corleone. How much?'

'Oh, I'd say a tenner would cover it ... for now.' Dylan sighed and slipped Benji a tenner from his wallet as Lou jumped down from the counter. Benji gave them both a bright smile, then surprised Lou by dashing forward and giving her a gentle hug around her middle. 'I won't have to worry about you any more now,' he said into her side, and then drew back looking embarrassed before running out as silently as he came.

'Little shit,' Dylan muttered, and then grunted when Lou punched him on the arm.

'Don't you dare insult my hero.'

'Babes, he's bleeding me dry here.' She rolled her eyes, and to his relief she was smiling. He moved towards her again, ready to pick up where they left off, but her hand went up against his chest to stop him.

'Lou, I love you. Please –'

'Why?'

'Why what?'

'Why do you love me?' She was staring at him intently and he could see he was being given a chance here, but the kiss had scrambled his brain; all coherent thought was a thing of the past.

'I … I … I just do,' he said lamely, running his hands through his hair, a confused expression on his face.

She moved forward and cupped his face in her hand. 'Your sense of humour, your laid-back nature, your unwavering support to anyone you consider the underdog, the love you have for your family, your loyalty to your friends, your ability to make me laugh so hard I snort, your endless optimism, your ambition, your drive to succeed, your ridiculously extensive knowledge of *Blackadder*, your gift for making even the most shy person feel at ease, your eyes, your hair, your stubble, your jaw, and last but certainly not least, your arse. Those are the things I love about you Dylan. I'm sorry but "I just do" isn't going to cut it for me to believe that you're serious.'

Dylan stood open-mouthed, trying to process everything Lou had just said and trying to get out actual words to salvage the situation. But his throat seemed to have closed over, and all he could do was watch helplessly as Lou dropped her eyes from his and her hand from his cheek and walked out of the kitchen.

Chapter 31

You're still a twp bugger, mind

Lou smiled as she looked up from the lectern at the front of the lecture theatre. Today's Grand Round was a very special one, completely unique in fact. Curious mutterings were spreading through the much larger than normal crowd. Practically the entire hospital staff had turned up for it. All the seats were taken, and people had crammed into the aisles and down the sides. As she surveyed the front row, she gave a little wave to an excited Benji, who shot out of his chair and waved back enthusiastically. His brothers seemed to be equally excited, and Sarah and Rob were having a job keeping them all in their seats. Lou turned her attention to Alun and continued waving, knowing how much it would piss him off. Her smile grew even wider as she saw him grunt and look away, shifting uncomfortably in his seat. Benji and Alun were flanked by Ash and Tom. Lou had drafted Ash and Tom into 'Alun duty' yesterday, which had involved basically kidnapping him and forcing him into the lecture theatre.

A lot had happened in the two weeks since the christening. Lou was back at work for a start. The chief executive had phoned her at home to request a meeting, which she had reluctantly attended. She'd been surprised that he wanted it to be in a conference room, but soon realized why when she arrived and was confronted by the entire Elderly Care department seated around the large table. The chief executive had started by apologizing for not taking the previous threats made by Mr Talbot seriously. Apparently they were treated in the context of complaints, so the aggression behind them was overlooked. Lou nodded along with this, thinking that the fact that Mr Talbot was drunk or high on the hospital grounds was also conveniently overlooked at the time, but thought better of adding any fuel to the fire.

As she knew by now that they would be, Dr Hudson and Miles were her staunch defenders, and both demanded that she be allowed back to complete the rotation. Miles even said that if he could pick anyone as a consultant colleague it would be Lou. And Dr Hudson added that, for the good of the Elderly Care department (which she pointed out had been flailing somewhat since Lou left, seeing as she had been doing the work of at least three registrars), they must do everything in their power to keep Dr Sands. For his part, Rich just sulked in a corner until called upon to withdraw his previous appraisal, which he begrudgingly did, saying that he'd 'got confused by the layout of the new online form'. (Dylan had already withdrawn his comments multiple times, and had become such a thorn in the side of the department that he was banned from the meeting.) To be honest, Lou didn't think that she even needed everyone to vouch for her: from the fear she could see in the managers' eyes when they talked about the attack, she knew that they would do anything to appease her, probably worried she would sue, or worse, go to the press.

So yesterday she had started back on the Elderly Care wards and fallen into her old routine easily. She was on reduced hours for two more weeks, and was loving every minute. But

259

before she could settle back in properly she felt that she needed to do this – hence the packed lecture theatre.

'Ahem,' she cleared her throat and the sound was amplified around the large space, causing everyone to fall silent.

~

BENJI'S EYES FLICKED UP TO LOUEY AS HE HEARD HER cough. He instantly stopped fidgeting and gave her a big smile. She smiled back and winked at him before starting her speech. She was back to the old Louey now: long, flowing, shiny hair like a princess, pink in her cheeks and on her lips, tall again, now that she wore those weird stilt-shoes, and colourful again. Her bright blue dress seemed to make her stand out from the other ladies in the room. It was like she was a splash of colour in a sea of greys and blacks, and it suited her.

'Ladies and gentlemen, thank you for coming to this very special Grand Round today.' Benji didn't exactly know what a 'Grand Round' was but it sounded pretty important and his chest swelled with pride. 'I'm not sure if all of you know this, but six weeks ago I was attacked in the hospital car park and I nearly died. In fact, without the people I'm going to thank today, I definitely would have done.' She stopped and blinked her eyes for a minute, and Benji noticed that they looked a little glassy. He was relieved when she managed to stem the tears. It was bad enough if he cried in front of Jack; he reckoned that to cry in front of this many people would have been mortifying.

'I'll start with my rescuers.'

Benji nudged Alun next to him. 'That's us,' he said in a stage whisper, and received a long-suffering sigh in response. Benji did not understand why Alun wouldn't be excited. When they'd called Benji up in assembly to give him a bravery certificate, he'd been beside himself. Then again, Alun seemed to be grumpy about most things – maybe he didn't have any other settings, kind of like when Benji had broken Daddy's computer and all it would do was show a flashing screen. Dad said it had 'crashed', and Benji thought that was a good description of Alun.

'Benji, honey, would you come up here?' Benji sprang out of his seat and ran to stand next to Louey. Louey curled her arm around him and gave him a squeeze. 'This young man was with me at the time and he was very brave. He –' Benji jumped up suddenly and pulled the mic down to his level.

'I whacked him in the willy with my marbles,' he said proudly, and a ripple of laughter went through the crowd as Lou wrestled the mic back from him.

'Right, okay ... well, I'm not condoning violence but at the time it did save my life, so, Benji, thank you.' She kissed his cheek and put a medal around his neck as the audience burst into applause.

'My other rescuer was less keen to attend today, but as with Benji, I owe him my life and that means that I get to be a pain in his arse forever. That's the saying, right, Ash?'

'I think you'll find the Chinese proverb is more like, "Save a life and you are responsible for that life forever," ' Ash shouted out, and the crowd (most of whom had been heavily proverbed by Ash before) gave a collective groan.

'Well, anyway. The next person who is apparently responsible for my life is Alun. Come up here, Alun.'

～

ALUN GLARED AT THE CRAZY BLONDE DOCTOR. HE WAS NOT going anywhere. It was bad enough to be dragged away from his comfortable armchair at home for this nonsense; he certainly wasn't going to be hauled up in front of all these people and be thanked for something any decent man would have done in his place. He felt something pulling on his hand, and saw that the kid had left his place at the front of the lecture theatre to try to get him to move. The determination and excitement in his little face weakened Alun's resolve, and when he looked back at the crazy blonde, the blinding smile she was directing at him melted it completely. He grunted and used his stick to get to his feet, ignoring offers of help from either side. He'd bashed a guy's head in for Christ's sake; he could bloody well manage to walk a few yards on his own. Still scowling at the crazy blonde, he made his way up to the front of the room and stood next to her, leaning heavily on his stick.

'Two years ago Alun suffered a massive stroke, and was unable to walk or talk for many weeks. He was not only brave enough to recover from that ordeal, but he then went on to save me by –'

The kid made another successful grab for the mic, and before Crazy Blonde could stop him, he shouted into it: 'He bashed him with his stick. It. Was. *Awesome*.' Crazy Blonde rolled her eyes and managed to wrestle the mic off the kid. And for the first time in a long time Alun felt his lips attempt to tip up in a small smile. He caught the kid staring at him, and watched as his eyes went wide, taking in his expression. Alun fought back a laugh: the kid was probably shocked to see him wear any expression that wasn't pissed off, but Alun couldn't help himself; the little bastard was ffwcin funny.

'Okay, Benji, I don't think we all need the gory details,' Crazy Blonde continued, then turned to Alun. 'Thank you, Alun.' He grunted in response and made a move to sit back down, but froze in shock as Crazy Blonde lurched forward and wrapped her arms around his neck, kissing him hard on his cheek.

The lecture theatre erupted into applause once again, and

Alun felt an unfamiliar emotion swell in his chest, one that he hadn't experienced in a long time. He'd always been a bit of an arsehole. It was why he never married, why his only surviving family that bothered with him was his long-suffering niece, and why moments of pride in his life had been few and far between. But standing there in front of all these people, a beautiful blonde wrapping her arms around him, he felt a surge of pride. All that beauty, intelligence, life and vitality; he'd had a hand in saving that, and if his life amounted to no more than that single act, he knew it was worth it for the woman in front of him.

Of course, when she finally let him go he managed to roll his eyes, grumble under his breath that he needed a bloody drink, and grunt at anyone in his way as he hobbled back to his seat. But when he looked back at her and her already dazzling smile cranked up a few more notches, he knew that he hadn't quite managed to blink away the wet in his eyes, or completely hide the small, pleased smile playing on his lips.

~

DYLAN WATCHED AS LOU SMILED AT THAT OLD BASTARD who was trying to hide how much her words meant to him. Back at full strength again, she lit up the entire, cavernous lecture theatre, drawing everyone's rapt attention. She began rattling off the names of all the others who had helped her that night, including every member of the resus team, surgical team and anaesthetic team that had worked on her. As the applause was dying down and Dylan thought she must have finished, he heard his name ring out in her clear, steady voice.

'And lastly a thank-you to someone who saved me in a different way. Who was stubborn enough not to let me recover with strangers, and who cared enough to move back in with his mother for me. Thanks again, Bronwen –' she nodded to his mum, who was sitting next to him in the middle of the theatre '– and thank you, Dylan. So now that I've got all the thank yous ... um, Dylan ... it's okay, you, um ... you don't have to come down here.' Lou stared in shock as Dylan walked over the tops of the lecture theatre's chairs, literally over people's heads, and then sprang down in front of her, snatching the mic out of her hands.

He took a deep breath, blocked out everyone else in the room, and concentrated on just her. 'Your laugh; your smile; your wit; your smartarse put downs; your compassion; your fierce devotion to those you care about; your courage; your strength; your ability to make me laugh, roll my eyes and want to strangle you all in one go; your generosity; your single-mindedness; your sleep-wear; your stubbornness; the way you've always loved me and looked after me, even if I was too twp to see it. The way you dance like a stripper in a bad Vegas nightclub; the way you strut through life like you're the leading role in your own personal Romantic Comedy; your hair, your eyes and your ... other stuff.' Dylan's eyes dropped down from hers for a second, then rose back to her face as he smiled sheepishly. 'Now, you had better agree to be my girlfriend after that, or "believe me, eternity in the company of Beelzebub and all his hellish instruments of death will be a picnic compared to five minutes with me and this pencil," ' he finished, producing one he had stashed in his pocket earlier.

Lou stepped forward and put her fingers over his mouth to stop him. She was flushed bright red with embarrassment, but her eyes were shining with what he hoped was happiness. '*Series Three*,' she whispered.

'Episode?'

' "*Ink and Incapability.*" '

Dylan dropped the mic, stepped forward and kissed her. To Lou's horror, this sparked off the most enthusiastic round of applause yet, and when she managed to pull away she saw that most everyone was standing as they clapped, with a fair few whistles and cheers to boot. As always, Dylan was completely impervious to embarrassment. He high-fived an excited Benji, before lifting Lou in the air and spinning her in a circle to more frantic applause. He even spotted Dr Hudson wiping away a tear in the crowd; seemed the old battleaxe had a heart after all.

The only person who didn't crack a smile was Alun. As the crowd started to disperse, Dylan felt a hand grasp his arm in a surprisingly strong grip.

'Don't fuck this up, lad,' Alun grunted out, and when Dylan looked down, taking in Alun's solemn expression, he instantly sobered.

'I won't,' he said with conviction. Alun searched his face for a moment and must have been satisfied with what he saw there, because he grunted and nodded his head.

'You're still a twp bugger, mind,' Alun added, clapping Dylan on the shoulder so hard he almost staggered to the side. Dylan was starting to understand how this guy had managed to floor someone half his age and twice his size.

'I'll take that as a compliment, mate,' he said, and could have sworn he saw another ghost of a smile on Alun's lips before he was back to scowling.

'Right,' Alun barked, drawing everyone's attention. 'Now that this *cach* is over, who's getting me a ffwcin drink?'

Epilogue

Not too shabby at all

DYLAN STROKED LOU'S HAIR AWAY FROM HER FACE, AND
smiled. She was lying with her head on his chest and her body
flung across his, as she tended to do in her sleep, pinning him to
the bed. As her eyes fluttered open and stared up into his, he
caught the flash of panic that she always shrugged off or tried to
hide when they woke up together like this.

It had been three months since the lecture theatre. Three
months since she'd finally given in and let him prove he loved
her. After the emptiness of being without her for so long, having
her so completely was almost too good to comprehend. It was all
so clear to him now; he'd never worked right without her, and
until she went away he hadn't ever had to try. He knew he
wasn't ideal boyfriend material, but he was getting there, and
he'd do everything in his power to ensure that she never went
away again. The flashbacks and dreams he'd had about their one
night together were nothing compared to the reality of having
her in his bed night after night.

There were of course teething problems. He'd found that
when it came to Lou he had a tendency to be a possessive arsehole, which was tricky when your girlfriend had a tendency to

prance around all day in short skirts and sky-high heels, drawing every male's attention in a five-mile radius. He'd actually tried to hide her more sexy shoes and shorter dresses. The trouble was that she had very few shoes that couldn't also be comfortably used by a burlesque queen, so his thievery had been extensive and fairly obvious. He knew he was being unreasonable, and that he couldn't just steal a suitcase full of her shoes and hide them in his house without some fallout. So he wasn't surprised when Lou had gone nuts, throwing her 'ugly' shoes at him and demanding he produce the ones he'd stolen.

She'd stormed out and Dylan had been terrified that he'd managed to screw things up already. But after she had ignored his calls and texts for a day and calmed down, she came back over to his house, sat him down, and they compromised. She wouldn't wear next-to-nothing in the house when people came over (Lou's cooked breakfasts were the stuff of legend, and usually drew a pretty good crowd on Saturday or Sunday mornings), but her daywear would stay the same. The compromise didn't quite work out the way he wanted though, as her idea of 'covering up' was to put a ridiculously short silk dressing gown over her insanely small pyjamas. And the way Ash's, Tom's, Rob's and even bloody Miles's eyes followed her around the kitchen as she made breakfast, from their carefully selected vantage point at the breakfast bar, suggested to Dylan that the clingy silk, which rode up frequently and generally exposed more than it hid, was compounding the problem. But he bit his lip. Lou was his at the end of the day. He'd known how she was before they got together and the last thing he wanted was to stifle her irrepressible personality. So what if some other guys got a bit of a show once in a while, or got hot under the collar over her in a meeting here and there? He was the one she came home to, and he was the one she slept with at night.

The other thing they argued about was money. She had a lot

of money. In fact, she had a shitload of money. Despite practically building a hospital in Africa, she had barely made a dent in her trust fund. Dylan was a traditional type of guy. He didn't want her to pay when they went out or for her to buy him drinks, and he went berserk when she tried to replace his ancient Ford Focus for him. That time he sat her down and told her how it made him feel and they reached another compromise.

This compromise seemed to involve her easing off on what she bought *him*; but as Christmas rolled around he wasn't surprised when she bought his sister a complete remodelling of her salon, and his delighted mum a new goddamn *bathroom* – *and* a hot tub for their garden (making them the envy of all the neighbours in the village). But he let that slide as well. He knew how much the love of his family meant to her, especially now, with Jimbo still away and her mother not speaking to her (although her dad had surprised them all by visiting her *without* the evil bitch in tow, a previously unheard of event according to Lou). Dylan still resented him for not protecting Lou during her childhood, but was careful what he said, as it was obvious that her dad's visits meant a lot to her.

'Hey,' she said, the fear in her eyes, which he hated so much, but which he knew he was responsible for, slowly receding.

She still had bad dreams about the stabbing, but he knew that far more frequently she had nightmares that she would wake up with him and he would do what he'd done that first morning and reject her. The very idea was ridiculous, and the fact that he could have been so unconsciously cruel as to cause that type of insecurity in this beautiful woman was almost too much to bear. He knew what he had to do and say to chase those demons away, but today he had something else he hoped would replace that memory.

That's why he had chosen this moment to do it. He leaned

away from her and almost swore when he felt her body tense next to him. Jerking open the drawer to his side-table he grabbed the small box out and turned to Lou, tucking her back into the crook of his arm.

'I love you, Louise Sands,' he said softly, the same words he had repeated every morning for three months. He flipped open the small box and took the ring from inside. Her left hand was lying against his chest, so he lifted it slightly and pushed the ring onto her finger. Lou froze for a moment, and then held her left hand out in front of her face, blinking rapidly.

'I'm sorry it's not a diamond or anything ... I mean ... I thought ... well, you've already got your fair share of diamonds and I ... Oh God, I've ballsed up again haven't I?'

Lou was still staring at her outstretched hand, her body completely frozen as she continued to blink rapidly. It was a simple platinum band, but instead of a diamond, a pink and white shell was resting in the setting. Suddenly her face crumpled and she fell forward into his chest, bursting into noisy tears.

'You hate it, don't you? I can get you another one. Just let me _'

'I bloody love it, you big idiot,' Lou shouted through her tears, punching him in the chest for good measure.

'Oh ... right ... um, why are you crying then?'

'I'm happy, okay?' she shouted again, still sobbing, and he looked up at the ceiling, seeking patience from over-emotional women.

'So you will then?'

'What?'

Crikey, she was making this painful. 'Bloody marry me?'

'Of course I'll bloody marry you!' she choked out, but managed to stem her tears long enough to give his bemused face a watery smile, and then an equally watery kiss.

'High maintenance,' he muttered under his breath as he

hugged her to him, letting her tears soak into his chest. She snorted, prodding his side in one of the weak spots she knew so well.

'Argh! Woman, you realize I've just proposed to you, right? You probably shouldn't assault the future father of your babies seconds after agreeing to marry him.'

He felt Lou smile against his chest at the mention of babies, and a second later she had propped herself up to look into his eyes.

'I love you,' she said softly.

'Love you too, even if you are a pain in arse.'

Lou just smiled even brighter at his insult, and then settled back down with her head on his chest.

'Do you really think I'm high maintenance?' she asked.

'Um ... yes.' Just as she was about to prod him again he caught her hand. 'But you wouldn't be nearly so much fun if you weren't, and anyway I think I'm up to the job of keeping you regularly serviced for the foreseeable future.' Lou rolled her eyes.

'You're such a romantic.'

As proposals went, Dylan knew he hadn't exactly chosen the most exciting setting or the most flowery of words, but he had done what he set out to accomplish. The next morning, when Lou's eyes blinked open, the fear he'd seen there for the last few weeks was replaced by contentment ... with an edge of irritation when she heard the loud banging emanating from the kitchen; his mum was yet to give up her key.

～

ALUN'S NIECE WATCHED THE BEAUTIFUL BLONDE LEAN heavily into the handsome dark-haired man as her uncle's casket was lowered into the ground. It was unusual nowadays to choose burial rather than a cremation, but Uncle Alun had selected this plot over thirty years ago. Planning for his death was one of his favourite pastimes. She often got the impression that he was just waiting it out, biding his time until the axe finally fell.

As she looked around the churchyard, she was again shocked by the sheer number of people. Angharad had always had a soft spot for her uncle. Given that he was a miserable, drunken old codger most of the time, her affection for him was a mystery to the rest of their family, who tended to steer well clear. In fact, Angharad could see very little of Uncle Alun's extended family in the cemetery. No, the throngs of people gathered at the graveside were here to pay their respects to the man who had saved the beautiful blonde.

Angharad had seen some of them before when they were visiting her uncle. She doubted that Alun had ever had such a busy social calendar in his life as he had over the last few years. He would grumble and grouse about the 'uffar gwirions*' that kept badgering him, but she knew better. She saw the small smile he tried to hide when the doorbell went, the light in his eyes and his renewed energy after a visitor would leave, or after he returned from his so called 'kidnappings' to their houses or sometimes the local pub (she knew they had offered to take him further afield, but when asked what he wanted to do he would invariably bark 'pub' and scowl furiously at any other suggestions).

Movement caught her eye from the other side of the grave, and she watched as one of Alun's most frequent visitors stepped forward and dropped his wooden stick in with the casket. The boy was tall for an eleven-year-old, his blond hair shining in the sun and a cheeky expression on his face. When his mother pulled him back from the edge, scowling at him, he just shrugged, and Angharad could just about hear him say, 'He needs it, Mum. What if someone pisses him off up there?'

Angharad stifled her laughter with some effort; no wonder Alun had liked the boy so much. The beautiful, dark-haired man who had his arm around the blonde was not so successful in tamping down his amusement, unashamedly letting out a loud bark of laughter and earning an annoyed look from the vicar.

'Luce, don't be a wuss,' she heard the blond boy say to a sniffling, pretty, dark-haired girl beside him. Despite his exasperated tone, the boy put his arm around her and drew her in for a hug, causing both sets of parents behind them to smile at each other. Movement caught Angharad's eye across the yard, and she watched as three miniature versions of the beautiful blonde and the handsome dark-haired man darted around the gravestones, playing hide-and-seek.

As she looked up, the beautiful blonde woman across from her caught her eye, and gave her a warm smile. Maybe Angharad's family was right, and Alun was just a miserable old bastard. But even if the only thing he ever really accomplished in his life was saving the beautiful woman opposite her, Angharad didn't think that was too shabby as lifetime achievements went. Not too shabby at all.

The End

Acknowledgments

I'll start by saying a massive thank you to my readers. I am honoured that you have taken the time to read my words. Thank you so much for making my dreams come true. I am also eternally grateful to the reviewers and bloggers that have taken a chance on me – your feedback has made all the difference to the books and is the reason I've been able to make writing not just a passion, but a career.

To my beta reading team, as ever your feedback in the early stages was invaluable and stopped me going off the rails.

A huge thank you to my readers for their ongoing support. Thanks also to Liz Jackson for her encouragement and proofreading, and Martin Ouvry for his fantastic copy-editing.

Last but not least thanks to my very own romantic hero. He's been married to me for twelve years now and he supports me unconditionally, to the extent that he'll read the manuscript multiple times, picking out the smallest of errors to assist me in my quest for perfection. I love you and the boys to the moon and back.

About the Author

Susie Tate is a contemporary romance author and doctor living in beautiful Dorset with her lovely husband, equally lovely (most of the time) three boys and properly lovely dog.

Please use any of the links below to connect with Susie. She really appreciates any feedback on her writing and would love to hear from anyone who has taken the time to read her books.

Official website:
http://www.susietate.com/

Join Facebook reader group:
<u>Susie's Book Badgers</u>

Find Susie on TikTok:
<u>Susie Tate Author</u>

Facebook Page:
https://www.facebook.com/susietateauthor